THE WORLD'S CLASSICS

A SICILIAN ROMANCE

ANN RADCLIFFE was born in London in 1764. Her father was in trade, but a great part of her youth was passed in the society of wealthy relatives in easy circumstances. At the age of 23 she married William Radcliffe, who later became proprietor and editor of the *English Chronicle*.

Her talents as a novelist were first recognized in 1790 with the publication of *A Sicilian Romance*, which Sir Walter Scott considered to be the first modern English example of the poetical novel. However, her fame rests on her *Romance of the Forest* (1791), *The Mysteries of Udolpho* (1794), and *The Italian* (1797, a romance of the Inquisition).

Mrs Radcliffe's method, which found a number of imitators, was to arouse terror and curiosity by events apparently supernatural. Many of her books were translated into French and Italian.

After 1797 she wrote very little. For the last twelve years of her life she suffered from spasmodic asthma, and succumbed to a sudden attack in 1823.

ALISON MILBANK was John Rylands Research Institute Fellow at the University of Manchester, and now lives and teaches in Cambridge. Her *Daughters of the House: Modes of the Gothic in Victorian Fiction* was published by Macmillan in 1992.

Julia & Hippolitus

Emila

Ferdinand

Madame de Menon

Louisa Bernini

Monta de Vellorno

THE WORLD'S CLASSICS

ANN RADCLIFFE

A Sicilian Romance

Edited by
ALISON MILBANK

Oxford   New York
OXFORD UNIVERSITY PRESS

Oxford University Press, Walton Street, Oxford OX2 6DP
Oxford New York Toronto
Delhi Bombay Calcutta Madras Karachi
Kuala Lumpur Singapore Hong Kong Tokyo
Nairobi Dar es Salaam Cape Town
Melbourne Auckland Madrid
and associated companies in
Berlin Ibadan

Oxford is a trade mark of Oxford University Press

Introduction, Note on the Text, Select Bibliography,
Explanatory Notes © Alison Milbank 1993
Chronology © Chloe Chard 1986

First Published as a World's Classics Paperback 1993

British Library Cataloguing in Publication Data
Data available

Library of Congress Cataloging in Publication Data
Radcliffe, Ann Ward, 1764–1823.
A Sicilian romance / Ann Radcliffe; edited by Alison Milbank.
p. cm.—(World's classics)
I. Milbank, Alison, 1954– . II. Title. III. Series.
PR5202S55 1992 823'.6—dc20 92–25480
ISBN 0–19–282212–8

3 5 7 9 10 8 6 4 2

Printed in Great Britain by
BPCC Paperbacks Ltd
Aylesbury, Bucks

ACKNOWLEDGEMENTS

I would like to thank Ros Ballaster for her generous assistance in the preparation of this edition.

CONTENTS

INTRODUCTION

Very little is known of Ann Radcliffe's life, beyond the bare facts of her upbringing as a shopkeeper's daughter in London and Bath, her childhood introduction through her uncle, Thomas Bentley, to the Piozzi and Wedgwood circles, and her marriage to the editor of *The English Chronicle*. Her diary, full of ample descriptions of the natural scenery of the south of England, is as carefully impersonal as that advocate of the general, Samuel Johnson, might have desired. This contrast between the spectacularly successful novels and their reclusive author made Radcliffe something of a mystery to her contemporaries. There was a tendency during her own lifetime to attribute to Radcliffe herself the experiences of her fictional heroines, and to inscribe her private and uneventful years of retirement with the Gothic markers of incarceration and insanity.

Her literary influence on the poets and dramatists of the early nineteenth century was extensive. 'Mother Radcliffe' was Keats's appellation for the great exponent of the Gothic romance, and the Romantics generally agreed in applauding the enchantment of her fictional world, addressing her as witch or necromancer, nurtured, in Thomas Mathias's words, by 'the Florentine muses in their secret solitary caverns'.[1] Such language stresses the originating power of her imagination, and presents her, not as holding her place within a tradition of novel writing, but as some miraculous birth, as uncanny as her own literary productions.

In complete contrast to this myth of the inspired prophetess, an alternative viewpoint on Radcliffe which dominates much twentieth-century criticism is one which tries to 'explain' her work as a precise employment of Gilpin's theories on the picturesque, and Edmund Burke's *A Philo-*

---

[1] Quoted by Walter Scott, 'Mrs Ann Radcliffe', in *Lives of the Novelists* (Edinburgh, 1825), 53.

sophical Enquiry into the Origin of our Ideas of the Sublime and Beautiful (1756). Effects in her novels will be 'ticked off' on the Burkean checklist of sublime stimuli, rather than explored for the particular nature of her response to the nexus of ideas on psychology, politics, and aesthetics bound up in that overloaded word, the sublime. The term implies vastness, awe, and an overwhelming sense of the power of natural forces or great art. Burke's particular contribution to its definition was twofold: to link it with Locke's psychology, and to identify terror as the true source of sublime effect. The early position of *A Sicilian Romance*—it is Radcliffe's second novel—and its less fully integrated aesthetic material, give us an opportunity to question both the Romantic and the rationalist assumptions of these two approaches, and to study the emergence of the Radcliffean novel's characteristic concerns with the power of the masculine order, sexual difference, and the interrelation of the aesthetic and the political. Such a focus will also set *A Sicilian Romance* in dialogue with recent feminist debates on sexual difference and the development of female identity—not in an attempt once again to explicate Radcliffe in terms of another master discourse, but to reveal the existence of Utopian strivings towards representation of the female as a project common to both the eighteenth-century novel and late twentieth-century feminist aesthetics.

Ann Radcliffe's first published work, *The Castles of Athlin and Dunbayne* (1789), is very evidently a response to earlier Gothic fictions, most notably Clara Reeve's *The Champion of Virtue* (1775), the title of which was altered to *The Old English Baron* in later editions. Both novels share a debt to Walpole's *The Castle of Otranto* (1764) in their focus upon the castle or great house as a field of force for its usurping tyrant, and as simultaneously a harbourer and revealer of secrets. While *The Castles of Athlin and Dunbayne* replicates the plots of murder, usurpation, and the unacknowledged heir of Reeve's tale, Radcliffe introduces the topos of the imprisoned woman deprived of her property rights, as well as the maiden endangered with abduction, to balance the focus of interest on the masculine tyrant. This latter figure of omnivorous desire and overreaching ambition dominates the Gothic novel from Walpole—whose protagonist murders in furtherance of his incestuous desires—to de Sade's monstrous libertines, Godwin's Falkland in *Caleb Williams* (1794), Matthew Lewis's Ambrosio in *The Monk* (1796), Charles Maturin's Melmoth, and beyond, although in the Victorian period his presence is either comical, as in the case of the egregious Willoughby in George Meredith's *The Egoist* (1879), or supernatural, as in Bram Stoker's vampire novel, *Dracula* (1897). As Franco Moretti has pointed out in his *Signs Taken for Wonders*, the power of capital, which Stoker's ubiquitous, untrammelled Count can be seen to incarnate, takes the place of the aristocratic tyrant as focus of dread and mystery in the nineteenth century, although it should be added that the aristocrat can quite easily metamorphose into the capitalist both in fiction and in reality.[2]

In contrast to this focus on the phallocentric power of the tyrannous nobleman, one can chart in *A Sicilian Romance* a shift away to a new concentration on his victims. In *The Castle of Otranto* the virtuous Isabella and Matilda flee from Manfred down a succession of subterranean passages, but when Manfred kills his daughter, thinking her to be Isabella whom he loves, she entreats *his* forgiveness for being discovered in a seemingly guilty meeting with Theodore, while Manfred's wife, Hippolita, threatened with divorce by her husband so that he can marry Isabella, accedes out of unquestioning wifely obedience. But in *A Sicilian Romance* Julia defies both the authority of her father and later that of the Church to assert her own freedom to marry as she chooses, or to live alone. And although the long-imprisoned Louisa Bernini is cowed into gratitude for the food the Marquis brings her, she is persuaded to escape his control with her daughter, and give her blessing to a union he opposes.

[2] Franco Moretti, *Signs Taken for Wonders: Essays in the Sociology of Literary Forms* (London, 1983).

This alteration in focus is not without its awkwardnesses, which are evident in the abrupt shifts in perspective once the action of the tale falls outside the castle walls, and attention is shifted from one group of pursuers to another, and from one characteristic Sicilian landscape to a further contrast, with little sense of progression between one frame and another. Yet only a year later the immensely more sophisticated *Romance of the Forest* can play effectively with the change from La Motte's to the heroine's viewpoint, and by *The Italian*, Radcliffe can again focus upon the machinations and mixed motives of the villain, the monk Schedoni, without upsetting the moral balance of the novel.

The mediation that enables this development is aesthetic—the employment of the sublime in a new and radical manner. It is undeniable that Radcliffe had read and absorbed the writing of Burke on this subject, but not in a mechanical way, as merely a source-book of sublime effects to energize a plot. She grasps what is most interesting in Burke's analysis of the sublime—his recognition of the pleasure the seemingly painful can incite, and that what is most sublime is that which threatens our very sense of self-preservation: 'Whatever is fitted in any sort to excite the ideas of pain, and danger, that is to say, whatever is in any sort terrible, or is conversant with terrible objects, or operates in a manner analogous to terror, is a source of the *sublime*; that is, it is productive of the strongest emotion which the mind is capable of feeling.'[3] The rhetorical sublime of the treatise attributed to Longinus, which had an enormous influence on eighteenth-century poetics following Boileau's translation of 1674, had as its site the masculine public arena of privileged equals, in which the orator 'transports' his hearers to new appreciations of their shared discourse. He 'not only persuades, but even throws an audience into transport . . . In most cases it is wholly in our

---

[3] Edmund Burke, *A Philosophical Enquiry into The Origin of our Ideas of the Sublime and Beautiful*, ed. Adam Phillips, World's Classics (Oxford, 1990), pt. 1, sect. 7; p. 36.

Resources

As you read this book you probably became aware of a need for more information in various areas. Here is a list of resources that can be helpful to you.

Campbell, Ross. *How to Really Love Your Teenager*. Scripture Press, 1987.

Crabb, Lawrence J. *The Marriage Builder*. Grand Rapids: Zondervan Publishing House, 1982.

Dobson, James. *Preparing for Adolescence*. Kingsway, 1982.

Lewis, Paul. *Forty Ways to Teach Your Child Values*. Wheaton, IL: Tyndale House, 1985.

Mace, David R. *Christian Response to the Sexual Revolution*. Nashville: Abingdon Press, 1970.

McDowell, Josh. *Evidence for Joy*. Word UK, 1985.

McDowell, Josh. *Love and Sex*. Tyndale House, 1985, distributed by Scripture Press.

McDowell, Josh. *His Image . . . My Image*. Here's Life Publishers, 1984, distributed by Scripture Press.

McDowell, Josh. *The Secret of Loving*. Here's Life Publishers, 1985, distributed by Scripture Press.

McDowell, Josh. *Why Shouldn't I? Teens Speak Out*. Here's Life Publishers, 1987, distributed by Scripture Press.

McDowell, Josh. Youth Video Series: *No! the Positive Answer*. Word UK, 1988/1989.

Stanley, Charles. *How to Keep Your Kids on Your Team*. Nashville: Oliver-Nelson, 1986.

power, either to resist or yield to persuasion. But the *Sublime*, endued with strength irresistible, strikes home, and triumphs over every hearer.'[4] Notably, the example of the biblical sublime that Longinus gives is from the act of creation in Genesis: 'God said: "Let there be light!" ' It is an act of divine power whose effect, as Boileau remarks, is instantaneous, just like that exercised on the audience by the orator. The analogy serves also to cast God himself in the role of orator, aligning him with the privileged circle of the rhetorically educated, who similarly partake of the creativity of the deity. In Burke, the model of the divine is that evoked in the Psalms or the book of Job—the all-powerful voice from the whirlwind who confirms the creature's weakness, and causes the earth itself to shake. The protagonist of the Burkean text is dramatized as a victim and a sufferer for whom the sublime is an experience which puts self-identity at risk: 'whilst we contemplate so vast an object [God], under the arm, as it were, of almighty power, and invested upon every side with omnipresence, we shrink into the minuteness of our own nature, and are, in a manner, annihilated before him'.[5] Such a procedure can be seen to reflect Burke's own political powerlessness as an Irishman, citizen of a conquered nation, of no family and with a Catholic mother, fighting for a living in the aristocratic world of English politics.

Radcliffe's sublime, as an analysis of *A Sicilian Romance* will illustrate, shares the interest in power and subjection of Burke's *Enquiry*, but she adds to it the emphasis on the natural sublime found in the meditative poetry of James Thomson's *The Seasons* (1726–30), which opens up the concept of the sublime as a democratic experience, since all people can respond to the beauties of the creation. The verse of Thomas Gray and William Collins, and especially the apocalyptic *Night Thoughts* of Edward Young (1742–5), all

---

[4] *Dionysius Longinus on the Sublime*, trans. William Smith (London, 1739), 3–4.

[5] Burke, *Enquiry*, pt. 2, sect. 5; p. 63.

have the effect of wresting the sublime away from its closed circle of the classically trained to a position where it acts as a unifying factor in the construction of a human subjectivity that is made one through its awareness of its weakness and status as God's creature. Such a subjectivity is one in which women can easily find a place. Samuel Monk, author of an important study on eighteenth-century theories of the sublime, has a great deal of fun at the expense of bluestockings like Mrs Montagu, Mrs Carter, and Anna Seward who so courted the sublime that they would, in the case of Mrs Carter, expose themselves voluntarily to the entertainment of hail, thunder, and pouring rain.[6] However, he makes the point that this taste for the chivalric, the Gothic, and the Ossianic takes the place, for women deprived of Greek and Latin, of classical education. They can be seen as establishing a rival cultural genealogy. Following the respected novelist Charlotte Smith, also a poet, who inserted her own poems into the text of her fictions, Radcliffe too aims to challenge the relegation of the romance or novel to the realm of low culture by her imitations of the Odes of Collins, and other 'graveyard' poets, which are interspersed throughout the texts of all her works. Moreover, in her epigraphs and quotations from Shakespeare, she aligns herself with his newly bestowed authority as the fount of a specifically English culture. (This was the period of his transformation into a 'classic' to rival the Greek and Roman originals.) It was the translator of Longinus, William Smith, Monk states, who was the first to use Shakespeare and Milton as exemplars of the sublime as well as classical authors such as Homer. Burke employs the two English authors strategically, although classical examples predominate. But in Radcliffe's posthumously published essay, 'On the Supernatural in Poetry', Shakespeare is the major point of reference, particularly the tragedies.

In Radcliffe's earliest fiction, *The Castles of Athlin and Dunbayne*, the sublime is invoked just two or three times in

---

[6] Samuel Monk, *The Sublime: A Study of Critical Theories in Eighteenth-Century England* (Ann Arbor, Mich., 1960), 216–17.

routine fashion to inscribe the 'lofty towers' of a baronial stronghold, or the 'delightful vallies of the Swiss cantons', although it begins to take on a more active role when the young Earl of Athlin stands observing the fury of a sea-storm, and is 'wrapt in the sublimity of the scene'.[7] It is in her next novel, *A Sicilian Romance*, that she both uses the term much more frequently and also provides, during the various peregrinations around the island, a fuller engagement with the concept, and with the picturesque with which it was intimately associated. (Literally, the term 'picturesque' means viewing a landscape as if it were a painting. It privileges roughness and asymmetry over smoothness and regularity, and it is the rocky outcrops and shadowy caverns of Salvator Rosa's work that set the standard for picturesque aesthetic appeal.) This sequence of alternating frantic chases and frozen tableaux has been described by David S. Durant as a procedure of 'deft substitution of geography for adventure' in its relentless symmetries, such as the Duke's search for Julia leading to the discovery of quite another errant couple, while that pair's pursuer encounters Julia and Madame de Menon.[8] Similarly, the Duke's enquiries for Julia which lead to the accidental discovery of the son he had formerly lost and searched for are mirrored by Julia's flight from banditti which causes her own family reunion, and the resolution of the Mazzini family mystery. Such parallels in the dreamlike journey sequences witness to some sense of purpose in the various repetitions.

The scenes in the second half of the story are narrated in the language of pictorial description, allowing the reader to 'frame' them either as the lowering crags and romantic chasms of Salvator Rosa, the dewy dawns and golden landscapes of Claude Lorrain, or the bright pastoral severities of Poussin or Dughet. A year was to elapse before the

---

[7] Ann Radcliffe, *The Castles of Athlin and Dunbayne: A Highland Story* (London, 1789), 186.

[8] David S. Durant, *Ann Radcliffe's Novels: Experiments in Setting*, Gothic Studies and Dissertations (New York, 1980), 54.

publication of William Gilpin's *Three Essays: On Picturesque Beauty; On Picturesque Travel; and on Sketching Landscape*, but such treatment was already common in travel literature, so that Henry Swinburne in 1780 could desire 'the powers of a Salvator or a Poussin' to illustrate the beauties of 'the sublime style' of northern Sicily.[9] In a fashion quite unlike the perspectives allowed her later villains, the Duke of Luovo is allowed to experience the effect of pictorial framing of a scene, as he is whisked in twenty pages from lush vineyards, through Salvatorean chasms, an isolated monastery, and the terrors of a ruined mansion, to a wild heath. What follows is yet another contrast:

About noon he found himself in a beautiful romantic country; and having reached the summit of some wild cliffs, he rested, to view the picturesque imagery of the scene below. A shadowy sequestered dell appeared buried deep among the rocks, and in the bottom was seen a lake, whose clear bosom reflected the impending cliffs, and the beautiful luxuriance of the overhanging shades.

But his attention was quickly called from the beauties of inanimate nature, to objects more interesting; for he observed two persons, whom he instantly recollected to be the same that he had formerly pursued over the plains. They were seated on the margin of the lake, under the shade of some high trees at the foot of the rocks, and seemed partaking of a repast which was spread upon the grass. (pp. 93–4)

It is the Duke's consciousness that constructs the Claudesque scene, but he immediately destroys his own effect, as aesthetic appreciation is quickly abandoned for pursuit, and he launches himself into the landscape. The small figures enjoying their *fête-champêtre* are literally put out of perspective as the tiny adjuncts of a pastoral picture when the Duke clatters over the rocks to break into a furious assault on the unknown male. Two sorts of control are evidenced here: the power of organizing one's view into a meaningful frame, followed by the urge to extend that control inside the image itself, and to deny its integrity.

[9] Henry Swinburne, *Travels in the Two Sicilies in the Years 1777, 1778, 1779 and 1780*, 4 vols. (London, 1790), iv. 169.

To contrast this impatient breaking of the aesthetic by the narrative, one can instance the scene in which Madame de Menon, former companion and governess to the Mazzini sisters, finds herself in similar romantic terrain. Unlike the Duke, with his very definite objective, Madame 'seemed without interest and without motive for exertion' (p. 103). The Duke, despite his Gothic responses to the vista into nothingness at the end of the ruined mansion, was able to sleep there soundly, but Madame has allowed her mind to become prey to imagination's 'wild and terrific images' in her fears about Julia's fate. That evening, she takes a walk:

Her thoughts, affected by the surrounding objects, gradually sunk into a pleasing and complacent melancholy, and she was insensibly led on. She still followed the course of the stream to where the deep shades retired, and the scene again opening to day, yielded to her a view so various and sublime, that she paused in thrilling and delightful wonder. A group of wild and grotesque rocks rose in a semicircular form, and their fantastic shapes exhibited Nature in her most sublime and striking attitudes. Here her vast magnificence elevated the mind of the beholder to enthusiasm. Fancy caught the thrilling sensation, and at her touch the towering steeps became shaded with unreal glooms; the caves more darkly frowned—the projecting cliffs assumed a more terrific aspect, and the wild overhanging shrubs waved to the gale in deeper murmurs. The scene inspired madame with reverential awe, and her thoughts involuntarily rose, 'from Nature up to Nature's God.' The last dying gleams of day tinted the rocks and shone upon the waters, which retired through a rugged channel and were lost afar among the receding cliffs. While she listened to their distant murmur, a voice of liquid and melodious sweetness arose from among the rocks; it sung an air, whose melancholy expression awakened all her attention, and captivated her heart. (p. 104)

Following irresistibly the voice of the 'syren', Madame, to her astonishment, finds the sequestered figure to be the very Julia she had believed lost. The picture evoked in this scene is the irregular sublime of Salvator Rosa, who drew the domiciles of witches and sibyls in such rocky terrain, rather than the more balanced orderliness of the beautiful landscape of the Duke's *coup d'œil*. Unlike the Duke, who keeps control of his gaze and of his intentions only to encounter disappointment and frustration, Madame de Menon gives herself up to the power of the sublime experience, and enters along the lines offered by the geometry of the picture rather than breaking the frame. So she does not force her way down the clattering rocks but follows the natural turnings of the mountain stream. Her active role is that of the imagination, which is enabled rather than paralysed by what she sees and hears in a manner described thus by Archibald Alison in his *Essays on the Nature and Principles of Taste*, published that same year: 'It is then, only, we feel the sublimity or beauty of their productions [i.e. Those of Claude, Handel, *et al.*], when our imaginations are kindled by their power, when we lose ourselves amid the number of images that pass before our minds, and when we waken at last from this play of fancy, as from a romantic dream.'[10] To be open to the sublimity of creation, he states, one must be 'vacant and unemployed' like Madame, whose voluntary passivity which makes her subject to the natural world allows a transference. There is movement 'from Nature up to Nature's God', from the natural to the transcendent, which then allows movement on the physical plane as Madame is literally 'transported' and able to realize her desire to find the lost Julia. Here the aesthetic of the sublime has had an actual, practical effect, as a female character is enabled, through her openness to its force, to appropriate also its imaginative authority. Her weakness is then transformed into power, whereas the Duke's refusal to accept a position of vulnerability makes him unable to benefit from the clues the picturesque landscape actually holds.

A similar principle is at work in the other encounters, or missed encounters, of the narrative. The Duke does indeed find his lost son, but only after he has long given up hope of finding him, whereas his determined pursuits of Julia are fruitless. More happily, Julia meets her brother Ferdinand,

---

[10] Archibald Alison, *Essays on the Nature and Principles of Taste* (London, 1789), 3.

then Hippolitus, her mother, and finally her brother again, all by chance. Not all these reunions are triggered by an abandonment to the sublime, but all do occur at points of weakness or constraint by others which are then followed immediately by bursts of empowerment, however temporary these may prove. In this way the Burkean sublime has become both a means of dramatizing human, and particularly female, subjection, and a catalyst to its overcoming. In the later novels, this is evidenced in the way in which the protagonists' acknowledgement of the sublime power of forces in nature and history beyond their control is followed by literary or musical creation, as an Emily St Aubert 'transposes' her immediate sensations into 'composition' of a more objective and universal character. Private feelings can become public, and female experience is enabled to reach out to claim representative human status. Hence the very general nature of the verses such heroines produce, which rarely bear subjectively upon their particular circumstances. It is notable that Charlotte Smith's Emmeline, in the novel of the same name of 1788, similarly sets herself in potentially sublime landscapes, such as the sea-shore, where she gives herself up to meditation. However, Smith's fiction eschews the 'high' discourse of the sublime in favour of the term 'romantic', and her descriptions of the sea are precise and realistic, lacking any desire for transposition into the power-relations of the aesthetic. Her interspersed poetry, similarly, is more frequently the outcome of masculine feeling, and finds immediate social expression.

Recent feminist literary criticism has witnessed a new understanding of the relevance of the sublime for women's writing, an awareness partly occasioned by the intense concentration around the concept in postmodern aesthetics. Patricia Yaegar discerns three strategies: first, the 'failed sublime', in which a moment of empowerment is undermined, often by a masculine counter-sublime.[11] Women are

---

[11] Patricia Yaegar, 'Toward a Female Sublime', in *Gender and Theory: Dialogues on Feminist Criticism*, ed. Linda Kauffman (Oxford, 1989), 191–3.

mediated narrative

thereby proved capable of greatness, but something in the social order intrudes to prevent their expression. A second mode is the 'sovereign sublime' of domination (of which the protagonist of de Sade's *Juliette* would be a good example), in which a woman appropriates the male sublime, but is thereby vulnerable to its structure of violence and appropriation. Last comes the 'pre-Oedipal sublime', in which the Oedipal battle of father and son (which is in fact the 'sovereign sublime' of Yaegar's second category) is a mask for an oral primordial desire to merge with the identity of the mother, rather than to possess her Oedipally. This desire leads to a blockage that is quickly refigured as an experience of inundation.

It is clear that Yaegar is working with a later Romantic model of the 'egotistical sublime' rather than the Longinian model or the victimized subjectivity of Burke. In the terms of these categories, Radcliffe is certainly not staging a stronger masculine counter-sublime, although, as we have seen, she presents the picturesque frame as the prelude to an omnivorous desire for control that begins with the gaze. Nor, as the example of Madame de Menon's 'transportation' illustrates, is Radcliffe's text Oedipal in its relation to the sublime, which is not wrested from others but bestowed. And indeed, in the group experiences of the La Luc circle in the Alps in *The Romance of the Forest*, and the St Aubert family in the Pyrenees in *The Mysteries of Udolpho*, the sublime is a communal effect. But, as a text famously concerned with the absent mother who disturbs her children's sleep with her spectral groans, is not *A Sicilian Romance* vulnerable to the third description of a pre-Oedipal identification with the maternal?

Running in parallel with the extensive body of psychoanalytical criticism of Gothic texts which privilege Oedipal wrestlings of sons and fathers, as well as incestuous relations between fathers and daughters, is a feminist discourse focusing on the attraction but also the threat to female identity caused by too close a relation to the all-embracing maternal body. Mothers are, of course, notoriously absent in Gothic texts, or rather, as Norman Holland and Leonora Sherman in an influential article would have it, displaced, so that the topos of the Gothic heroine fleeing the tyrant through the passages of an ancient castle can be seen to represent both female anxieties about male penetration, and the need to flee the recesses of the castle as maternal body, with its blurrings of inside and outside, self and not-self, into individuation.[12] Julia Kristeva has paid great attention to the pre-Oedipal stage of one's first attempts to distinguish the 'me' from the 'not me', and has described this as a procedure of 'abjection'.[13] One becomes aware of something which appears like a weight of meaninglessness, and which threatens to overcome any emerging sense of identity. Throwing this off by means of feelings of nausea and disgust for bodily fluids and excrement, the child begins to move towards a sense of himself or herself as a separate entity, independent of the mother, who is herself 'abjected'. However, in moving beyond total identification with the mother the child loses and represses the experience, and it is the argument of a critic of the Gothic such as Claire Kahane that the novels of Radcliffe offer a 'vital imaginary space' figured as a precipice 'on the edge of maternal blackness to which every Gothic heroine is fatefully drawn'.[14] The sublime here is the location of the repressed and unrepresented mother, and it tempts the heroine to return to a complete identification with this buried experience.

The element in *A Sicilian Romance* that can be seen to give substance to this psychoanalytic reading of the mother is the way in which her children register the clues to the presence of the marchioness as uncanny, and proof of ghostly invasion. As Margaret Doody puts it: 'The irony of

[12] Norman Holland and Leonora Sherman, 'Gothic Possibilities', *New Literary History*, 8/2 (Winter 1977), 279–94.

[13] Julia Kristeva, *Powers of Horror: An Essay on Abjection*, trans. Leon S. Roudiez (New York, 1982).

[14] Claire Kahane, 'The Gothic Mirror', in *The Mother Tongue: Essays in Feminist Psychoanalytic Interpretation*, ed. Shirley Nelson Garner, Claire Kahane, and Madelon Sprengnether (Ithaca, NY, and London, 1985), 340.

the tale is that the children are guilty while innocent: they have not rescued their mother, they have feared what they would love.'[15] This fear culminates in the scene in which the Marquis's son, Ferdinand, penetrates alone the neglected part of the castle under his sister's apartments, whence cries and groans had been heard. He follows a shadowy figure up a staircase:

He had not proceeded very far, when the stones of a step which his foot had just quitted, loosened by his weight, gave way; and dragging with them those adjoining, formed a chasm in the staircase that terrified even Ferdinand, who was left tottering on the suspended half of the steps, in momentary expectation of falling to the bottom with the stone on which he rested. (p. 41)

Unable to move either up or down, Ferdinand is with great difficulty eventually rescued by his sisters. Unknown to him, he has been following his father, and his failure to complete the pursuit, as well as his terrors on the broken staircase, have all the force of a symbolic castration. In orthodox Freudian interpretation of this stage of human development, the boy (or girl) recognizes the power of the phallus, and accepts the law of the father. Further, he now realizes that his mother does not, after all, possess the phallus or its authority. As Jacques Lacan has it, she is defined as 'lack' itself, a hole or gap, registered in A Sicilian Romance as the gap in the staircase. It is after this event that the Marquis takes his son into his (supposed) confidence, and tells him of an ancestral crime that has resulted in the haunting by a deposed enemy, thus separating him from his sisters, who are not to be party to the secret.

However, the mother missing from the centre of A Sicilian Romance is more than the archaic plenitude of infant identification. She is denied her true place in the narrative, and her place in human society. It is indeed the law of the father (which, as the novel points out, is absolute in his Sicilian

---

[15] Margaret Anne Doody, 'Deserts, Ruins, and Troubled Waters: Female Dreams in Fiction and the Development of the Gothic Novel', Genre, 10 (1977), 529–72, 569.

domain) that causes the burial of the mother in the vaults of his castle. But this repression does not—as psychoanalytic theory would have it—enable the individuation and maturation of the children. While this situation holds, any attempts at personal choice of mate, or sexual fulfilment, are nullified. Rather, the children are condemned to wander blindly until they rediscover their maternal origin, after which all these things are possible, and, indeed, enabled by Julia remaining in the underground room with her mother, where Hippolitus rescues them both. Kristeva is content to allow the location of the feminine in the gaps and discontinuities of language, to locate the abject in the 'linings of the sublime', in which the subject loses herself in the 'raptures of a bottomless memory'.[16] But one can find a more creative analogy with the further project of *A Sicilian Romance*—the rescue of the maternal from this chasm—in the writings of another French feminist philosopher, Luce Irigaray. In one key text, Irigaray uses the example of Antigone to describe the situation of the female, and argues that if women are cut off from their own becoming, and from any model of their own transcendence, then they are buried alive in our culture, as Antigone was by Creon when she was left in a cave to die.[17] Irigaray moves to release the mother ('the dark continent of a dark continent') from silence and the cave, and the assimilation of *ventre* (womb) and *antre* (cave), into representation, so that children may learn to 'imagine' their mothering, and to establish a maternal genealogy which patriarchy obscures.[18]

While many commentators on *A Sicilian Romance* are content to note that Julia's discovery of her mother in the subterranean vault is a return to the womb, their discussion rarely goes further. Pierre Arnaud, however, takes this insight to its Freudian conclusion, that Louisa Mazzini's

---

[16] Kristeva, *Powers of Horror*, 12.

[17] Luce Irigaray, *Speculum of the Other Woman*, trans. Gillian C. Gill (Ithaca, NY, 1985), 214–26.

[18] Luce Irigaray, *Le Corps-à-corps avec la mère* (Montreal, 1981), 61.

rescue 'symbolizes the *rebirth* of the heroine; it is also the symbol of return to the mother's womb before birth and above all the substitution of the daughter for the mother' (my translation).[19] This viewpoint Irigaray would describe as witnessing to the fact that 'our western culture rests on the murder of the mother': since for the male imagination there can only be one woman, the wife subsumes the mother, and the female itself is sacrificed as the mode of exchange between men, which enables them to represent, while woman herself remains unrepresented.[20] In such an economy there can be no place for a genealogy of women, or a recognition of the maternal as a place of origin. In Radcliffe's *Sicilian Romance*, however, there are moves towards a testing out of what it might mean to acknowledge the mother, and to establish social networks built upon this Utopian project. Not only do Madame de Menon and Hippolitus's sister, the nun Cornelia, reveal hidden sexual unions that establish alternative occluded narratives of female desire frustrated by masculine ambition or aggression, but it is the witness of another woman, again Madame de Menon, that helps to re-establish and prove Louisa Mazzini's stolen identity while that of the Marchioness confirms the legality of Madame de Menon's marriage. It was while the mother, Louisa, was hidden from sight that Maria de Vellorno, the Marquis's second wife, could substitute for her and also, by her figuratively incestuous passion for Julia's lover Hippolitus, deny the separateness of the roles of mother and daughter. The deaths of the Marquis and his second consort are therefore necessary to allow a new and larger social grouping to emerge, in which a broader range of familial relations are displayed, and sibling and parental affections can reach expression. This will be a feature of the endings of Radcliffe's other novels, seen especially in the La Luc circle in *The Romance of the Forest* and the late

---

[19] Pierre Arnaud, *Ann Radcliffe et le fantastique: Essai de psychobiographie* (Paris, 1976), 122.

[20] Irigaray, *Le Corps-à-corps avec la mère*, 62.

introduction of the Count de Villefort's family in the narrative of *The Mysteries of Udolpho*. The model is both that of Samuel Richardson, who arranges a new moral order based on the aesthetic of Clarissa Harlowe's death in the novel named after her, and of Rousseau, who can be seen to attempt a similar moral challenge to contemporary values in the philosophical *Émile* and *La Nouvelle Héloïse*. In the latter novel Rousseau attempts to negotiate between the lover Julie and the wife and mother, without subsuming all these roles under the maternal. The death of Julie witnesses to the failure of this project, as she cannot live out the fullness of all these roles. She dies as mother, in trying to rescue her child, but leaves evidence of her inability to forget her former lover. These novels witness in differing ways to the substitution of a bourgeois ethic that stresses individual virtue based on social affections for the aristocratic code of honour represented by the Duke, the Marquis, and equally the abbot of the convent where Julia hopes to find refuge.

In *A Sicilian Romance*, in contrast to the crisis of identity and threat to the boundaries of the self that Kristeva and others locate in the abjected maternal, the rediscovery of the mother leads to the creation of a female self of value. There is, indeed, a moment when Julia is subsumed into her mother's situation. She has the choice of revealing her presence in the cave to the Marquis when he comes to bring food, and thus being able to escape the fate of the marchioness, even if this means exchanging immolation for a forced marriage. Instead, she chooses to share her mother's imprisonment in an act of deliberate—if desperate—choice. And this move to be 'with' the mother and her imprisonment is what allows the rescue of both of them by Julia's lover and their reunion with Ferdinand in the firelight of the lighthouse. Julia's identification with her mother's situation is no infantile regression to the womb: instead it precipitates her maturation and sexual union. The child can now understand himself or herself as the product of the union of male and female—of a truly sexual union—and understand that the mother is also a lover. And the opening of what had hitherto been a hermetically closed womblike space and symbolically an occluded and forbidden origin will allow change in terms of both individual sexual fulfilment and social mobility, as the absolutist power of the male aristocrat is cancelled.

Like the womb, the cave of Louisa's incarceration holds a mediating position between nature and culture, since it is actually part of the vaults of the castle, which can be entered either from the house or the natural landscape outside. As Irigaray has it, in her rereading of Plato's equally womblike cave in *The Republic*, the cave (*antre*) puns also with *entre*, meaning 'between'. There is something particularly Sicilian about such an arrangement; as Radcliffe would have read in the travellers' descriptions of the subterranean gardens of the Capuchin monastery near Syracuse and the use of interconnecting caves for burial chambers. Thomas Warton distinguishes Sicily for its 'caverns hung with ivy-twine' in his 'Ode XVII', while Tasso's Aurora in his pastoral, *Amin-ta*, lives in a cave on the same island.[21] Sicily, with its layers of lava forming curious involutions and burying whole houses and villages, is the appropriate setting for a story so concerned with the interpenetration of inside and outside, and the permeable cave. Indeed, the reviewer of The *Critical Review* suggested drily that 'if the author again engages in this task we would advise her not to introduce so many caverns with such peculiar concealments';[22] and certainly the novel is structured on a rigid axis of what Talfourd's *Memoir* noted as a vertical 'bird's eye view' of people and events crossed by dreamlike sequences of pursuits along subter-ranean passages.[23] The symmetry seems to invite a dualistic

[21] Thomas Warton (the younger), 'Ode for His Majesty's Birthday, June 4th, 1786', *Poetical Works* (London, 1790), 100-1.

[22] '*A Sicilian Romance*', *Critical Review or Annals of Literature*, 1 (1791), 350.

[23] T. N. Talfourd, in *Gaston de Blondeville, or the Court of Henry III, Keeping Festival in Ardenne, A Romance, St Alban's Abbey, A Metrical Tale; With Some Poetical Pieces. By Anne Radcliffe, Author of 'The Mysteries of Udolpho', 'Romance of the Forest', &c. To Which is Prefixed a Memoir of the Author, With Extracts From Her Journals. In Four Volumes* (London, 1826), i. 10.

analysis of the grid in terms of mind–body, male–female oppositions. That the overarching viewpoint is presented as masculine I argued above, but tried to suggest that the female cave is not merely a figure of the body, or the natural, but holds an essential mediating position on which culture and history rely. The learned visitor to the ruined castle of the Mazzinis, whose historicizing eye frames the narrative, is unable to piece together the story of its dissolution without the witness of the cave.

To anyone familiar with the literature of Radcliffe's time on the topography of Sicily, there is a puzzling omission from her account of the island, and that is the absence of any but the briefest mention of Mount Etna. For this was the site of the sublime for literary visitors such as Henry Swinburne or Patrick Brydone. It is clear from this omission that Radcliffe wishes to revise the location of the sublime in the purely vertical, and the purely powerful. The novel does not substitute the cavern for the mountain as privileged location, but argues for mediation between the high and the low: the transcendent can only be viewed through the material, the immanent. It is experience of the feminine situation of confinement and powerlessness, whether in mansion or cave, that allows a movement to the transcendent. In this way the divine is refigured in a way that will admit some correspondence between the female and itself. 'From Nature up to Nature's God' enables she who is equated with the natural to modulate to the spiritual.

More than Radcliffe's later and more complex literary productions, *A Sicilian Romance* reveals its place in a tradition of writings by women novelists about imprisonment. Most notably, it shows strong similarities to Sophia Lee's *The Recess, or: A Tale of Other Times* (1785). In that novel, the unrecognized daughters of Mary, Queen of Scots are confined to an underground life for the whole of their childhood and adolescence:

This Recess could not be called a cave, because it was compos'd of many rooms; and the stones were obviously united by labor; yet every room was distinct, and divided from the rest by a vaulted passage with many stairs, while our light proceeded from casements of painted glass so infinitely above our reach we could never seek a world beyond.[24]

Like the cave where Louisa Mazzini is incarcerated, this place too is part of an architectural structure, forming the subterranean part of the great house that had formerly been a convent. Yet there are ways leading from it directly into the world outside. Commentators on this novel too are quick to speak of the recess as a womb—'a dense fluid medium which renders all objects indistinct and indefinite, constantly altering in its dimensions—almost as if everything in *The Recess* were in the process of being born, attempting to achieve a clear and definite form'.[25]

The daughters leave their subterranean home for what proves to be a tragic engagement in romance and politics, each hitching her star to a different lord, Leicester and Essex respectively. Their lovers fail them, not least because of the phallic power of the mother-usurper, Elizabeth I, who, again like Maria de Vellorno in *A Sicilian Romance*, wishes to subsume all sexual roles—mother, daughter, lover, virgin, bride—to herself, and holds her male courtiers in incestuous erotic thrall. The heroines' true mother, Mary, the rival queen, remains incarcerated (for a much longer period than was historically the case), and her daughters can gain only a mere sight of her as she paces the courtyard of her prison. (This is a scene repeated with some variations in Radcliffe's novel, when Louisa recounts how she managed a glimpse from a window of her offspring, but could not speak to them.) Although it is the absence of the unacknowledged mother that leads to the appalling sufferings of her daughters, and precludes their own secure social and sexual positioning at the court of Elizabeth, the recess of the novel's title is more ambiguous in its function than Radcliffe's vault. Talfourd's *Memoir* states that the young Ann

---

[24] Sophia Lee, *The Recess, or: A Tale of Other Times*, Arno reprint of 1785 ed., introd. Devendra P. Varma (New York, 1972), i. 3.
[25] Ibid., p. xix.

Radcliffe was a great admirer of *The Recess*, and she was probably acquainted with the Lee sisters when all three were resident at Bath, but hers is no tame imitation of the earlier novel. Life in Lee's recess is ordered and nurtured by a governess and a tutor who sublimated their love for each other in parenting the girls when they discovered that their feelings for each other were unwittingly incestuous. The recess does not enable sexual fulfilment but protects its inhabitants from erotic forces. It hides the truth of their actual paternity from Matilda and Elinor, and, later in the narrative, when the daughters seek to escape capture by fleeing to its safety, it proves an actual prison where death and rape are variously plotted.

Like their famous mother, the heroines of *The Recess* follow a trajectory of abandonment to romantic fatalism, being the spoil or prey of a series of powerful men, in a series of extreme adventures which end in madness, death, or disillusion. There is no way in which they can 'be with' their mother, either actually or symbolically, nor, conversely, can they escape identification with her fate. But in the breathless turnings of the passages of *A Sicilian Romance*, Ann Radcliffe can be seen to be setting herself the task of finding resources for the motherless heroine, both in terms of providing her with the relation to the mother hitherto denied her, and by staking out, as a political act, the aesthetic space of the sublime as a place where the experience of being a woman can be dramatized, affirmed, and transcended.

NOTE ON THE TEXT

The text used for this volume is that of the new edition of 1821, which was the last to appear in Radcliffe's own lifetime. *A Sicilian Romance* went through five earlier editions: in 1790, 1792, 1796, 1809, and 1818 respectively, as well as a Minerva Press edition of 1820. Radcliffe's death in 1823 led to a flurry of editions in the following years, while the nineteenth century saw editions in 1848 and 1887, as well as a number of cheap reprints. Differences between the first edition and that of 1821 are minor, consisting mainly in the alteration of lower to upper case for the initial letters of names and titles. There is some evidence of a desire to remove unnecessary commas, and to modernize spellings, but these tasks are not consistently carried out. As part of what makes the novel interesting is its less finished quality in relation to the later fiction, variations in spelling have been retained, so that Etna, for example, appears both as 'Ætna' and in its modernized form. Significant changes of wording are indicated in the explanatory notes.

SELECT BIBLIOGRAPHY

J. and A. Aikin, *Miscellaneous Pieces in Prose* (London, 1773).

Archibald Alison, *Essays on the Nature and Principles of Taste* (Dublin, 1790).

Pierre Arnaud, *Ann Radcliffe et le fantastique: Essai de psychobiographie* (Paris, 1976).

Gillian Beer, ' "Our unnatural no-voice": The Heroic Epistle, Pope, and Women's Gothic', *Yearbook of English Studies*, 12 (1982), 125–51.

Patrick Brydone, *A Tour Thro' Sicily and Malta. In a Series of Letters to William Beckford* (London, 1775).

Edmund Burke, *A Philosophical Enquiry into the Origin of our Ideas of the Sublime and Beautiful*, ed. Adam Phillips, World's Classics (Oxford, 1990).

Margaret Anne Doody, 'Deserts, Ruins, and Troubled Waters: Female Dreams in Fiction and the Development of the Gothic Novel', *Genre*, 10 (1977), 529–72.

David S. Durant, *Ann Radcliffe's Novels: Experiments in Setting* (New York, 1980).

Norman Holland and Leonora Sherman, 'Gothic Possibilities', *New Literary History*, 8/2 (Winter 1977), 279–94.

Luce Irigaray, *Le Corps-à-corps avec la mère* (Montreal, 1981).

—— *Speculum of the Other Woman*, trans. Gillian C. Gill (Ithaca, NY, 1985).

Julia Kristeva, *Powers of Horror: An Essay on Abjection*, trans. Leon S. Roudiez (New York, 1982).

Ellen Moers, *Literary Women* (London, 1977).

Samuel H. Monk, *The Sublime: A Study of Critical Theories in Eighteenth-Century England* (Ann Arbor, Mich., 1960).

Elizabeth Nollen, 'Ann Radcliffe's *A Sicilian Romance*: A New Source for Jane Austen's *Sense and Sensibility*', *English Language Notes*, 22/2 (Dec. 1984), 30–7.

Melvin P. Palmer, 'Madame D'Aulnoy in England', *Comparative Literature*, 27/3 (Summer 1975), 237–53.

David Punter, *The Literature of Terror: A History of Gothic Fictions from 1765 to the Present Day* (London, 1980).

Eino Railo, *The Haunted Castle: A Study of the Elements of English Romanticism* (London and New York, 1927).

Sir Walter Scott, 'Mrs Ann Radcliffe', in *The Lives of the Novelists* (Edinburgh, 1825).

Nelson C. Smith, 'Sense, Sensibility and Ann Radcliffe', *Studies in English Literature 1500–1900*, 13/4 (Autumn 1973), 577–91.

Henry Swinburne, *Travels in the Two Sicilies in the Years 1777, 1778, 1779 and 1780*, 2nd edn. (London, 1790).

Malcolm Ware, *Sublimity in the Novels of Ann Radcliffe* (Uppsala and Copenhagen, 1963).

Patricia Yaegar, 'Toward a Female Sublime', in *Gender and Theory: Dialogues on Feminist Criticism*, ed. Linda Kauffman (Oxford, 1989), 191–212.

A CHRONOLOGY OF ANN RADCLIFFE

1764   (9 July) Born in London, daughter of William and Ann Ward (née Oates).

1787   Married William Radcliffe.

1789   *The Castles of Athlin and Dunbayne: A Highland Story*. Published anonymously.

1790   *A Sicilian Romance* (2 vols.). Published anonymously.

1791   *The Romance of the Forest, Interspersed with Some Pieces of Poetry* (3 vols.). Published anonymously, but acknowledged as the work of Radcliffe in the second edition (1792).

1794   *The Mysteries of Udolpho: A Romance, Interspersed with Some Pieces of Poetry* (4 vols.).

1795   *A Journey Made in the Summer of 1794, through Holland and the Western Frontier of Germany, with a Return down the Rhine, to which Are Added Observations during a Tour to the Lakes of Lancashire, Westmoreland and Cumberland.*

1797   *The Italian; or, The Confessional of the Black Penitents: A Romance* (3 vols.).

1815   *The Poems of Mrs. Ann Radcliffe* (an unauthorized reprint of the poems in the novels).

1823   (7 February) Died.

1826   'Of the Supernatural in Poetry', *New Monthly Magazine and Literary Journal*, 16, 145–52.
Gaston de Blondeville; or, The Court of Henry III, Keeping Festival in Ardenne: A Romance and *St. Alban's Abbey: A Metrical Tale* (published together in 4 vols.).

A SICILIAN ROMANCE

'I could a tale unfold'*

On the northern shore of Sicily are still to be seen the magnificent remains of a castle, which formerly belonged to the noble house of Mazzini.* It stands in the centre of a small bay, and upon a gentle acclivity,* which, on one side, slopes towards the sea, and on the other rises into an eminence crowned by dark woods. The situation is admirably beautiful and picturesque, and the ruins have an air of ancient grandeur, which, contrasted with the present solitude of the scene, impresses the traveller with awe and curiosity.* During my travels abroad I visited this spot. As I walked over the loose fragments of stone, which lay scattered through the immense area of the fabrick, and surveyed the sublimity and grandeur of the ruins, I recurred, by a natural association of ideas, to the times when these walls stood proudly in their original splendour, when the halls were the scenes of hospitality and festive magnificence, and when they resounded with the voices of those whom death had long since swept from the earth. 'Thus,' said I, 'shall the present generation—he who now sinks in misery—and he who now swims in pleasure, alike pass away and be forgotten.' My heart swelled with the reflection; and, as I turned from the scene with a sigh, I fixed my eyes upon a friar, whose venerable figure, gently bending towards the earth, formed no uninteresting object in the picture. He observed my emotion; and, as my eye met his, shook his head and pointed to the ruin. 'These walls,' said he, 'were once the seat of luxury and vice. They exhibited a singular instance of the retribution of Heaven, and were from that period forsaken, and abandoned to decay.' His words excited my curiosity, and I enquired further concerning their meaning.

'A solemn history belongs to this castle,' said he, 'which is too long and intricate for me to relate. It is, however, contained in a manuscript in our library,* of which I could, perhaps, procure you a sight. A brother of our order, a descendant of the noble house of Mazzini, collected and recorded the most striking incidents relating to his family, and the history thus formed, he left as a legacy to our convent. If you please, we will walk thither.'

I accompanied him to the convent,* and the friar introduced me to his superior, a man of an intelligent mind and benevolent heart, with whom I passed some hours in interesting conversation. I believe my sentiments pleased him; for, by his indulgence, I was permitted to take abstracts of the history before me, which, with some further particulars obtained in conversation with the abate, I have arranged in the following pages.

CHAPTER I

TOWARDS the close of the sixteenth century, this castle was in the possession of Ferdinand, fifth marquis of Mazzini, and was for some years the principal residence of his family. He was a man of a voluptuous and imperious character. To his first wife, he married Louisa Bernini, second daughter of the Count della Salario, a lady yet more distinguished for the sweetness of her manners and the gentleness of her disposition, than for her beauty. She brought the marquis one son and two daughters, who lost their amiable mother in early childhood. The arrogant and impetuous character of the marquis operated powerfully upon the mild and susceptible nature of his lady: and it was by many persons believed, that his unkindness and neglect put a period to her life. However this might be, he soon afterwards married Maria de Vellorno, a young lady eminently beautiful, but of a character very opposite to that of her predecessor. She was a woman of infinite art, devoted to pleasure, and of an unconquerable spirit. The marquis, whose heart was dead to paternal tenderness, and whose present lady was too volatile to attend to domestic concerns, committed the education of his daughters to the care of a lady, completely qualified for the undertaking, and who was distantly related to the late marchioness.

He quitted Mazzini soon after his second marriage, for the gaieties and splendour of Naples, whither his son accompanied him. Though naturally of a haughty and overbearing disposition, he was governed by his wife. His passions were vehement, and she had the address to bend them to her own purpose; and so well to conceal her influence, that he thought himself most independent when he was most enslaved. He paid an annual visit to the castle of Mazzini; but the marchioness seldom attended him, and he staid only to give such general directions concerning the education of his daughters, as his pride, rather than his affection, seemed to dictate.

Emilia, the elder, inherited much of her mother's disposition. She had a mild and sweet temper, united with a clear and comprehensive mind. Her younger sister, Julia, was of a more lively cast. An extreme sensibility subjected her to frequent uneasiness; her temper was warm, but generous; she was quickly irritated, and quickly appeased; and to a reproof, however gentle, she would often weep, but was never sullen. Her imagination was ardent, and her mind early exhibited symptoms of genius. It was the particular care of Madame de Menon to counteract those traits in the disposition of her young pupils, which appeared inimical to their future happiness; and for this task she had abilities which entitled her to hope for success. A series of early misfortunes had entendered* her heart, without weakening the powers of her understanding. In retirement she had acquired tranquillity, and had almost lost the consciousness of those sorrows which yet threw a soft and not unpleasing shade over her character. She loved her young charge with maternal fondness, and their gradual improvement and respectful tenderness repaid all her anxiety. Madame excelled in music and drawing. She had often forgot her sorrows in these amusements, when her mind was too much occupied to derive consolation from books, and she was assiduous to impart to Emilia and Julia a power so valuable as that of beguiling the sense of affliction. Emilia's taste led her to drawing, and she soon made rapid advances in that art. Julia was uncommonly susceptible of the charms of harmony.* She had feelings which trembled in unison to all its various and enchanting powers.

The instructions of madame she caught with astonishing quickness, and in a short time attained to a degree of excellence in her favorite study, which few persons have ever exceeded. Her manner was entirely her own. It was not in the rapid intricacies of execution, that she excelled so much in as in that delicacy of taste, and in those enchanting powers of expression, which seem to breathe a soul through the sound, and which take captive the heart of the hearer. The lute was her favorite instrument, and its tender notes accorded well with the sweet and melting tones of her voice.

The castle of Mazzini was a large irregular fabrick, and seemed suited to receive a numerous train of followers, such as, in those days, served the nobility, either in the splendour of peace, or the turbulence of war. Its present family inhabited only a small part of it; and even this part appeared forlorn and almost desolate from the spaciousness of the apartments, and the length of the galleries which led to them. A melancholy stillness reigned through the halls, and the silence of the courts, which were shaded by high turrets, was for many hours together undisturbed by the sound of any foot-step. Julia, who discovered an early taste for books, loved to retire in an evening to a small closet in which she had collected her favorite authors. This room formed the western angle of the castle: one of its windows looked upon the sea, beyond which was faintly seen, skirting the horizon, the dark rocky coast of Calabria; the other opened towards a part of the castle, and afforded a prospect of the neighbouring woods. Her musical instruments were here deposited, with whatever assisted her favorite amusements. This spot, which was at once elegant, pleasant, and retired, was embellished with many little ornaments of her own invention, and with some drawings executed by her sister. The cioset was adjoining her chamber, and was separated from the apartments of madame only by a short gallery. This gallery opened into another, long and winding, which led to the grand staircase, terminating in the north hall, with which the chief apartments of the north side of the edifice communicated.

Madame de Menon's apartment opened into both galleries. It was in one of these rooms that she usually spent the mornings, occupied in the improvement of her young charge. The windows looked towards the sea, and the room was light and pleasant. It was their custom to dine in one of the lower apartments, and at table they were always joined by a dependant of the marquis's, who had resided many years in the castle, and who instructed the young ladies in the Latin tongue, and in geography. During the fine evenings of summer, this little party frequently supped in a pavilion, which was built on an eminence in the woods belonging to the castle. From this spot the eye had an almost boundless range of sea and land. It commanded the straits of Messina, with the opposite shores of Calabria, and a great extent of the wild and picturesque scenery of Sicily.* Mount Etna,* crowned with eternal snows, and shooting from among the clouds, formed a grand and sublime picture in the background of the scene. The city of Palermo was also distinguishable; and Julia, as she gazed on its glittering spires, would endeavour in imagination to depicture its beauties, while she secretly sighed for a view of that world, from which she had hitherto been secluded by the mean jealousy of the marchioness, upon whose mind the dread of rival beauty operated strongly to the prejudice of Emilia and Julia. She employed all her influence over the marquis to detain them in retirement; and, though Emilia was now twenty, and her sister eighteen, they had never passed the boundaries of their father's domains.*

Vanity often produces unreasonable alarm; but the marchioness had in this instance just grounds for apprehension; the beauty of her lord's daughters has seldom been exceeded. The person of Emilia was finely proportioned. Her complexion was fair, her hair flaxen, and her dark blue eyes were full of sweet expression. Her manners were dignified and elegant, and in her air was a feminine softness, a tender timidity which irresistibly attracted the heart of the beholder. The figure of Julia was light and graceful—her step was airy—her mien animated, and her smile enchanting. Her eyes were dark, and full of fire, but tempered with modest sweetness. Her features were finely turned—every laughing grace played round her mouth, and her countenance quickly discovered all the various emotions of her soul. The dark auburn hair, which curled in beautiful profusion in her neck, gave a finishing charm to her appearance.

Thus lovely, and thus veiled in obscurity, were the daughters of the noble Mazzini. But they were happy, for they knew not enough of the world seriously to regret the want of its enjoyments, though Julia would sometimes sigh for the airy image which her fancies painted, and a painful curiosity would arise concerning the busy scenes from which she was excluded. A return to her customary amusements, however, would chase the ideal image from her mind, and restore her usual happy complacency. Books, music, and painting, divided the hours of her leisure, and many beautiful summer-evenings were spent in the pavilion, where the refined conversation of madame, the poetry of Tasso,* the lute of Julia, and the friendship of Emilia, combined to form a species of happiness, such as elevated and highly susceptible minds are alone capable of receiving or communicating. Madame understood and practised all the graces of conversation, and her young pupils perceived its value, and caught the spirit of its character.

Conversation may be divided into two classes—the familiar and the sentimental.* It is the province of the familiar, to diffuse cheerfulness and ease—to open the heart of man to man, and to beam a temperate sunshine upon the mind.—Nature and art must conspire to render us susceptible of the charms, and to qualify us for the practice of the second class of conversation, here termed sentimental, and in which Madame de Menon particularly excelled. To good sense, lively feeling, and natural delicacy of taste, must be united an expansion of mind, and a refinement of thought, which is the result of high cultivation. To render this sort of conversation irresistibly attractive, a knowledge of the world is requisite, and that enchanting ease, that elegance of manner, which is to be acquired only by frequenting the higher circles of polished life. In sentimental conversation, subjects interesting to the heart, and to the imagination, are brought forward; they are discussed in a kind of sportive way, with animation and refinement, and are never continued longer than politeness allows. Here fancy flourishes,—the sensibilities expand—and wit, guided by delicacy and embellished by taste—points to the heart.

Such was the conversation of Madame de Menon; and the pleasant gaiety of the pavilion seemed peculiarly to adapt it for the scene of social delights. On the evening of a very sultry day, having supped in their favorite spot, the coolness of the hour, and the beauty of the night, tempted this happy party to remain there later than usual. Returning home, they were surprised by the appearance of a light through the broken window-shutters of an apartment, belonging to a division of the castle which had for many years been shut up. They stopped to observe it, when it suddenly disappeared, and was seen no more. Madame de Menon, disturbed at this phænomenon, hastened into the castle, with a view of enquiring into the cause of it, when she was met in the north hall by Vincent.* She related to him what she had seen, and ordered an immediate search to be made for the keys of those apartments. She apprehended that some person had penetrated that part of the edifice with an intention of plunder; and, disdaining a paltry fear where her duty was concerned, she summoned the servants of the castle, with an intention of accompanying them thither. Vincent smiled at her apprehensions, and imputed what she had seen to an illusion, which the solemnity of the hour had impressed upon her fancy. Madame, however, persevered in her purpose; and, after a long and repeated search, a massey key, covered with rust, was produced. She then proceeded to the southern side of the edifice, accompanied by Vincent, and followed by the servants, who were agitated with impatient wonder. The key was applied to an iron gate, which opened into a court that separated this division from the other parts of the castle. They entered this court, which was overgrown with grass and weeds, and ascended some steps that led to a large door, which they vainly endeavoured to open. All the different keys of the castle were applied to the lock, without effect, and they were at length compelled to quit the place, without having either satisfied their curiosity, or quieted their fears. Everything, however, was still, and the light did not reappear. Madame concealed her apprehensions, and the family retired to rest.

This circumstance dwelt on the mind of Madame de Menon, and it was some time before she ventured again to spend an evening in the pavilion. After several months passed, without further disturbance or discovery, another occurrence renewed the alarm. Julia had one night remained in her closet later than usual. A favorite book had engaged her attention beyond the hour of customary repose, and every inhabitant of the castle, except herself, had long been lost in sleep. She was roused from her forgetfulness, by the sound of the castle clock, which struck one. Surprised at the lateness of the hour, she rose in haste, and was moving to her chamber, when the beauty of the night attracted her to the window. She opened it; and observing a fine effect of moonlight upon the dark woods, leaned forwards. In that situation she had not long remained, when she perceived a light faintly flash through a casement in the uninhabited part of the castle. A sudden tremor seized her, and she with difficulty supported herself. In a few moments it disappeared, and soon after a figure, bearing a lamp, proceeded from an obscure door belonging to the south tower; and stealing along the outside of the castle walls, turned round the southern angle, by which it was afterwards hid from the view. Astonished and terrified at what she had seen, she hurried to the apartment of Madame de Menon, and related the circumstance. The servants were immediately roused, and the alarm became general. Madame arose and descended into the north hall, where the domestics were already assembled. No one could be found of courage sufficient to enter into the courts; and the orders of madame were disregarded, when opposed to the effects of superstitious terror. She perceived that Vincent was absent, but as she was ordering him to be called, he entered the hall. Surprised to find the family thus assembled, he was told the occasion. He immediately ordered a party of the servants to attend him round the castle walls; and with some reluctance, and more fear, they obeyed him. They all returned to the hall, without having witnessed any extraordinary appearance; but though their fears were not confirmed, they were by no means dissipated. The appearance of a light in a part of the castle which had for several years been shut up, and to which time and circumstance had given an air of singular desolation, might reasonably be supposed to excite a strong degree of surprise and terror. In the minds of the vulgar, any species of the wonderful is received with avidity; and the servants did not hesitate in believing the southern division of the castle to be inhabited by a supernatural power. Too much agitated to sleep, they agreed to watch for the remainder of the night. For this purpose they arranged themselves in the east gallery, where they had a view of the south tower from which the light had issued. The night, however, passed without any further disturbance; and the morning dawn, which they beheld with inexpressible pleasure, dissipated for a while the glooms of apprehension. But the return of evening renewed the general fear, and for several successive nights the domestics watched the southern tower. Although nothing remarkable was seen, a report was soon raised, and believed, that the southern side of the castle was haunted. Madame de Menon, whose mind was superior to the effects of superstition, was yet disturbed and perplexed, and she determined, if the light reappeared, to inform the marquis of the circumstance, and request the keys of those apartments.

The marquis, immersed in the dissipations of Naples, seldom remembered the castle, or its inhabitants. His son, who had been educated under his immediate care, was the sole object of his pride, as the marchioness was that of his affection. He loved her with romantic fondness, which she repaid with seeming tenderness, and secret perfidy. She allowed herself a free indulgence in the most licentious pleasures, yet conducted herself with an art so exquisite as to elude discovery, and even suspicion. In her amours she was equally inconstant as ardent, till the young Count Hippolitus* de Vereza attracted her attention. The natural fickleness of her disposition seemed then to cease, and upon him she centered all her desires.

The count Vereza lost his father in early childhood. He was now of age, and had just entered upon the possession of his estates. His person was graceful, yet manly; his mind accomplished, and his manners elegant; his countenance expressed a happy union of spirit, dignity, and benevolence, which formed the principal traits of his character. He had a sublimity of thought, which taught him to despise the voluptuous vices of the Neapolitans, and led him to higher pursuits. He was the chosen and early friend of young Ferdinand, the son of the marquis, and was a frequent visitor in the family. When the marchioness first saw him, she treated him with great distinction, and at length made such advances, as neither the honor nor the inclinations of the count permitted him to notice. He conducted himself toward her with frigid indifference, which served only to inflame the passion it was meant to chill. The favors of the marchioness had hitherto been sought with avidity, and accepted with rapture; and the repulsive* insensibility which she now experienced, roused all her pride, and called into action every refinement of coquetry.

It was about this period that Vincent was seized with a disorder which increased so rapidly, as in a short time to assume the most alarming appearance. Despairing of life, he desired that a messenger might be dispatched to inform the marquis of his situation, and to signify his earnest wish to see him before he died. The progress of his disorder defied every art of medicine, and his visible distress of mind seemed to accelerate his fate. Perceiving his last hour approaching, he requested to have a confessor. The confessor was shut up with him a considerable time, and he had already received extreme unction, when Madame de Menon was summoned to his bedside. The hand of death was now upon him, cold damps hung upon his brows, and he, with difficulty, raised his heavy eyes to madame as she entered the apartment. He beckoned her towards him, and desiring that no person might be permitted to enter the room, was for a few moments silent. His mind appeared to labour under oppressive remembrances; he made several attempts to speak, but either resolution or strength failed him. At length, giving madame a look of unutterable anguish, 'Alas, madam,' said he, 'Heaven grants not the prayer of such a wretch as I am. I must expire long before the marquis can arrive. Since I shall see him no more, I would impart to you a secret which lies heavy at my heart, and which makes my last moments dreadful, as they are without hope.' 'Be comforted,' said madame, who was affected by the energy of his manner, 'we are taught to believe that forgiveness is never denied to sincere repentance.' 'You, madam, are ignorant of the enormity of my crime, and of the secret—the horrid secret which labours at my breast. My guilt is beyond remedy in this world, and I fear will be without pardon in the next; I therefore hope little from confession even to a priest. Yet some good it is still in my power to do; let me disclose to you that secret which is so mysteriously connected with the southern apartments of this castle.'—'What of them!' exclaimed madame, with impatience. Vincent returned no answer; exhausted by the effort of speaking, he had fainted. Madame rung for assistance, and by proper applications, his senses were recalled. He was, however, entirely speechless, and in this state he remained till he expired, which was about an hour after he had conversed with madame.

The perplexity and astonishment of madame, were by the late scene heightened to a very painful degree. She recollected the various particulars relative to the southern division of the castle, the many years it had stood uninhabited—the silence which had been observed concerning it—the appearance of the light and the figure—the fruitless search for the keys, and the reports so generally believed; and thus remembrance presented her with a combination of circumstances, which served only to increase her wonder, and heighten her curiosity. A veil of mystery enveloped that part of the castle, which it now seemed impossible should ever be penetrated, since the only person who could have removed it, was no more.

The marquis arrived on the day after that on which Vincent had expired. He came attended by servants only, and alighted at the gates of the castle with an air of impatience, and a countenance expressive of strong emotion. Madame, with the young ladies, received him in the hall. He hastily saluted his daughters, and passed on to the oak parlour, desiring madame to follow him. She obeyed, and the marquis enquired with great agitation after Vincent. When told of his death, he paced the room with hurried steps, and was for some time silent. At length seating himself, and surveying madame with a scrutinizing eye, he asked some questions concerning the particulars of Vincent's death. She mentioned his earnest desire to see the marquis, and repeated his last words. The marquis remained silent, and madame proceeded to mention those circumstances relative to the southern division of the castle, which she thought it of so much importance to discover. He treated the affair very lightly, laughed at her conjectures, represented the appearances she described as the illusions of a weak and timid mind, and broke up the conversation, by going to visit the chamber of Vincent, in which he remained a considerable time.

On the following day Emilia and Julia dined with the marquis. He was gloomy and silent; their efforts to amuse him seemed to excite displeasure rather than kindness; and when the repast was concluded, he withdrew to his own apartment, leaving his daughters in a state of sorrow and surprise.

Vincent was to be interred, according to his own desire, in the church belonging to the convent of St Nicholas. One of the servants, after receiving some necessary orders concerning the funeral, ventured to inform the marquis of the appearance of the lights in the south tower. He mentioned the superstitious reports that prevailed amongst the household, and complained that the servants would not cross the courts after it was dark. 'And who is he that has commissioned you with this story?' said the marquis, in a tone of displeasure; 'are the weak and ridiculous fancies of women and servants to be obtruded upon my notice? Away—appear no more before me, till you have learned to speak what it is proper for me to hear.' Robert withdrew abashed, and it was some time before any person ventured to renew the subject with the marquis.

The majority of young Ferdinand now drew near, and the marquis determined to celebrate the occasion with festive magnificence at the castle of Mazzini. He, therefore, summoned the marchioness and his son from Naples, and very splendid preparations were ordered to be made. Emilia and Julia dreaded the arrival of the marchioness, whose influence they had long been sensible of, and from whose presence they anticipated a painful restraint. Beneath the gentle guidance of Madame de Menon, their hours had passed in happy tranquillity, for they were ignorant alike of the sorrows and the pleasures of the world. Those did not oppress, and these did not inflame them. Engaged in the pursuits of knowledge, and in the attainment of elegant accomplishments, their moments flew lightly away, and the flight of time was marked only by improvement. In madame was united the tenderness of the mother, with the sympathy of a friend; and they loved her with a warm and inviolable affection.

The purposed visit of their brother, whom they had not seen for several years, gave them great pleasure. Although their minds retained no very distinct remembrance of him, they looked forward with eager and delightful expectation to his virtues and his talents; and hoped to find in his company, a consolation for the uneasiness which the presence of the marchioness would excite. Neither did Julia contemplate with indifference the approaching festival. A new scene was now opening to her, which her young imagination painted in the warm and glowing colours of delight. The near approach of pleasure frequently awakens the heart to emotions, which would fail to be excited by a more remote and abstracted observance. Julia, who, in the distance, had considered the splendid gaieties of life with tranquillity, now lingered with impatient hope through the moments which withheld her from their enjoyments. Emilia, whose feelings were less lively, and whose imagination was less powerful, beheld the approaching festival with calm consideration, and almost regretted the interruption of those tranquil pleasures, which she knew to be more congenial with her powers and disposition.

In a few days the marchioness arrived at the castle. She was followed by a numerous retinue, and accompanied by Ferdinand, and several of the Italian noblesse, whom pleasure attracted to her train. Her entrance was proclaimed by the sound of music, and those gates which had long rusted on their hinges, were thrown open to receive her. The courts and halls, whose aspect so lately expressed only gloom and desolation, now shone with sudden splendour, and echoed the sounds of gaiety and gladness. Julia surveyed the scene from an obscure window; and as the triumphal strains filled the air, her breast throbbed; her heart beat quick with joy, and she lost her apprehensions from the marchioness in a sort of wild delight hitherto unknown to her. The arrival of the marchioness seemed indeed the signal of universal and unlimited pleasure. When the marquis came out to receive her, the gloom that lately clouded his countenance, broke away in smiles of welcome, which the whole company appeared to consider as invitations to joy.

The tranquil heart of Emilia was not proof against a scene so alluring, and she sighed at the prospect, yet scarcely knew why. Julia pointed out to her sister, the graceful figure of a young man who followed the marchioness, and she expressed her wishes that he might be her brother. From the contemplation of the scene before them, they were summoned to meet the marchioness. Julia trembled with apprehension, and for a few moments wished the castle was in its former state. As they advanced through the saloon,* in which they were presented, Julia was covered with blushes; but Emilia, tho' equally timid, preserved her graceful dignity. The marchioness received them with a mingled smile of condescension and politeness, and immediately the whole attention of the company was attracted by their elegance and beauty. The eager eyes of Julia sought in vain to discover her brother, of whose features she had no recollection in those of any of the persons then present. At length her father presented him, and she perceived, with a sigh of regret, that he was not the youth she had observed from the window. He advanced with a very engaging air, and she met him with an unfeigned welcome. His figure was tall and majestic; he had a very noble and spirited carriage; and his countenance expressed at once sweetness and dignity. Supper was served in the east hall, and the tables were spread with a profusion of delicacies. A band of music played during the repast, and the evening concluded with a concert in the saloon.

CHAPTER II

THE day of the festival, so long and so impatiently looked for by Julia, was now arrived. All the neighbouring nobility were invited, and the gates of the castle were thrown open for a general rejoicing. A magnificent entertainment, consisting of the most luxurious and expensive dishes, was served in the halls. Soft music floated along the vaulted roofs, the walls were hung with decorations, and it seemed as if the hand of a magician had suddenly metamorphosed this once gloomy fabric into the palace of a fairy. The marquis, notwithstanding the gaiety of the scene, frequently appeared abstracted from its enjoyments, and in spite of all his efforts at cheerfulness, the melancholy of his heart was visible in his countenance.

In the evening there was a grand ball: the marchioness, who was still distinguished for her beauty, and for the winning elegance of her manners, appeared in the most splendid attire. Her hair was ornamented with a profusion of jewels, but was so disposed as to give an air rather of voluptuousness than of grace, to her figure. Although conscious of her charms, she beheld the beauty of Emilia and Julia with a jealous eye, and was compelled secretly to acknowledge, that the simple elegance with which they were adorned, was more enchanting than all the studied artifice of splendid decoration. They were dressed alike in light Sicilian habits, and the beautiful luxuriance of their flowing hair was restrained only by bandellets* of pearl. The ball was opened by Ferdinand and the lady Matilda Constanza. Emilia danced with the young Marquis della Fazelli, and acquitted herself with the ease and dignity so natural to her. Julia experienced a various emotion of pleasure and fear when the Count de Vereza, in whom she recollected the cavalier she had observed from the window, led her forth. The grace of her step, and the elegant symmetry of her figure, raised in the assembly a gentle murmur of applause, and the soft blush which now stole over her cheek, gave an additional charm to her appearance. But when the music changed, and she danced to the soft Sicilian measure, the airy grace of her movement, and the unaffected tenderness of her air, sunk attention into silence, which continued for some time after the dance had ceased. The marchioness observed the general admiration with seeming pleasure, and secret uneasiness. She had suffered a very painful solicitude, when the Count de Vereza selected her for his partner in the dance, and she pursued him through the evening with an eye of jealous scrutiny. Her bosom, which before glowed only with love, was now torn by the agitation of other passions more violent and destructive. Her thoughts were restless, her mind wandered from the scene before her, and it required all her address to preserve an apparent ease. She saw, or fancied she saw, an impassioned air in the count, when he addressed himself to Julia, that corroded her heart with jealous fury.

At twelve the gates of the castle were thrown open, and the company quitted it for the woods, which were splendidly illuminated. Arcades of light lined the long vistas, which were terminated by pyramids of lamps that presented to the eye one bright column of flame. At irregular distances buildings were erected, hung with variegated lamps, disposed in the gayest and most fantastic forms. Collations were spread under the trees; and music, touched by unseen hands, breathed around. The musicians were placed in the most obscure and embowered spots, so as to elude the eye and strike the imagination. The scene appeared enchanting. Nothing met the eye but beauty and romantic splendour; the ear received no sounds but those of mirth and melody. The younger part of the company formed themselves into groups, which at intervals glanced through the woods, and were again unseen. Julia seemed the magic queen of the place. Her heart dilated with pleasure, and diffused over her features an expression of pure and complacent delight. A generous, frank, and exalted sentiment sparkled in her eyes, and animated her manner. Her bosom glowed with benevolent affections; and she seemed anxious to impart to all around her, a happiness as unmixed as that she experienced. Wherever she moved, admiration followed her steps. Ferdinand was as gay as the scene around him. Emilia was pleased; and the marquis seemed to have left his melancholy in the castle. The marchioness alone was wretched. She supped with a select party, in a pavilion on the sea-shore, which was fitted up with peculiar elegance. It was hung with white silk, drawn up in festoons, and richly fringed with gold. The sofas were of the same materials, and alternate wreaths of lamps and of roses entwined the columns. A row of small lamps placed about the cornice, formed an edge of light round the roof which, with the other numerous lights, was reflected in a blaze of splendour from the large mirrors that adorned the room. The Count Muriani was of the party;—he complimented the marchioness on the beauty of her daughters; and after lamenting with gaiety the captives which their charms would enthral, he mentioned the Count de Vereza. 'He is certainly of all others the man most deserving the lady Julia. As they danced, I thought they exhibited a perfect model of the beauty of either sex; and if I mistake not, they are inspired with a mutual admiration.' The marchioness, endeavouring to conceal her uneasiness, said, 'Yes, my lord, I allow the count all the merit you adjudge him, but from the little I have seen of his disposition, he is too volatile for a serious attachment.' At that instant the count entered the pavilion: 'Ah,' said Muriani, laughingly, 'you was the subject of our conversation, and seem to be come in good time to receive the honors allotted you. I was interceding with the marchioness for her interest in your favor, with the lady Julia; but she absolutely refuses it; and though she allows you merit, alleges, that you are by nature fickle and inconstant. What say you—would not the beauty of lady Julia bind your unsteady heart?'

'I know not how I have deserved that character of the marchioness,' said the count with a smile, 'but that heart must be either fickle or insensible in an uncommon degree, which can boast of freedom in the presence of lady Julia.' The marchioness, mortified by the whole conversation, now felt the full force of Vereza's reply, which she imagined he pointed with particular emphasis.

The entertainment concluded with a grand firework, which was exhibited on the margin of the sea, and the company did not part till the dawn of morning. Julia retired from the scene with regret. She was enchanted with the new world that was now exhibited to her, and she was not cool enough to distinguish the vivid glow of imagination from the colours of real bliss. The pleasure she now felt she believed would always be renewed, and in an equal degree, by the objects which first excited it. The weakness of humanity is never willingly perceived by young minds. It is painful to know, that we are operated upon by objects whose impressions are variable as they are indefinable—and that what yesterday affected us strongly, is to-day but imperfectly felt, and to-morrow perhaps shall be disregarded. When at length this unwelcome truth is received into the mind, we at first reject, with disgust, every appearance of good, we disdain to partake of a happiness which we cannot always command, and we not unfrequently sink into a temporary despair. Wisdom or accident, at length, recal us from our error, and offers to us some object capable of producing a pleasing, yet lasting effect, which effect, therefore, we call happiness. Happiness has this essential difference from what is commonly called pleasure, that virtue forms its basis, and virtue being the offspring of reason, may be expected to produce uniformity of effect.

The passions which had hitherto lain concealed in Julia's heart, touched by circumstance, dilated to its power, and afforded her a slight experience of the pain and delight which flow from their influence. The beauty and accomplishments of Vereza raised in her a new and various* emotion, which reflection made her fear to encourage, but which was too pleasing to be wholly resisted. Tremblingly alive to a sense of delight, and unchilled by disappointment, the young heart welcomes every feeling, not simply painful, with a romantic expectation that it will expand into bliss.

Julia sought with eager anxiety to discover the sentiments of Vereza towards her; she revolved each circumstance of the day, but they afforded her little satisfaction; they reflected only a glimmering and uncertain light, which instead of guiding, served only to perplex her. Now she remembered some instance of particular attention, and then some mark of apparent indifference. She compared his conduct with that of the other young noblesse; and thought each appeared equally desirous of the favor of every lady present. All the ladies, however, appeared to her to court the admiration of Vereza, and she trembled lest he should be too sensible of the distinction. She drew from these reflections no positive inference; and though distrust rendered pain the predominate sensation, it was so exquisitely interwoven with delight, that she could not wish it exchanged for her former ease. Thoughtful and restless, sleep fled from her eyes, and she longed with impatience for the morning, which should again present Vereza, and enable her to pursue the enquiry. She rose early, and adorned herself with unusual care. In her favorite closet she awaited the hour of breakfast, and endeavoured to read, but her thoughts wandered from the subject. Her lute and favorite airs lost half their power to please; the day seemed to stand still—she became melancholy, and thought the breakfast-hour would never arrive. At length the clock struck the signal, the sound vibrated on every nerve, and trembling she quitted the closet for her sister's apartment. Love taught her disguise. Till then Emilia had shared all her thoughts; they now descended to the breakfast-room in silence, and Julia almost feared to meet her eye. In the breakfast-room they were alone. Julia found it impossible to support a conversation with Emilia, whose observations interrupting the course of her thoughts, became uninteresting and tiresome. She was therefore about to retire to her closet, when the marquis entered. His air was haughty, and his look severe. He coldly saluted his daughters, and they had scarcely time to reply to his general enquiries, when the marchioness entered, and the company soon after assembled. Julia, who had awaited with so painful an impatience for the moment which should present Vereza to her sight, now sighed that it was arrived. She scarcely dared to lift her timid eyes from the ground, and when by accident they met his, a soft tremour seized her; and apprehension lest he should discover her sentiments, served only to render her confusion conspicuous. At length, a glance from the marchioness recalled her bewildered thoughts; and other fears superseding those of love, her mind, by degrees, recovered its dignity. She could distinguish in the behaviour of Vereza no symptoms of particular admiration, and she resolved to conduct herself towards him with the most scrupulous care.

This day, like the preceding one, was devoted to joy. In the evening there was a concert, which was chiefly performed by the nobility. Ferdinand played the violoncello, Vereza the German flute, and Julia the piana-forte,* which she touched with a delicacy and execution that engaged every auditor. The confusion of Julia may be easily imagined, when Ferdinand, selecting a beautiful duet, desired Vereza would accompany his sister. The pride of conscious excellence, however, quickly overcame her timidity, and enabled her to exert all her powers. The air was simple and pathetic, and she gave it those charms of expression so peculiarly her own. She struck the chords of her piana-forte in beautiful accompaniment, and towards the close of the second stanza, her voice resting on one note, swelled into a tone so exquisite, and from thence descended to a few simple notes, which she touched with such impassioned tenderness that every eye wept to the sounds. The breath of the flute trembled, and Hippolitus entranced, forgot to play. A pause of silence ensued at the conclusion of the piece, and continued till a general sigh seemed to awaken the audience from their enchantment. Amid the general applause, Hippolitus was silent. Julia observed his behaviour, and gently raising her eyes to his, there read the sentiments which she had inspired. An exquisite emotion thrilled her heart, and she experienced one of those rare moments which illuminate life with a ray of bliss, by which the darkness of its general shade is contrasted.* Care, doubt, every disagreeable sensation vanished, and for the remainder of the evening she was conscious only of delight. A timid respect marked the manner of Hippolitus, more flattering to Julia than the most ardent professions. The evening concluded with a ball, and Julia was again the partner of the count.

When the ball broke up, she retired to her apartment, but not to sleep. Joy is as restless as anxiety or sorrow. She seemed to have entered upon a new state of existence;—those fine springs of affection which had hitherto lain concealed, were now touched, and yielded to her a happiness more exalted than any her imagination had ever painted. She reflected on the tranquillity of her past life, and comparing it with the emotions of the present hour, exulted in the difference. All her former pleasures now appeared insipid; she wondered that they ever had power to affect her, and that she had endured with content the dull uniformity to which she had been condemned. It was now only that she appeared to live. Absorbed in the single idea of being beloved, her imagination soared into the regions of romantic bliss, and bore her high above the possibility of evil. Since she was beloved by Hippolitus, she could only be happy.

From this state of entranced delight, she was awakened by the sound of music immediately under her window. It was a lute touched by a masterly hand. After a wild and melancholy symphony, a voice of more than magic expression swelled into an air so pathetic and tender, that it seemed to breathe the very soul of love. The chords of the lute were struck in low and sweet accompaniment. Julia listened, and distinguished the following words;

SONNET*

Still is the night-breeze!—not a lonely sound
    Steals through the silence of this dreary hour;
O'er these high battlements Sleep reigns profound,
    And sheds on all, his sweet oblivious power.

On all but me—I vainly ask his dews
    To steep in short forgetfulness my cares.
Th' affrighted god still flies when Love pursues,
    Still—still denies the wretched lover's prayers.

An interval of silence followed, and the air was repeated; after which the music was heard no more. If before Julia believed that she was loved by Hippolitus, she was now confirmed in the sweet reality. But sleep at length fell upon her senses, and the airy forms of ideal bliss no longer fleeted before her imagination. Morning came, and she arose light and refreshed. How different were her present sensations from those of the preceding day. Her anxiety had now evaporated in joy, and she experienced that airy dance of spirits which accumulates delight from every object; and with a power like the touch of enchantment, can transform a gloomy desert into a smiling Eden. She flew to the breakfast-room, scarcely conscious of motion; but, as she entered it, a soft confusion overcame her; she blushed, and almost feared to meet the eyes of Vereza. She was presently relieved, however, for the Count was not there. The company assembled—Julia watched the entrance of every person with painful anxiety, but he for whom she looked did not appear. Surprised and uneasy, she fixed her eyes on the door, and whenever it opened, her heart beat with an expectation which was as often checked by disappointment. In spite of all her efforts, her vivacity sunk into languor, and she then perceived that love may produce other sensations than those of delight. She found it possible to be unhappy, though loved by Hippolitus; and acknowledged with a sigh of regret, which was yet new to her, how tremblingly her peace depended upon him. He neither appeared nor was mentioned at breakfast; but though delicacy prevented her enquiring after him, conversation soon became irksome to her, and she retired to the apartment of Madame de Menon. There she employed herself in painting, and endeavoured to beguile the time till the hour of dinner, when she hoped to see Hippolitus. Madame was, as usual, friendly and cheerful, but she perceived a reserve in the conduct of Julia, and penetrated without difficulty into its cause. She was, however, ignorant of the object of her pupil's admiration. The hour so eagerly desired by Julia at length arrived, and with a palpitating heart she entered the hall. The Count was not there, and in the course of conversation, she learned that he had that morning sailed for Naples. The scene which so lately appeared enchanting to her eyes, now changed its hue; and in the midst of society, and surrounded by gaiety, she was solitary and dejected. She accused herself of having suffered her wishes to mislead her judgment; and the present conduct of Hippolitus convinced her, that she had mistaken admiration for a sentiment more tender. She believed, too, that the musician who had addressed her in his sonnet, was not the Count; and thus at once was dissolved all the ideal fabric of her happiness. How short a period often reverses the character of our sentiments, rendering that which yesterday we despised, to-day desirable. The tranquil state which she had so lately delighted to quit, she now reflected upon with regret. She had, however, the consolation of believing that her sentiments towards the Count were unknown, and the sweet consciousness that her conduct had been governed by a nice sense of propriety.

The public rejoicings at the castle closed with the week; but the gay spirit of the marchioness forbade a return to tranquillity; and she substituted diversions more private, but in splendour scarcely inferior to the preceding ones. She had observed the behaviour of Hippolitus on the night of the concert with chagrin, and his departure with sorrow; yet, disdaining to perpetuate misfortune by reflection, she sought to lose the sense of disappointment in the hurry of dissipation. But her efforts to erase him from her remembrance were ineffectual. Unaccustomed to oppose the bent of her inclinations, they now maintained unbounded sway; and she found too late, that in order to have a due command of our passions, it is necessary to subject them to early obedience. Passion, in its undue influence, produces weakness as well as injustice. The pain which now recoiled upon her heart from disappointment, she had not strength of mind to endure, and she sought relief from its pressure in afflicting the innocent. Julia, whose beauty she imagined had captivated the count, and confirmed him in indifference towards herself, she incessantly tormented by the exercise of those various and splenetic little arts which elude the eye of the common observer, and are only to be known by those who have felt them. Arts, which individually are inconsiderable, but in the aggregate amount to a cruel and decisive effect.

From Julia's mind the idea of happiness was now faded. Pleasure had withdrawn her beam from the prospect, and the objects no longer illumined by her ray, became dark and colourless. As often as her situation would permit, she withdrew from society, and sought the freedom of solitude, where she could indulge in melancholy thoughts, and give a loose to that despair which is so apt to follow the disappointment of our first hopes.

Week after week elapsed, yet no mention was made of returning to Naples. The marquis at length declared it his intention to spend the remainder of the summer in the castle. To this determination the marchioness submitted with decent resignation, for she was here surrounded by a croud* of flatterers, and her invention supplied her with continual diversions: that gaiety which rendered Naples so dear to her, glittered in the woods of Mazzini, and resounded through the castle.

The apartments of Madame de Menon were spacious and noble. The windows opened upon the sea, and commanded a view of the straits of Messina, bounded on one side by the beautiful shores of the isle of Sicily, and on the other by the high mountains of Calabria. The straits, filled with vessels whose gay streamers glittered to the sun-beam, presented to the eye an ever-moving scene.* The principal room opened upon a gallery that overhung the grand terrace of the castle, and it commanded a prospect which for beauty and extent has seldom been equalled. These were formerly considered the chief apartments of the castle; and when the Marquis quitted them for Naples, were allotted for the residence of Madame de Menon, and her young charge. The marchioness, struck with the prospect which the windows afforded, and with the pleasantness of the gallery, determined to restore the rooms to their former splendour. She signified this intention to madame, for whom other apartments were provided. The chambers of Emilia and Julia forming part of the suite, they were also claimed by the marchioness, who left Julia only her favorite closet. The rooms to which they removed were spacious, but gloomy; they had been for some years uninhabited; and though preparations had been made for the reception of their new inhabitants, an air of desolation reigned within them that inspired melancholy sensations. Julia observed that her chamber, which opened beyond madame's, formed a part of the southern building, with which, however, there appeared no means of communication. The late mysterious circumstances relating to this part of the fabric, now arose to her imagination, and conjured up a terror which reason could not subdue. She told her emotions to madame, who, with more prudence than sincerity, laughed at her fears. The behaviour of the marquis, the dying words of Vincent, together with the preceding circumstances of alarm, had sunk deep in the mind of madame, but she saw the necessity of confining to her own breast doubts which time only could resolve.

Julia endeavoured to reconcile herself to the change, and a circumstance soon occurred which obliterated her present sensations, and excited others far more interesting. One day that she was arranging some papers in the small drawers of a cabinet that stood in her apartment, she found a picture which fixed all her attention. It was a miniature of a lady, whose countenance was touched with sorrow, and expressed an air of dignified resignation. The mournful sweetness of her eyes, raised towards Heaven with a look of supplication, and the melancholy languor that shaded her features, so deeply affected Julia, that her eyes were filled with involuntary tears. She sighed and wept, still gazing on the picture, which seemed to engage her by a kind of fascination. She almost fancied that the portrait breathed, and that the eyes were fixed on hers with a look of penetrating softness. Full of the emotions which the miniature had excited, she presented it to madame, whose mingled sorrow and surprise increased her curiosity. But what were the various sensations which pressed upon her heart, on learning that she had wept over the resemblance of her mother! Deprived of a mother's tenderness before she was sensible of its value, it was now only that she mourned the event which lamentation could not recall. Emilia, with an emotion as exquisite, mingled her tears with those of her sister. With eager impatience they pressed madame to disclose the cause of that sorrow which so emphatically marked the features of their mother.

'Alas! my dear children,' said madame, deeply sighing, 'you engage me in a task too severe, not only for your peace, but for mine; since in giving you the information you require, I must retrace scenes of my own life, which I wish for ever obliterated. It would, however, be both cruel and unjust to withhold an explanation so nearly interesting to you, and I will sacrifice my own ease to your wishes.

'Louisa de Bernini, your mother, was, as you well know, the only daughter of the Count de Bernini. Of the misfortunes of your family, I believe you are yet ignorant. The chief estates of the count were situated in the *Val di Demona*, a valley deriving its name from its vicinity to Mount Ætna, which vulgar tradition has peopled with devils. In one of those dreadful eruptions of Ætna, which deluged this valley with a flood of fire, a great part of your grandfather's domains in that quarter were laid waste. The count was at that time with a part of his family at Messina, but the countess and her son, who were in the country, were destroyed. The remaining property of the count was proportionably inconsiderable, and the loss of his wife and son deeply affected him. He retired with Louisa, his only surviving child, who was then near fifteen, to a small estate near Cattania. There was some degree of relationship between your grandfather and myself; and your mother was attached to me by the ties of sentiment, which, as we grew up, united us still more strongly than those of blood. Our pleasures and our tastes were the same; and a similarity of misfortunes might, perhaps, contribute to cement our early friendship. I, like herself, had lost a parent in the eruption of Ætna. My mother had died before I understood her value; but my father, whom I revered and tenderly loved, was destroyed by one of those terrible events; his lands were buried beneath the lava, and he left an only son and myself to mourn his fate, and encounter the evils of poverty. The count, who was our nearest surviving relation, generously took us home to his house, and declared that he considered us as his children. To amuse his leisure hours, he undertook to finish the education of my brother, who was then about seventeen, and whose rising genius promised to reward the labours of the count. Louisa and myself often shared the instruction of her father, and at those hours Orlando* was generally of the party. The tranquil retirement of the count's situation, the rational employment of his time between his own studies, the education of those whom he called his children, and the conversation of a few select friends, anticipated the effect of time, and softened the asperities of his distress into a tender complacent melancholy. As for Louisa and myself, who were yet new in life, and whose spirits possessed the happy elasticity of youth, our minds gradually shifted from suffering to tranquillity, and from tranquillity to happiness. I have sometimes thought that when my brother has been reading to her a delightful passage, the countenance of Louisa discovered a tender interest, which seemed to be excited rather by the reader than by the author. These days, which were surely the most enviable of our lives, now passed in serene enjoyments, and in continual gradations of improvement.

'The count designed my brother for the army, and the time now drew nigh when he was to join the Sicilian regiment, in which he had a commission. The absent thoughts, and dejected spirits of my cousin, now discovered to me the secret which had long been concealed even from herself; for it was not till Orlando was about to depart, that she perceived how dear he was to her peace. On the eve of his departure, the count lamented, with fatherly yet manly tenderness, the distance which was soon to separate us. "But we shall meet again," said he, "when the honors of war shall have rewarded the bravery of my son." Louisa grew pale, a half suppressed sigh escaped her, and, to conceal her emotion, she turned to her harpsichord.

'My brother had a favorite dog, which, before he set off, he presented to Louisa, and committing it to her care, begged she would be kind to it, and sometimes remember its master. He checked his rising emotion, but as he turned from her, I perceived the tear that wetted his cheek. He departed, and with him the spirit of our happiness seemed to evaporate. The scenes which his presence had formerly enlivened, were now forlorn and melancholy, yet we loved to wander in what were once his favorite haunts. Louisa forbore to mention my brother even to me, but frequently, when she thought herself unobserved, she would steal to her harpsichord, and repeat the strain which she had played on the evening before his departure.

'We had the pleasure to hear from time to time that he was well: and though his own modesty threw a veil over his conduct, we could collect from other accounts that he had behaved with great bravery. At length the time of his return approached, and the enlivened spirits of Louisa declared the influence he retained in her heart. He returned, bearing public testimony of his valour in the honors which had been conferred upon him. He was received with universal joy; the count welcomed him with the pride and fondness of a father, and the villa became again the seat of happiness. His person and manners were much improved; the elegant beauty of the youth was now exchanged for the graceful dignity of manhood, and some knowledge of the world was added to that of the sciences. The joy which illumined his countenance when he met Louisa, spoke at once his admiration and his love; and the blush which her observation of it brought upon her cheek, would have discovered, even to an uninterested spectator, that this joy was mutual.

'Orlando brought with him a young Frenchman, a brother officer, who had rescued him from imminent danger in battle, and whom he introduced to the count as his preserver. The count received him with gratitude and distinction, and he was for a considerable time an inmate at the villa. His manners were singularly pleasing, and his understanding was cultivated and refined. He soon discovered a partiality for me, and he was indeed too pleasing to be seen with indifference. Gratitude for the valuable life he had preserved, was perhaps the groundwork of an esteem which soon increased into the most affectionate love. Our attachment grew stronger as our acquaintance increased; and at length the chevalier de Menon asked me of the count, who consulted my heart, and finding it favorable to the connection, proceeded to make the necessary enquiries concerning the family of the stranger. He obtained a satisfactory and pleasing account of it. The chevalier was the second son of a French gentleman of large estates in France, who had been some years deceased. He had left several sons; the family-estate, of course, devolved to the eldest, but to the two younger he had bequeathed considerable property. Our marriage was solemnized in a private manner at the villa, in the presence of the count, Louisa, and my brother. Soon after the nuptials, my husband and Orlando were remanded to their regiments. My brother's affections were now unalterably fixed upon Louisa, but a sentiment of delicacy and generosity still kept him silent. He thought, poor as·he was, to solicit the hand of Louisa, would be to repay the kindness of the count with ingratitude. I have seen the inward struggles of his heart, and mine has bled for him. The count and Louisa so earnestly solicited me to remain at the villa during the campaign, that at length my husband consented. We parted—O! let me forget that period!—Had I accompanied him, all might have been well; and the long, long years of affliction which followed had been spared me.'

The horn now sounded the signal for dinner, and interrupted the narrative of Madame. Her beauteous auditors wiped the tears from their eyes, and with extreme reluctance

descended to the hall. The day was occupied with company
and diversions, and it was not till late in the evening that
they were suffered to retire. They hastened to madame
immediately upon their being released; and too much interested for sleep, and too importunate to be repulsed, solicited
the sequel of her story. She objected the lateness of the
hour, but at length yielded to their entreaties. They drew
their chairs close to hers; and every sense being absorbed
in the single one of hearing, followed her through the course
of her narrative.

'My brother again departed without disclosing his sentiments; the effort it cost him was evident, but his sense of
honor surmounted every opposing consideration. Louisa
again drooped, and pined in silent sorrow. I lamented
equally for my friend and my brother; and have a thousand
times accused that delicacy as false, which withheld them
from the happiness they might so easily and so innocently
have obtained. The behaviour of the count, at least to my
eye, seemed to indicate the satisfaction which this union
would have given him. It was about this period that the
marquis Mazzini first saw and became enamoured of Louisa.
His proposals were very flattering, but the count forbore to
exert the undue authority of a father; and he ceased to press
the connection, when he perceived that Louisa was really
averse to it. Louisa was sensible of the generosity of his
conduct, and she could scarcely reject the alliance without
a sigh, which her gratitude paid to the kindness of her
father.

'But an event now happened which dissolved at once our
happiness, and all our air-drawn schemes for futurity. A
dispute, which it seems originated in a trifle, but soon
increased to a serious degree, arose between the *Chevalier
de Menon* and my brother. It was decided by the sword, and
my dear brother fell by the hand of my husband. I shall
pass over this period of my life. It is too painful for
recollection. The effect of this event upon Louisa was such
as may be imagined. The world was now become indifferent
to her, and as she had no prospect of happiness for herself,

she was unwilling to withhold it from the father who had deserved so much of her. After some time, when the marquis renewed his addresses, she gave him her hand. The characters of the marquis and his lady were in their nature too opposite to form a happy union. Of this Louisa was very soon sensible; and though the mildness of her disposition made her tamely submit to the unfeeling authority of her husband, his behaviour sunk deep in her heart, and she pined in secret. It was impossible for her to avoid opposing the character of the marquis to that of him upon whom her affections had been so fondly and so justly fixed. The comparison increased her sufferings, which soon preyed upon her constitution, and very visibly affected her health. Her situation deeply afflicted the count, and united with the infirmities of age to shorten his life.

'Upon his death, I bade adieu to my cousin, and quitted Sicily for Italy, where the Chevalier de Menon had for some time expected me. Our meeting was very affecting. My resentment towards him was done away, when I observed his pale and altered countenance, and perceived the melancholy which preyed upon his heart. All the airy vivacity of his former manner was fled, and he was devoured by unavailing grief and remorse. He deplored with unceasing sorrow the friend he had murdered, and my presence seemed to open afresh the wounds which time had begun to close. His affliction, united with my own, was almost more than I could support, but I was doomed to suffer, and endure yet more. In a subsequent engagement my husband, weary of existence, rushed into the heat of battle, and there obtained an honorable death. In a paper which he left behind him, he said it was his intention to die in that battle; that he had long wished for death, and waited for an opportunity of obtaining it without staining his own character by the cowardice of suicide, or distressing me by an act of butchery. This event gave the finishing stroke to my afflictions;—yet let me retract;—another misfortune awaited me when I least expected one. The *Chevalier de Menon* died without a will, and his brothers refused to give up his estate, unless I could produce a witness of my marriage. I returned to Sicily, and, to my inexpressible sorrow, found that your mother had died during my stay abroad, a prey, I fear, to grief. The priest who performed the ceremony of my marriage, having been threatened with punishment for some ecclesiastical offences, had secretly left the country; and thus was I deprived of those proofs which were necessary to authenticate my claims to the estates of my husband. His brothers, to whom I was an utter stranger, were either too prejudiced to believe, or believing, were too dishonorable to acknowledge the justice of my claims. I was therefore at once abandoned to sorrow and to poverty; a small legacy from the count de Bernini being all that now remained to me.

'When the marquis married Maria de Vellorno, which was about this period, he designed to quit Mazzini for Naples. His son was to accompany him, but it was his intention to leave you, who were both very young, to the care of some person qualified to superintend your education. My circumstances rendered the office acceptable, and my former friendship for your mother made the duty pleasing to me. The marquis was, I believe, glad to be spared the trouble of searching further for what he had hitherto found it difficult to obtain—a person whom inclination as well as duty would bind to his interest.'

Madame ceased to speak, and Emilia and Julia wept to the memory of the mother, whose misfortunes this story recorded. The sufferings of madame, together with her former friendship for the late marchioness, endeared her to her pupils, who from this period endeavoured by every kind and delicate attention to obliterate the traces of her sorrows. Madame was sensible of this tenderness, and it was productive in some degree of the effect desired. But a subject soon after occurred, which drew off their minds from the consideration of their mother's fate to a subject more wonderful and equally interesting.

One night that Emilia and Julia had been detained by company, in ceremonial restraint, later than usual, they were induced, by the easy conversation of madame, and by the pleasure which a return to liberty naturally produces, to defer the hour of repose till the night was far advanced. They were engaged in interesting discourse, when madame, who was then speaking, was interrupted by a low hollow sound, which arose from beneath the apartment, and seemed like the closing of a door. Chilled into a silence, they listened and distinctly heard it repeated. Deadly ideas crowded upon their imaginations, and inspired a terror which scarcely allowed them to breathe. The noise lasted only for a moment, and a profound silence soon ensued. Their feelings at length relaxed, and suffered them to move to Emilia's apartment, when again they heard the same sounds. Almost distracted with fear, they rushed into madame's apartment, where Emilia sunk upon the bed and fainted. It was a considerable time ere the efforts of madame recalled her to sensation. When they were again tranquil, she employed all her endeavours to compose the spirits of the young ladies, and dissuade them from alarming the castle. Involved in dark and fearful doubts, she yet commanded her feelings, and endeavoured to assume an appearance of composure. The late behaviour of the marquis had convinced her that he was nearly connected with the mystery which hung over this part of the edifice; and she dreaded to excite his resentment by a further mention of alarms, which were perhaps only ideal, and whose reality she had certainly no means of proving.

Influenced by these considerations, she endeavoured to prevail on Emilia and Julia to await in silence some confirmation of their surmises; but their terror made this a very difficult task. They acquiesced, however, so far with her wishes, as to agree to conceal the preceding circumstances from every person but their brother, without whose protecting presence they declared it utterly impossible to pass another night in the apartments. For the remainder of this night they resolved to watch. To beguile the tediousness of the time they endeavoured to converse, but the minds of Emilia and Julia were too much affected by the late occurrence to wander from the subject. They compared this with the foregoing circumstance of the figure and the light which had appeared; their imaginations kindled wild conjectures, and they submitted their opinions to madame, entreating her to inform them sincerely, whether she believed that disembodied spirits were ever permitted to visit this earth.

'My children,' said she, 'I will not attempt to persuade you that the existence of such spirits is impossible. Who shall say that any thing is impossible to God? We know that he has made us, who are embodied spirits; he, therefore, can make unembodied spirits.* If we cannot understand how such spirits exist, we should consider the limited powers of our minds, and that we cannot understand many things which are indisputably true. No one yet knows why the magnetic needle points to the north; yet you, who have never seen a magnet, do not hesitate to believe that it has this tendency, because you have been well assured of it, both from books and in conversation. Since, therefore, we are sure that nothing is impossible to God, and that such beings *may* exist, though we cannot tell how, we ought to consider by what evidence their existence is supported. I do not say that spirits *have* appeared; but if several discreet unprejudiced persons were to assure me that they had seen one, I should not be proud or bold enough to reply—'it is impossible.' Let not, however, such considerations disturb your minds. I have said thus much, because I was unwilling to impose upon your understandings; it is now your part to exercise your reason, and preserve the unmoved confidence of virtue. Such spirits, if indeed they have ever been seen, can have appeared only by the express permission of God, and for some very singular purposes; be assured that there are no beings who act unseen by him; and that, therefore, there are none from whom innocence can ever suffer harm.'

No further sounds disturbed them for that time; and before the morning dawned, weariness insensibly overcame apprehension, and sunk them in repose.

When Ferdinand learned the circumstances relative to the southern side of the castle, his imagination seized with avidity each appearance of mystery, and inspired him with an irresistible desire to penetrate the secrets of his desolate part of the fabric. He very readily consented to watch with his sisters in Julia's apartment; but as his chamber was in a remote part of the castle, there would be some difficulty in passing unobserved to her's. It was agreed, however, that when all was hushed, he should make the attempt. Having thus resolved, Emilia and Julia waited the return of night with restless and fearful impatience.

At length the family retired to rest. The castle clock had struck one, and Julia began to fear that Ferdinand had been discovered, when a knocking was heard at the door of the outer chamber.

Her heart beat with apprehensions, which reason could not justify. Madame rose, and enquiring who was there, was answered by the voice of Ferdinand. The door was cheerfully opened. They drew their chairs round him, and endeavoured to pass the time in conversation; but fear and expectation attracted all their thoughts to one subject, and madame alone preserved her composure. The hour was now come when the sounds had been heard the preceding night, and every ear was given to attention. All, however, remained quiet, and the night passed without any new alarm.

The greater part of several succeeding nights were spent in watching, but no sounds disturbed their silence. Ferdinand, in whose mind the late circumstances had excited a degree of astonishment and curiosity superior to common obstacles, determined, if possible, to gain admittance to those recesses of the castle, which had for so many years been hid from human eye. This, however, was a design which he saw little probability of accomplishing, for the keys of that part of the edifice were in the possession of the marquis, of whose late conduct he judged too well to believe he would suffer the apartments to be explored. He racked his invention for the means of getting access to them, and at length recollected that Julia's chamber formed a part of these buildings, it occurred to him, that according to the mode of building in old times, there might formerly have been a communication between them. This consideration suggested to him the possibility of a concealed door in her apartment, and he determined to survey it on the following night with great care.

CHAPTER III

THE castle was buried in sleep when Ferdinand again joined his sisters in madame's apartment. With anxious curiosity they followed him to the chamber. The room was hung with tapestry. Ferdinand carefully sounded the wall which communicated with the southern buildings. From one part of it a sound was returned, which convinced him there was something less solid than stone. He removed the tapestry, and behind it appeared, to his inexpressible satisfaction, a small door. With a hand trembling through eagerness, he undrew the bolts, and was rushing forward, when he perceived that a lock withheld his passage. The keys of madame and his sisters were applied in vain, and he was compelled to submit to disappointment at the very moment when he congratulated himself on success, for he had with him no means of forcing the door.

He stood gazing on the door, and inwardly lamenting, when a low hollow sound was heard from beneath. Emilia and Julia seized his arm; and almost sinking with apprehension, listened in profound silence. A footstep was distinctly heard, as if passing through the apartment below, after which all was still. Ferdinand, fired by this confirmation of the late report, rushed on to the door, and again tried to burst his way, but it resisted all the efforts of his strength. The ladies now rejoiced in that circumstance which they so lately lamented; for the sounds had renewed their terror, and though the night passed without further disturbance, their fears were very little abated.

Ferdinand, whose mind was wholly occupied with wonder, could with difficulty await the return of night. Emilia and Julia were scarcely less impatient. They counted the minutes as they passed; and when the family retired to rest, hastened with palpitating hearts to the apartment of madame. They were soon after joined by Ferdinand, who brought with him tools for cutting away the lock of the door. They paused a few moments in the chamber in fearful silence, but no sound disturbed the stillness of night. Ferdinand applied a knife to the door, and in a short time separated the lock. The door yielded, and disclosed a large and gloomy gallery. He took a light. Emilia and Julia, fearful of remaining in the chamber, resolved to accompany him, and each seizing an arm of madame, they followed in silence. The gallery was in many parts falling to decay, the ceiling was broke, and the window-shutters shattered, which, together with the dampness of the walls, gave the place an air of wild desolation.

They passed lightly on, for their steps ran in whispering echoes through the gallery, and often did Julia cast a fearful glance around.

The gallery terminated in a large old stair-case, which led to a hall below; on the left appeared several doors which seemed to lead to separate apartments. While they hesitated which course to pursue, a light flashed faintly up the stair-case, and in a moment after passed away; at the same time was heard the sound of a distant footstep. Ferdinand drew his sword and sprang forward; his companions, screaming with terror, ran back to madame's apartment.

Ferdinand descended a large vaulted hall; he crossed it towards a low arched door, which was left half open, and through which streamed a ray of light. The door opened upon a narrow winding passage; he entered, and the light retiring, was quickly lost in the windings of the place. Still he went on. The passage grew narrower, and the frequent fragments of loose stone made it now difficult to proceed. A low door closed the avenue, resembling that by which he had entered. He opened it, and discovered a square room, from whence rose a winding stair-case, which led up the south tower of the castle. Ferdinand paused to listen; the sound of steps was ceased, and all was profoundly silent. A door on the right attracted his notice; he tried to open it, but it was fastened. He concluded, therefore, that the person, if indeed a human being it was that bore the light he had seen, had passed up the tower. After a momentary hesitation, he determined to ascend the stair-case, but its ruinous condition made this an adventure of some difficulty. The steps were decayed and broken, and the looseness of the stones rendered a footing very insecure. Impelled by an irresistible curiosity, he was undismayed, and began the ascent. He had not proceeded very far, when the stones of a step which his foot had just quitted, loosened by his weight, gave way; and dragging with them those adjoining, formed a chasm in the stair-case that terrified even Ferdinand, who was left tottering on the suspended half of the steps, in momentary expectation of falling to the bottom with the stone on which he rested. In the terror which this occasioned, he attempted to save himself by catching at a kind of beam which projected over the stairs, when the lamp dropped from his hand, and he was left in total darkness. Terror now usurped the place of every other interest, and he was utterly perplexed how to proceed. He feared to go on, lest the steps above, as infirm as those below, should yield to his weight;—to return was impracticable, for the darkness precluded the possibility of discovering a means. He determined, therefore, to remain in this situation till light should dawn through the narrow grates in the walls, and enable him to contrive some method of letting himself down to the ground.

He had remained here above an hour, when he suddenly heard a voice from below. It seemed to come from the passage leading to the tower, and perceptibly drew nearer. His agitation was now extreme, for he had no power of defending himself, and while he remained in this state of torturing expectation, a blaze of light burst upon the stair-case beneath him. In the succeeding moment he heard his own name sounded from below. His apprehensions instantly vanished, for he distinguished the voices of madame and his sisters.

They had awaited his return in all the horrors of apprehension, till at length all fear for themselves was lost in their concern for him; and they, who so lately had not dared to enter this part of the edifice, now undauntedly searched it in quest of Ferdinand. What were their emotions when they discovered his perilous situation!

The light now enabled him to take a more accurate survey of the place. He perceived that some few stones of the steps which had fallen still remained attached to the wall, but he feared to trust to their support only. He observed, however, that the wall itself was partly decayed, and consequently rugged with the corners of half-worn stones. On these small projections he contrived, with the assistance of the steps already mentioned, to suspend himself, and at length gained the unbroken part of the stairs in safety. It is difficult to determine which individual of the party rejoiced most at this escape. The morning now dawned, and Ferdinand desisted for the present from farther enquiry.

The interest which these mysterious circumstances excited in the mind of Julia, had withdrawn her attention from a subject more dangerous to its peace. The image of Vereza, notwithstanding, would frequently intrude upon her fancy; and, awakening the recollection of happy emotions, would call forth a sigh which all her efforts could not suppress. She loved to indulge the melancholy of her heart in the solitude of the woods. One evening she took her lute to a favorite spot on the seashore, and resigning herself to a pleasing sadness, touched some sweet and plaintive airs. The purple flush of evening was diffused over the heavens. The sun, involved in clouds of splendid and innumerable hues, was setting o'er the distant waters, whose clear bosom glowed with rich reflection. The beauty of the scene, the soothing murmur of the high trees, waved by the light air which overshadowed her, and the soft shelling of the waves that flowed gently in upon the shores, insensibly sunk her mind into a state of repose.* She touched the chords of her lute in sweet and wild melody, and sung the following ode:

EVENING*

Evening veil'd in dewy shades,
  Slowly sinks upon the main;

See th'empurpled glory fades,
  Beneath her sober, chasten'd reign.

Around her car* the pensive Hours,
  In sweet illapses* meet the sight,
Crown'd their brows with closing flow'rs
  Rich with chrystal dews of night.

Her hands, the dusky hues arrange
  O'er the fine tints of parting day;
Insensibly the colours change,
  And languish into soft decay.

Wide o'er the waves her shadowy veil she draws.
  As faint they die along the distant shores;
Through the still air I mark each solemn pause,
  Each rising murmur which the wild wave pours.

A browner shadow spreads upon the air,
  And o'er the scene a pensive grandeur throws;
The rocks—the woods a wilder beauty wear,
  And the deep wave in softer music flows;

And now the distant view where vision fails,
  Twilight and grey obscurity pervade;
Tint following tint each dark'ning object veils,
  Till all the landscape sinks into the shade.

Oft from the airy steep of some lone hill,
  While sleeps the scene beneath the purple glow:
And evening lives o'er all serene and still,
  Wrapt let me view the magic world below!

And catch the dying gale that swells remote,
  That steals the sweetness from the shepherd's flute:
The distant torrent's melancholy note
  And the soft warblings of the lover's lute.

Still through the deep'ning gloom of bow'ry shades
  To Fancy's eye fantastic forms appear;
Low whisp'ring echoes steal along the glades
  And thrill the ear with wildly-pleasing fear.

Parent of shades!—of silence!—dewy airs!
  Of solemn musing, and of vision wild!
To thee my soul her pensive tribute bears,
  And hails thy gradual step, thy influence mild.

Having ceased to sing, her fingers wandered over the lute in melancholy symphony, and for some moments she remained lost in the sweet sensations which the music and the scenery had inspired. She was awakened from her reverie, by a sigh that stole from among the trees, and directing her eyes whence it came, beheld—Hippolitus! A thousand sweet and mingled emotions pressed upon her heart, yet she scarcely dared to trust the evidence of sight. He advanced, and throwing himself at her feet: 'Suffer me,' said he, in a tremulous voice, 'to disclose to you the sentiments which you have inspired, and to offer you the effusions of a heart filled only with love and admiration.' 'Rise, my lord,' said Julia, moving from her seat with an air of dignity, 'that attitude is neither becoming you to use, or me to suffer. The evening is closing, and Ferdinand will be impatient to see you.'

'Never will I rise, madam,' replied the count, with an impassioned air, 'till'—He was interrupted by the marchioness, who at this moment entered the grove. On observing the position of the count she was retiring. 'Stay, madam,' said Julia, almost sinking under her confusion. 'By no means,' replied the marchioness, in a tone of irony, 'my presence would only interrupt a very agreeable scene. The count, I see, is willing to pay you his earliest respects.' Saying this she disappeared, leaving Julia distressed and offended, and the count provoked at the intrusion. He attempted to renew the subject, but Julia hastily followed the steps of the marchioness, and entered the castle.

The scene she had witnessed, raised in the marchioness a tumult of dreadful emotions. Love, hatred, and jealousy, raged by turns in her heart, and defied all power of controul. Subjected to their alternate violence, she experienced a misery more acute than any she had yet known. Her imagination, invigorated by opposition, heightened to her the graces of Hippolitus; her bosom glowed with more intense passion, and her brain was at length exasperated almost to madness.

In Julia this sudden and unexpected interview excited a mingled emotion of love and vexation, which did not soon subside. At length, however, the delightful consciousness of Vereza's love bore her high above every other sensation; again the scene more brightly glowed, and again her fancy overcame the possibility of evil.

During the evening a tender and timid respect distinguished the behaviour of the count towards Julia, who, contented with the certainty of being loved, resolved to conceal her sentiments till an explanation of his abrupt departure from Mazzini, and subsequent absence, should have dissipated the shadow of mystery which hung over this part of his conduct. She observed that the marchioness pursued her with steady and constant observation, and she carefully avoided affording the count an opportunity of renewing the subject of the preceding interview, which, whenever he approached her, seemed to tremble on his lips.

Night returned, and Ferdinand repaired to the chamber of Julia to pursue his enquiry. Here he had not long remained, when the strange and alarming sounds which had been heard on the preceding night were repeated. The circumstance that now sunk in terror the minds of Emilia and Julia, fired with new wonder that of Ferdinand, who seizing a light, darted through the discovered door, and almost instantly disappeared.

He descended into the same wild hall he had passed on the preceding night. He had scarcely reached the bottom of the stair-case, when a feeble light gleamed across the hall, and his eye caught the glimpse of a figure retiring through the low arched door which led to the south tower. He drew his sword and rushed on. A faint sound died away along the passage, the windings of which prevented his seeing the figure he pursued. Of this, indeed, he had obtained so slight a view, that he scarcely knew whether it bore the impression of a human form. The light quickly disappeared, and he heard the door that opened upon the tower suddenly close. He reached it, and forcing it open, sprang forward; but the place was dark and solitary, and there was no appearance of any person having passed along it. He looked up the tower, and the chasm which the stair-case exhibited, convinced him that no human being could have passed up. He stood silent and amazed; examining the place with an eye of strict enquiry, he perceived a door, which was partly concealed by hanging stairs, and which till now had escaped his notice. Hope invigorated curiosity, but his expectation was quickly disappointed, for this door also was fastened. He tried in vain to force it. He knocked, and a hollow sullen sound ran in echoes through the place, and died away at a distance. It was evident that beyond this door were chambers of considerable extent, but after long and various attempts to reach them, he was obliged to desist, and he quitted the tower as ignorant and more dissatisfied than he had entered it. He returned to the hall, which he now for the first time deliberately surveyed. It was a spacious and desolate apartment, whose lofty roof rose into arches supported by pillars of black marble. The same substance inlaid the floor, and formed the stair-case. The windows were high and gothic. An air of proud sublimity,* united with singular wildness, characterized the place, at the extremity of which arose several gothic arches, whose dark shade veiled in obscurity the extent beyond. On the left hand appeared two doors, each of which was fastened, and on the right the grand entrance from the courts. Ferdinand determined to explore the dark recess which terminated his view, and as he traversed the hall, his imagination, affected by the surrounding scene, often multiplied the echoes of his footsteps into uncertain sounds of strange and fearful import.

He reached the arches, and discovered beyond a kind of inner hall, of considerable extent, which was closed at the farther end by a pair of massy folding-doors, heavily ornamented with carving. They were fastened by a lock, and defied his utmost strength.

As he surveyed the place in silent wonder, a sullen groan arose from beneath the spot where he stood. His blood ran cold at the sound, but silence returning, and continuing unbroken, he attributed his alarm to the illusion of a fancy, which terror had impregnated. He made another effort to force the door, when a groan was repeated more hollow, and more dreadful than the first. At this moment all his courage forsook him; he quitted the door, and hastened to the stair-case, which he ascended almost breathless with terror.

He found Madame de Menon and his sisters awaiting his return in the most painful anxiety; and, thus disappointed in all his endeavours to penetrate the secret of these buildings, and fatigued with fruitless search, he resolved to suspend farther enquiry.

When he related the circumstances of his late adventure, the terror of Emilia and Julia was heightened to a degree that overcame every prudent consideration. Their apprehension of the marquis's displeasure was lost in a stronger feeling, and they resolved no longer to remain in apartments which offered only terrific images to their fancy. Madame de Menon almost equally alarmed, and more perplexed, by this combination of strange and unaccountable circumstances, ceased to oppose their design. It was resolved, therefore, that on the following day madame should acquaint the marchioness with such particulars of the late occurrence as their purpose made it necessary she should know, concealing their knowledge of the hidden door, and the incidents immediately dependant on it; and that madame should entreat a change of apartments.

Madame accordingly waited on the marchioness. The marchioness having listened to the account at first with surprise, and afterwards with indifference, condescended to reprove madame for encouraging superstitious belief in the minds of her young charge. She concluded with ridiculing as fanciful the circumstances related, and with refusing, on account of the numerous visitants at the castle, the request preferred to her.

It is true the castle was crowded with visitors; the former apartments of Madame de Menon were the only ones unoccupied, and these were in magnificent preparation for the pleasure of the marchioness, who was unaccustomed to sacrifice her own wishes to the comfort of those around her. She therefore treated lightly the subject, which, seriously attended to, would have endangered her new plan of delight.

But Emilia and Julia were too seriously terrified to obey the scruples of delicacy, or to be easily repulsed. They prevailed on Ferdinand to represent their situation to the marquis.

Meanwhile Hippolitus, who had passed the night in a state of sleepless anxiety, watched, with busy impatience, an opportunity of more fully disclosing to Julia the passion which glowed in his heart. The first moment in which he beheld her, had awakened in him an admiration which had since ripened into a sentiment more tender. He had been prevented formally declaring his passion by the circumstance which so suddenly called him to Naples. This was the dangerous illness of the Marquis de Lomelli, his near and much-valued relation. But it was a task too painful to depart in silence, and he contrived to inform Julia of his sentiments in the air which she heard so sweetly sung beneath her window.

When Hippolitus reached Naples, the marquis was yet living, but expired a few days after his arrival, leaving the count heir to the small possessions which remained from the extravagance of their ancestors.

The business of adjusting his rights had till now detained him from Sicily, whither he came for the sole purpose of declaring his love. Here unexpected obstacles awaited him. The jealous vigilance of the marchioness conspired with the delicacy of Julia, to withhold from him the opportunity he so anxiously sought.

When Ferdinand entered upon the subject of the southern buildings to the marquis, he carefully avoided mentioning the hidden door. The marquis listened for some time to the relation in gloomy silence, but at length assuming an air of displeasure, reprehended Ferdinand for yielding his confidence to those idle alarms, which he said were the suggestions of a timid imagination. 'Alarms,' continued he, 'which will readily find admittance to the weak mind of a woman, but which the firmer nature of man should disdain.—Degenerate boy! Is it thus you reward my care? Do I live to see my son the sport of every idle tale a woman may repeat? Learn to trust reason and your senses, and you will then be worthy of my attention.'

The marquis was retiring, and Ferdinand now perceived it necessary to declare, that he had himself witnessed the sounds he mentioned. 'Pardon me, my lord,' said he, 'in the late instance I have been just to your command—my senses have been the only evidences I have trusted. I have heard those sounds which I cannot doubt.' The marquis appeared shocked. Ferdinand perceived the change, and urged the subject so vigorously, that the marquis, suddenly assuming a look of grave importance, commanded him to attend him in the evening in his closet.

Ferdinand in passing from the marquis met Hippolitus. He was pacing the gallery in much seeming agitation, but observing Ferdinand, he advanced to him. 'I am ill at heart,' said he, in a melancholy tone, 'assist me with your advice. We will step into this apartment, where we can converse without interruption.'

'You are not ignorant,' said he, throwing himself into a chair, 'of the tender sentiments which your sister Julia has inspired. I entreat you by that sacred friendship which has so long united us, to afford me an opportunity of pleading my passion. Her heart, which is so susceptible of other impressions, is, I fear, insensible to love. Procure me, however, the satisfaction of certainty upon a point where the tortures of suspence are surely the most intolerable.'

'Your penetration,' replied Ferdinand, 'has for once forsaken you, else you would now be spared the tortures of which you complain, for you would have discovered what I have long observed, that Julia regards you with a partial eye.'

'Do not,' said Hippolitus, 'make disappointment more terrible by flattery; neither suffer the partiality of friendship to mislead your judgment. Your perceptions are affected by the warmth of your feelings, and because you think I deserve her distinction, you believe I possess it. Alas! you deceive yourself, but not me!'

'The very reverse,' replied Ferdinand; 'tis you who deceive yourself, or rather it is the delicacy of the passion which animates you, and which will ever operate against your clear perception of a truth in which your happiness is so deeply involved. Believe me, I speak not without reason:—she loves you.'

At these words Hippolitus started from his seat, and clasping his hands in fervent joy, 'Enchanting sounds!' cried he, in a voice tenderly impassioned; '*could* I but believe ye!—could I *but* believe ye—this world were paradise!'

During this exclamation, the emotions of Julia, who sat in her closet adjoining, can with difficulty be imagined. A door which opened into it from the apartment where this conversation was held, was only half closed. Agitated with the pleasure this declaration excited, she yet trembled with apprehension lest she should be discovered. She hardly dared to breathe, much less to move across the closet to the door, which opened upon the gallery, whence she might probably have escaped unnoticed, lest the sound of her step should betray her. Compelled, therefore, to remain where she was, she sat in a state of fearful distress, which no colour of language can paint.

'Alas!' resumed Hippolitus, 'I too eagerly admit the possibility of what I wish. If you mean that I should really believe you, confirm your assertion by some proof.'—'Readily,' rejoined Ferdinand.

The heart of Julia beat quick.

'When you was so suddenly called to Naples upon the illness of the Marquis Lomelli, I marked her conduct well, and in that read the sentiments of her heart. On the following morning, I observed in her countenance a restless anxiety which I had never seen before. She watched the entrance of every person with an eager expectation, which was as often succeeded by evident disappointment. At dinner your departure was mentioned:—she spilt the wine she was carrying to her lips, and for the remainder of the day

was spiritless and melancholy. I saw her ineffectual struggles
to conceal the oppression at her heart. Since that time she
has seized every opportunity of withdrawing from company.
The gaiety with which she was so lately charmed—charmed
her no longer; she became pensive, retired, and I have often
heard her singing in some lonely spot, the most moving and
tender airs. Your return produced a visible and instantaneous alteration; she has now resumed her gaiety; and the
soft confusion of her countenance, whenever you approach,
might alone suffice to convince you of the truth of my
assertion.'

'O! talk for ever thus!' sighed Hippolitus. 'These words
are so sweet, so soothing to my soul, that I could listen till
I forgot I had a wish beyond them. Yes!—Ferdinand, these
circumstances are not to be doubted, and conviction opens
upon my mind a flow of extacy I never knew till now. O!
lead me to her, that I may speak the sentiments which swell
my heart.'

They arose, when Julia, who with difficulty had supported
herself, now impelled by an irresistible fear of instant
discovery, rose also, and moved softly towards the gallery.
The sound of her step alarmed the count, who, apprehensive
lest his conversation had been overheard, was anxious to be
satisfied whether any person was in the closet. He rushed
in, and discovered Julia! She caught at a chair to support
her trembling frame; and overwhelmed with mortifying
sensations, sunk into it, and hid her face in her robe.
Hippolitus threw himself at her feet, and seizing her hand,
pressed it to his lips in expressive silence. Some moments
passed before the confusion of either would suffer them to
speak. At length recovering his voice, 'Can you, madam,'
said he, 'forgive this intrusion, so unintentional? or will it
deprive me of that esteem which I have but lately ventured
to believe I possessed, and which I value more than existence
itself. O! speak my pardon! Let me not believe that a single
accident has destroyed my peace for ever.'—'If your peace,
sir, depends upon a knowledge of my esteem,' said Julia, in
a tremulous voice, 'that peace is already secure. If I wished

even to deny the partiality I feel, it would now be useless; and since I no longer wish this, it would also be painful.' Hippolitus could only weep his thanks over the hand he still held. 'Be sensible, however, of the delicacy of my situation,' continued she, rising, 'and suffer me to withdraw.' Saying this she quitted the closet, leaving Hippolitus overcome with this sweet confirmation of his wishes, and Ferdinand not yet recovered from the painful surprize which the discovery of Julia had excited. He was deeply sensible of the confusion he had occasioned her, and knew that apologies would not restore the composure he had so cruelly yet unwarily disturbed.

Ferdinand awaited the hour appointed by the marquis in impatient curiosity. The solemn air which the marquis assumed when he commanded him to attend, had deeply impressed his mind. As the time drew nigh, expectation increased, and every moment seemed to linger into hours. At length he repaired to the closet, where he did not remain long before the marquis entered. The same chilling solemnity marked his manner. He locked the door of the closet, and seating himself, addressed Ferdinand as follows:—

'I am now going to repose in you a confidence which will severely prove the strength of your honour. But before I disclose a secret, hitherto so carefully concealed, and now reluctantly told, you must swear to preserve on this subject an eternal silence. If you doubt the steadiness of your discretion—now declare it, and save yourself from the infamy, and the fatal consequences, which may attend a breach of your oath;—if, on the contrary, you believe yourself capable of a strict integrity—now accept the terms, and receive the secret I offer.' Ferdinand was awed by this exordium*—the impatience of curiosity was for a while suspended, and he hesitated whether he should receive the secret upon such terms. At length he signified his consent, and the marquis arising, drew his sword from the scabbard.—'Here,' said he, offering it to Ferdinand, 'seal your vows—swear by this sacred pledge of honor never to repeat what I shall now reveal.' Ferdinand vowed upon the sword, and raising his eyes to heaven, solemnly swore. The marquis then resumed his seat, and proceeded.

'You are now to learn that, about a century ago, this castle was in the possession of Vincent, third marquis of Mazzini, my grandfather. At that time there existed an inveterate hatred between our family and that of della Campo. I shall not now revert to the origin of the animosity, or relate the particulars of the consequent feuds—suffice it to observe, that by the power of our family, the della Campos were unable to preserve their former consequence in Sicily, and they have therefore quitted it for a foreign land to live in unmolested security. To return to my subject.—My grandfather, believing his life endangered by his enemy, planted spies upon him. He employed some of the numerous banditti who sought protection in his service,* and after some weeks past in waiting for an opportunity, they seized Henry della Campo, and brought him secretly to this castle. He was for some time confined in a close chamber of the southern buildings, where he expired; by what means I shall forbear to mention. The plan had been so well conducted, and the secrecy so strictly preserved, that every endeavour of his family to trace the means of his disappearance proved ineffectual. Their conjectures, if they fell upon our family, were supported by no proof; and the della Campos are to this day ignorant of the mode of his death. A rumour had prevailed long before the death of my father, that the southern buildings of the castle were haunted. I disbelieved the fact, and treated it accordingly. One night, when every human being of the castle, except myself, was retired to rest, I had such strong and dreadful proofs of the general assertion, that even at this moment I cannot recollect them without horror. Let me, if possible, forget them. From that moment I forsook those buildings; they have ever since been shut up, and the circumstance I have mentioned, is the true reason why I have resided so little at the castle.'

Ferdinand listened to this narrative in silent horror. He remembered the temerity with which he had dared to penetrate those apartments—the light, and figure he had seen— and, above all, his situation in the stair-case of the tower. Every nerve thrilled at the recollection; and the terrors of remembrance almost equalled those of reality.

The marquis permitted his daughters to change their apartments, but he commanded Ferdinand to tell them, that, in granting their request, he consulted their ease only, and was himself by no means convinced of its propriety. They were accordingly reinstated in their former chambers, and the great room only of madame's apartments was reserved for the marchioness, who expressed her discontent to the marquis in terms of mingled censure and lamentation. The marquis privately reproved his daughters, for what he termed the idle fancies of a weak mind; and desired them no more to disturb the peace of the castle with the subject of their late fears. They received this reproof with silent submission—too much pleased with the success of their suit to be susceptible of any emotion but joy.

Ferdinand, reflecting on the late discovery, was shocked to learn, what was now forced upon his belief, that he was the descendant of a murderer. He now knew that innocent blood had been shed in the castle, and that the walls were still the haunt of an unquiet spirit, which seemed to call aloud for retribution on the posterity of him who had disturbed its eternal rest. Hippolitus perceived his dejection, and entreated that he might participate his uneasiness; but Ferdinand, who had hitherto been frank and ingenuous, was now inflexibly reserved. 'Forbear,' said he, 'to urge a discovery of what I am not permitted to reveal; this is the only point upon which I conjure you to be silent, and this even to you, I cannot explain.' Hippolitus was surprized, but pressed the subject no farther.

Julia, though she had been extremely mortified by the circumstances attendant on the discovery of her sentiments to Hippolitus, experienced, after the first shock had subsided, an emotion more pleasing than painful. The late conversation had painted in strong colours the attachment of her lover. His diffidence—his slowness to perceive the effect of his merit—his succeeding rapture, when conviction was at length forced upon his mind; and his conduct upon discovering Julia, proved to her at once the delicacy and the strength of his passion, and she yielded her heart to sensations of pure and unmixed delight. She was roused from this state of visionary happiness, by a summons from the marquis to attend him in the library. A circumstance so unusual surprized her, and she obeyed with trembling curiosity. She found him pacing the room in deep thought, and she had shut the door before he perceived her. The authoritative severity in his countenance alarmed her, and prepared her for a subject of importance. He seated himself by her, and continued a moment silent. At length, steadily observing her, 'I sent for you, my child,' said he, 'to declare the honor which awaits you. The Duke de Luovo has solicited your hand. An alliance so splendid was beyond my expectation. You will receive the distinction with the gratitude it claims, and prepare for the celebration of the nuptials.'

This speech fell like the dart of death upon the heart of Julia. She sat motionless—stupified and deprived of the power of utterance. The marquis observed her consternation; and mistaking its cause, 'I acknowledge,' said he, 'that there is somewhat abrupt in this affair; but the joy occasioned by a distinction so unmerited on your part, ought to overcome the little feminine weakness you might otherwise indulge. Retire and compose yourself; and observe,' continued he, in a stern voice, 'this is no time for finesse.'* These words roused Julia from her state of horrid stupefaction. 'O! sir,' said she, throwing herself at his feet, 'forbear to enforce authority upon a point where to obey you would be worse than death; if, indeed, to obey you were possible.'—'Cease,' said the marquis, 'this affectation, and practice what becomes you.'—'Pardon me, my lord,' she replied, 'my distress is, alas! unfeigned. I cannot love the duke.'—'Away!' interrupted the marquis, 'nor tempt my rage with objections thus childish and absurd.'—'Yet hear me, my lord,' said Julia, tears swelling in her eyes, 'and pity the sufferings of a child, who never till this moment has dared to dispute your commands.'

'Nor shall she now,' said the marquis. 'What—when wealth, honor, and distinction, are laid at my feet, shall they be refused, because a foolish girl—a very baby, who knows not good from evil, cries, and says she cannot love! Let me not think of it—My just anger may, perhaps, out-run discretion, and tempt me to chastise your folly.—Attend to what I say—accept the duke, or quit this castle for ever, and wander where you will.' Saying this, he burst away, and Julia, who had hung weeping upon his knees, fell prostrate upon the floor. The violence of the fall completed the effect of her distress, and she fainted. In this state she remained a considerable time. When she recovered her senses, the recollection of her calamity burst upon her mind with a force that almost again overwhelmed her. She at length raised herself from the ground, and moved towards her own apartment, but had scarcely reached the great gallery, when Hippolitus entered it. Her trembling limbs would no longer support her; she caught at a bannister to save herself; and Hippolitus, with all his speed, was scarcely in time to prevent her falling. The pale distress exhibited in her countenance terrified him, and he anxiously enquired concerning it. She could answer him only with her tears, which she found it impossible to suppress; and gently disengaging herself, tottered to her closet. Hippolitus followed her to the door, but desisted from further importunity. He pressed her hand to his lips in tender silence, and withdrew, surprized and alarmed.

Julia, resigning herself to despair, indulged in solitude the excess of her grief. A calamity, so dreadful as the present, had never before presented itself to her imagination. The union proposed would have been hateful to her, even if she had no prior attachment; what then must have been her distress, when she had given her heart to him who deserved all her admiration, and returned all her affection.

The Duke de Luovo was of a character very similar to that of the marquis. The love of power was his ruling

passion;—with him no gentle or generous sentiment melior-
ated the harshness of authority, or directed it to acts of
beneficence. He delighted in simple undisguised tyranny.
He had been twice married, and the unfortunate women
subjected to his power, had fallen victims to the slow but
corroding hand of sorrow. He had one son, who some years
before had escaped the tyranny of his father, and had not
been since heard of. At the late festival the duke had seen
Julia; and her beauty made so strong an impression upon
him, that he had been induced now to solicit her hand. The
marquis, delighted with the prospect of a connection so
flattering to his favorite passion, readily granted his consent,
and immediately sealed it with a promise.

Julia remained for the rest of the day shut up in her
closet, where the tender efforts of Madame and Emilia were
exerted to soften her distress. Towards the close of evening
Ferdinand entered. Hippolitus, shocked at her absence, had
requested him to visit her, to alleviate her affliction, and,
if possible, to discover its cause. Ferdinand, who tenderly
loved his sister, was alarmed by the words of Hippolitus,
and immediately sought her. Her eyes were swelled with
weeping, and her countenance was but too expressive of the
state of her mind. Ferdinand's distress, when told of his
father's conduct, was scarcely less than her own. He had
pleased himself with the hope of uniting the sister of his
heart with the friend whom he loved. An act of cruel
authority now dissolved the fairy dream of happiness which
his fancy had formed, and destroyed the peace of those most
dear to him. He sat for a long time silent and dejected; at
length, starting from his melancholy reverie, he bad Julia
good-night, and returned to Hippolitus, who was waiting
for him with anxious impatience in the north hall.

Ferdinand dreaded the effect of that despair, which the
intelligence he had to communicate would produce in the
mind of Hippolitus. He revolved* some means of softening
the dreadful truth; but Hippolitus, quick to apprehend the
evil which love taught him to fear, seized at once upon the
reality. 'Tell me all,' said he, in a tone of assumed firmness.

'I am prepared for the worst.' Ferdinand related the decree of the marquis, and Hippolitus soon sunk into an excess of grief which defied, as much as it required, the powers of alleviation.

Julia, at length, retired to her chamber, but the sorrow which occupied her mind withheld the blessings of sleep. Distracted and restless she arose, and gently opened the window of her apartment. The night was still, and not a breath disturbed the surface of the waters. The moon shed a mild radiance over the waves, which in gentle undulations flowed upon the sands. The scene insensibly tranquilized her spirits. A tender and pleasing melancholy diffused itself over her mind; and as she mused, she heard the dashing of distant oars. Presently she perceived upon the light surface of the sea a small boat. The sound of the oars ceased, and a solemn strain of harmony (such as fancy wafts from the abodes of the blessed) stole upon the silence of night. A chorus of voices now swelled upon the air, and died away at a distance. In the strain Julia recollected the midnight hymn to the virgin, and holy enthusiasm filled her heart. The chorus was repeated, accompanied by a solemn striking of oars. A sigh of exstacy stole from her bosom. Silence returned. The divine melody she had heard calmed the tumult of her mind, and she sunk in sweet repose.

She arose in the morning refreshed by light slumbers; but the recollection of her sorrows soon returned with new force, and sickening faintness overcame her. In this situation she received a message from the marquis to attend him instantly. She obeyed, and he bade her prepare to receive the duke, who that morning purposed to visit the castle. He commanded her to attire herself richly, and to welcome him with smiles. Julia submitted in silence. She saw the marquis was inflexibly resolved, and she withdrew to indulge the anguish of her heart, and prepare for this detested interview.

The clock had struck twelve, when a flourish of trumpets announced the approach of the duke. The heart of Julia sunk at the sound, and she threw herself on a sopha,* overwhelmed with bitter sensations. Here she was soon disturbed by a message from the marquis. She arose, and tenderly embracing Emilia, their tears for some moments flowed together. At length, summoning all her fortitude, she descended to the hall, where she was met by the marquis. He led her to the saloon in which the duke sat, with whom having conversed a short time, he withdrew. The emotion of Julia at this instant was beyond any thing she had before suffered; but by a sudden and strange exertion of fortitude, which the force of desperate calamity sometimes affords us, but which inferior sorrow toils after in vain, she recovered her composure, and resumed her natural dignity. For a moment she wondered at herself, and she formed the dangerous resolution of throwing herself upon the generosity of the duke, by acknowledging her reluctance to the engagement, and soliciting him to withdraw his suit.

The duke approached her with an air of proud condescension; and taking her hand, placed himself beside her. Having paid some formal and general compliments to her beauty, he proceeded to profess himself her admirer. She listened for some time to his professions, and when he appeared willing to hear her, she addressed him—'I am justly sensible, my lord, of the distinction you offer me, and must lament that respectful gratitude is the only sentiment I can return. Nothing can more strongly prove my confidence in your generosity, than when I confess to you, that parental authority urges me to give my hand whither my heart cannot accompany it.'

She paused—the duke continued silent.—' 'Tis you only, my lord, who can release me from a situation so distressing; and to your goodness and justice I appeal, certain that necessity will excuse the singularity of my conduct, and that I shall not appeal in vain.'

The duke was embarrassed—a flush of pride overspread his countenance, and he seemed endeavouring to stifle the feelings that swelled his heart. 'I had been prepared, madam,' said he, 'to expect a very different reception, and had certainly no reason to believe that the Duke de Luovo was likely to sue in vain. Since, however, madam, you acknowledge that you have already disposed of your affections, I shall certainly be very willing, if the marquis will release me from our mutual engagements, to resign you to a more favored lover.'

'Pardon me, my lord,' said Julia, blushing, 'suffer me to'——'I am not easily deceived, madam,' interrupted the duke,—'your conduct can be attributed only to the influence of a prior attachment; and though for so young a lady, such a circumstance is somewhat extraordinary, I have certainly no right to arraign your choice. Permit me to wish you a good morning.' He bowed low, and quitted the room. Julia now experienced a new distress; she dreaded the resentment of the marquis, when he should be informed of her conversation with the duke, of whose character she now judged too justly not to repent the confidence she had reposed in him.

The duke, on quitting Julia, went to the marquis, with whom he remained in conversation some hours. When he had left the castle, the marquis sent for his daughter, and poured forth his resentment with all the violence of threats, and all the acrimony of contempt. So severely did he ridicule the idea of her disposing of her heart, and so dreadfully did he denounce vengeance on her disobedience, that she scarcely thought herself safe in his presence. She stood trembling and confused, and heard his reproaches without the power to reply. At length the marquis informed her, that the nuptials would be solemnized on the third day from the present; and as he quitted the room, a flood of tears came to her relief, and saved her from fainting.

Julia passed the remainder of the day in her closet with Emilia. Night returned, but brought her no peace. She sat long after the departure of Emilia; and to beguile recollection, she selected a favorite author, endeavouring to revive those sensations his page had once excited. She opened to a passage, the tender sorrow of which was applicable to her own situation, and her tears flowed wean.* Her grief was soon suspended by apprehension. Hitherto a deadly silence had reigned through the castle, interrupted only by the wind, whose low sound crept at intervals through the galleries. She now thought she heard a footstep near her door, but presently all was still, for she believed she had been deceived by the wind. The succeeding moment, however, convinced her of her error, for she distinguished the low whisperings of some persons in the gallery. Her spirits, already weakened by sorrow, deserted her: she was seized with an universal terror, and presently afterwards a low voice called her from without, and the door was opened by Ferdinand.

She shrieked, and fainted. On recovering, she found herself supported by Ferdinand and Hippolitus, who had stolen this moment of silence and security to gain admittance to her presence. Hippolitus came to urge a proposal which despair only could have suggested. 'Fly,' said he, 'from the authority of a father who abuses his power, and assert the liberty of choice, which nature assigned you. Let the desperate situation of my hopes plead excuse for the apparent boldness of this address, and let the man who exists but for you be the means of saving you from destruction. Alas! madam, you are silent, and perhaps I have forfeited, by this proposal, the confidence I so lately flattered myself I possessed. If so, I will submit to my fate in silence, and will to-morrow quit a scene which presents only images of distress to my mind.'

Julia could speak but with her tears. A variety of strong and contending emotions struggled at her breast, and suppressed the power of utterance. Ferdinand seconded the proposal of the count. 'It is unnecessary,' my sister, said he, 'to point out the misery which awaits you here. I love you too well tamely to suffer you to be sacrificed to ambition, and to a passion still more hateful. I now glory in calling Hippolitus my friend—let me ere long receive him as a brother. I can give no stronger testimony of my esteem for his character, than in the wish I now express. Believe me he has a heart worthy of your acceptance—a heart noble and expansive as your own.'—'Ah, cease,' said Julia, 'to dwell upon a character of whose worth I am fully sensible. Your kindness and his merit can never be forgotten by her whose misfortunes you have so generously suffered to interest you.' She paused in silent hesitation. A sense of delicacy made her hesitate upon the decision which her heart so warmly prompted. If she fled with Hippolitus, she would avoid one evil, and encounter another. She would escape the dreadful destiny awaiting her, but must, perhaps, sully the purity of that reputation, which was dearer to her than existence. In a mind like hers, exquisitely susceptible of the pride of honor, this fear was able to counteract every other consideration, and to keep her intentions in a state of painful suspense. She sighed deeply, and continued silent. Hippolitus was alarmed by the calm distress which her countenance exhibited. 'O! Julia,' said he, 'relieve me from this dreadful suspense!—speak to me—explain this silence.' She looked mournfully upon him—her lips moved, but no sounds were uttered. As he repeated his question, she waved her hand, and sunk back in her chair. She had not fainted, but continued some time in a state of stupor not less alarming. The importance of the present question, operating upon her mind, already harassed by distress, had produced a temporary suspension of reason. Hippolitus hung over her in an agony not to be described, and Ferdinand vainly repeated her name. At length uttering a deep sigh, she raised herself, and, like one awakened from a dream, gazed around her. Hippolitus thanked God fervently in his heart. 'Tell me but that you are well,' said he, 'and that I may dare to hope, and we will leave you to repose.'—'My sister,' said Ferdinand, 'consult only your own wishes, and leave the rest to me. Suffer a confidence in me to dissipate the doubts with which you are agitated.'—'Ferdinand,' said Julia, emphatically, 'how shall I express the gratitude your kindness has excited?'—'Your gratitude,' said he, 'will be best shown in consulting your own wishes; for be assured, that whatever procures your happiness, will most effectually establish mine. Do not suffer the prejudices of education to render you miserable. Believe me, that a choice which involves the happiness or misery of your whole life, ought to be decided only by yourself.'

'Let us forbear for the present,' said Hippolitus, 'to urge the subject. Repose is necessary for you,' addressing Julia, 'and I will not suffer a selfish consideration any longer to with-hold you from it.—Grant me but this request—that at this hour to-morrow night, I may return hither to receive my doom.' Julia having consented to receive Hippolitus and Ferdinand, they quitted the closet. In turning into the grand gallery, they were surprised by the appearance of a light, which gleamed upon the wall that terminated their view. It seemed to proceed from a door which opened upon a back stair-case. They pushed on, but it almost instantly disappeared, and upon the stair-case all was still. They then separated, and retired to their apartments, somewhat alarmed by this circumstance, which induced them to suspect that their visit to Julia had been observed.

Julia passed the night in broken slumbers, and anxious consideration. On her present decision hung the crisis of her fate. Her consciousness of the influence of Hippolitus over her heart, made her fear to indulge its predilection, by trusting to her own opinion of its fidelity. She shrunk from the disgraceful idea of an elopement; yet she saw no means of avoiding this, but by rushing upon the fate so dreadful to her imagination.

On the following night, when the inhabitants of the castle were retired to rest, Hippolitus, whose expectation had lengthened the hours into ages, accompanied by Ferdinand, revisited the closet. Julia, who had known no interval of rest since they last left her, received them with much agitation. The vivid glow of health had fled her cheek, and was succeeded by a languid delicacy, less beautiful, but more interesting. To the eager enquiries of Hippolitus, she returned no answer, but faintly smiling through her tears, presented him her hand, and covered her face with her robe. 'I receive it,' cried he, 'as the pledge of my happiness;— yet—yet let your voice ratify the gift.' 'If the present concession does not sink me in your esteem,' said Julia, in a low tone, 'this hand is yours.'— 'The concession, my love, (for by that tender name I may now call you) would, if possible, raise you in my esteem; but since that has been long incapable of addition, it can only heighten my opinion of myself, and increase my gratitude to you: gratitude which I will endeavour to shew by an anxious care of your happiness, and by the tender attentions of a whole life. From this blessed moment,' continued he, in a voice of rapture, 'permit me, in thought, to hail you as my wife. From this moment let me banish every vestige of sorrow;—let me dry those tears,' gently pressing her cheek with his lips, 'never to spring again.'—The gratitude and joy which Ferdinand expressed upon this occasion, united with the tenderness of Hippolitus to soothe the agitated spirits of Julia, and she gradually recovered her complacency.

They now arranged their plan of escape; in the execution of which, no time was to be lost, since the nuptials with the duke were to be solemnized on the day after the morrow. Their scheme, whatever it was that should be adopted, they, therefore, resolved to execute on the following night. But when they descended from the first warmth of enterprize, to minuter examination, they soon found the difficulties of the undertaking. The keys of the castle were kept by Robert, the confidential servant of the marquis, who every night deposited them in an iron chest in his chamber. To obtain them by stratagem seemed impossible, and Ferdinand feared to tamper with the honesty of this man, who had been many years in the service of the marquis. Dangerous as was the attempt, no other alternative appeared, and they were therefore compelled to rest all their hopes upon the experiment. It was settled, that if the keys could be procured, Ferdinand and Hippolitus should meet Julia in the closet; that they should convey her to the seashore, from whence a boat, which was to be kept in waiting, would carry them to the opposite coast of Calabria, where the marriage might be solemnized without danger of interruption. But, as it was necessary that Ferdinand should not appear in the affair, it was agreed that he should return to the castle immediately upon the embarkation of his sister. Having thus arranged their plan of operation, they separated till the following night, which was to decide the fate of Hippolitus and Julia.

Julia, whose mind was soothed by the fraternal kindness of Ferdinand, and the tender assurances of Hippolitus, now experienced an interval of repose. At the return of day she awoke refreshed, and tolerably composed. She selected a few clothes which were necessary, and prepared them for her journey. A sentiment of generosity justified her in the reserve she preserved to Emilia and Madame de Menon, whose faithfulness and attachment she could not doubt, but whom she disdained to involve in the disgrace that must fall upon them, should their knowledge of her flight be discovered.

In the mean time the castle was a scene of confusion. The magnificent preparations which were making for the nuptials, engaged all eyes, and busied all hands. The marchioness had the direction of the whole; and the alacrity with which she acquitted herself, testified how much she was pleased with the alliance, and created a suspicion, that it had not been concerted without some exertion of her influence. Thus was Julia designed the joint victim of ambition and illicit love.

The composure of Julia declined with the day, whose hours had crept heavily along. As the night drew on, her anxiety for the success of Ferdinand's negociation with Robert increased to a painful degree. A variety of new emotions pressed at her heart, and subdued her spirits. When she bade Emilia good night, she thought she beheld her for the last time. The ideas of the distance which would separate them, of the dangers she was going to encounter, with a train of wild and fearful anticipations, crouded upon her mind, tears sprang in her eyes, and it was with difficulty she avoided betraying her emotions. Of madame, too, her heart took a tender farewell. At length she heard the marquis retire to his apartment, and the doors belonging to the several chambers of the guests successively close. She marked with trembling attention the gradual change from bustle to quiet, till all was still.

She now held herself in readiness to depart at the moment in which Ferdinand and Hippolitus, for whose steps in the gallery she eagerly listened, should appear. The castle clock struck twelve. The sound seemed to shake the pile. Julia felt it thrill upon her heart. 'I hear you,' sighed she, 'for the last time.' The stillness of death succeeded. She continued to listen; but no sound met her ear. For a considerable time she sat in a state of anxious expectation not to be described. The clock chimed the successive quarters; and her fear rose to each additional sound. At length she heard it strike one. Hollow was that sound, and dreadful to her hopes; for neither Hippolitus nor Ferdinand appeared. She grew faint with fear and disappointment. Her mind, which for two hours had been kept upon the stretch of expectation, now resigned itself to despair. She gently opened the door of her closet, and looked upon the gallery; but all was lonely and silent. It appeared that Robert had refused to be accessary to their scheme; and it was probable that he had betrayed it to the marquis. Overwhelmed with bitter reflections, she threw herself upon the sopha in the first distraction of despair. Suddenly she thought she heard a noise in the gallery; and as she started from her posture to listen to the sound, the door of her closet was gently opened by Ferdinand. 'Come, my love,' said he, 'the keys are ours, and we have not a moment to lose; our delay has been unavoidable; but this is no time for explanation.' Julia, almost fainting, gave her hand to Ferdinand, and Hippolitus, after some short expression of his thankfulness, followed. They passed the door of madame's chamber; and treading the gallery with slow and silent steps, descended to the hall. This they crossed towards a door, after opening which, they were to find their way, through various passages, to a remote part of the castle, where a private door opened upon the walls. Ferdinand carried the several keys. They fastened the hall door after them, and proceeded through a narrow passage terminating in a stair-case.

They descended, and had hardly reached the bottom, when they heard a loud noise at the door above, and presently the voices of several people. Julia scarcely felt the ground she trod on, and Ferdinand flew to unlock a door that obstructed their way. He applied the different keys, and at length found the proper one; but the lock was rusted, and refused to yield. Their distress was not now to be conceived. The noise above increased; and it seemed as if the people were forcing the door. Hippolitus and Ferdinand vainly tried to turn the key. A sudden crash from above convinced them that the door had yielded, when making another desperate effort, the key broke in the lock. Trembling and exhausted, Julia gave herself up for lost. As she hung upon Ferdinand, Hippolitus vainly endeavoured to sooth her—the noise suddenly ceased. They listened, dreading to hear the sounds renewed; but, to their utter astonishment, the silence of the place remained undisturbed. They had now time to breathe, and to consider the possibility of effecting their escape; for from the marquis they had no mercy to hope. Hippolitus, in order to ascertain whether the people had quitted the door above, began to ascend the passage, in which he had not gone many steps when the noise was renewed with increased violence. He instantly retreated; and making a desperate push at the door below, which obstructed their passage, it seemed to yield, and by another effort of Ferdinand, burst open. They had not an instant to lose; for they now heard the steps of persons descending the stairs. The avenue they were in opened into a kind of chamber, whence three passages branched, of which they immediately chose the first. Another door now obstructed their passage; and they were compelled to wait while Ferdinand applied the keys. 'Be quick,' said Julia, 'or we are lost. O! if this lock too is rusted!'—'Hark!' said Ferdinand. They now discovered what apprehension had before prevented them from perceiving, that the sounds of pursuit were ceased, and all again was silent. As this could happen only by the mistake of their pursuers, in taking the wrong *route*, they resolved to preserve their advantage, by concealing the light, which Ferdinand now covered with his cloak. The door was opened, and they passed on; but they were perplexed in the intricacies of the place, and wandered about in vain endeavour to find their way. Often did they pause to listen, and often did fancy give them sounds of fearful import. At length they entered on the passage which Ferdinand knew led directly to a door that opened on the woods. Rejoiced at this certainty, they soon reached the spot which was to give them liberty.

Ferdinand turned the key; the door unclosed, and, to their infinite joy, discovered to them the grey dawn. 'Now, my love,' said Hippolitus, 'you are safe, and I am happy.'— Immediately a loud voice from without exclaimed, 'Take, villain, the reward of your perfidy!' At the same instant Hippolitus received a sword in his body, and uttering a deep sigh, fell to the ground. Julia shrieked and fainted; Ferdinand drawing his sword, advanced towards the assassin, upon whose countenance the light of his lamp then shone, and discovered to him his father! The sword fell from his grasp, and he started back in an agony of horror. He was instantly surrounded, and seized by the servants of the marquis, while the marquis himself denounced vengeance upon his head, and ordered him to be thrown into the dungeon of the castle. At this instant the servants of the count, who were awaiting his arrival on the seashore, hearing the tumult, hastened to the scene, and there beheld their beloved master lifeless and weltering in his blood. They conveyed the bleeding body, with loud lamentations, on board the vessel which had been prepared for him, and immediately set sail for Italy.

Julia, on recovering her senses, found herself in a small room, of which she had no remembrance, with her maid weeping over her. Recollection, when it returned, brought to her mind an energy of grief, which exceeded even all former conceptions of sufferings. Yet her misery was heightened by the intelligence which she now received. She learned that Hippolitus had been borne away lifeless by his

people, that Ferdinand was confined in a dungeon by order
of the marquis, and that herself was a prisoner in a remote
room, from which, on the day after the morrow, she was to
be removed to the chapel of the castle, and there sacrificed
to the ambition of her father, and the absurd love of the
Duke de Luovo.

This accumulation of evil subdued each power of resistance, and reduced Julia to a state little short of distraction.
No person was allowed to approach her but her maid, and
the servant who brought her food. Emilia, who, though
shocked by Julia's apparent want of confidence, severely
sympathized in her distress, solicited to see her; but the
pain of denial was so sharply aggravated by rebuke, that she
dared not again to urge the request.

In the mean time Ferdinand, involved in the gloom of a
dungeon, was resigned to the painful recollection of the past,
and a horrid anticipation of the future. From the resentment
of the marquis, whose passions were wild and terrible, and
whose rank gave him an unlimited power of life and death*
in his own territories, Ferdinand had much to fear. Yet
selfish apprehension soon yielded to a more noble sorrow.
He mourned the fate of Hippolitus, and the sufferings of
Julia. He could attribute the failure of their scheme only to
the treachery of Robert, who had, however, met the wishes
of Ferdinand with strong apparent sincerity, and generous
interest in the cause of Julia. On the night of the intended
elopement, he had consigned the keys to Ferdinand, who,
immediately on receiving them, went to the apartment of
Hippolitus. There they were detained till after the clock had
struck one by a low noise, which returned at intervals, and
convinced them that some part of the family was not yet
retired to rest. This noise was undoubtedly occasioned by
the people whom the marquis had employed to watch, and
whose vigilance was too faithful to suffer the fugitives to
escape. The very caution of Ferdinand defeated its purpose;
for it is probable, that had he attempted to quit the castle
by the common entrance, he might have escaped. The keys
of the grand door, and those of the courts, remaining in the

possession of Robert, the marquis was certain of the intended place of their departure; and was thus enabled to defeat their hopes at the very moment when they exulted in their success.

When the marchioness learned the fate of Hippolitus, the resentment of jealous passion yielded to emotions of pity. Revenge was satisfied, and she could now lament the sufferings of a youth whose personal charms had touched her heart as much as his virtues had disappointed her hopes. Still true to passion, and inaccessible to reason, she poured upon the defenceless Julia her anger for that calamity of which she herself was the unwilling cause. By a dextrous adaptation of her powers, she had worked upon the passions of the marquis so as to render him relentless in the pursuit of ambitious purposes, and insatiable in revenging his disappointment. But the effects of her artifices exceeded her intention in exerting them; and when she meant only to sacrifice a rival to her love, she found she had given up its object to revenge.

CHAPTER IV

THE nuptial morn, so justly dreaded by Julia, and so impatiently awaited by the marquis, now arrived. The marriage was to be celebrated with a magnificence which demonstrated the joy it occasioned to the marquis. The castle was fitted up in a style of grandeur superior to any thing that had been before seen in it. The neighbouring nobility were invited to an entertainment which was to conclude with a splendid ball and supper, and the gates were to be thrown open to all who chose to partake of the bounty of the marquis. At an early hour the duke, attended by a numerous retinue, entered the castle. Ferdinand heard from his dungeon, where the rigour and the policy of the marquis still confined him, the loud clattering of hoofs in the courtyard above, the rolling of the carriage wheels, and all the tumultuous bustle which the entrance of the duke occasioned. He too well understood the cause of this uproar, and it awakened in him sensations resembling those which the condemned criminal feels, when his ears are assailed by the dreadful sounds that precede his execution. When he was able to think of himself, he wondered by what means the marquis would reconcile his absence to the guests. He, however, knew too well the dissipated character of the Sicilian nobility, to doubt that whatever story should be invented would be very readily believed by them; who, even if they knew the truth, would not suffer a discovery of their knowledge to interrupt the festivity which was offered them.

The marquis and marchioness received the duke in the outer hall, and conducted him to the saloon, where he partook of the refreshments prepared for him, and from thence retired to the chapel. The marquis now withdrew to lead Julia to the altar, and Emilia was ordered to attend at the door of the chapel, in which the priest and a numerous company were already assembled. The marchioness, a prey to the turbulence of succeeding passions, exulted in the near completion of her favorite scheme.—A disappointment, however, was prepared for her, which would at once crush the triumph of her malice and her pride. The marquis, on entering the prison of Julia, found it empty! His astonishment and indignation upon the discovery almost overpowered his reason. Of the servants of the castle, who were immediately summoned, he enquired concerning her escape, with a mixture of fury and sorrow which left them no opportunity to reply. They had, however, no information to give, but that her woman had not appeared during the whole morning. In the prison were found the bridal habiliments* which the marchioness herself had sent on the preceding night, together with a letter addressed to Emilia, which contained the following words:

'Adieu, dear Emilia; never more will you see your wretched sister, who flies from the cruel fate now prepared for her, certain that she can never meet one more dreadful.—In happiness or misery—in hope or despair—whatever may be your situation—still remember me with pity and affection. Dear Emilia, adieu!—You will always be the sister of my heart—may you never be the partner of my misfortunes!'

While the marquis was reading this letter, the marchioness, who supposed the delay occasioned by some opposition from Julia, flew to the apartment. By her orders all the habitable parts of the castle were explored, and she herself assisted in the search. At length the intelligence was communicated to the chapel, and the confusion became universal. The priest quitted the altar, and the company returned to the saloon.

The letter, when it was given to Emilia, excited emotions which she found it impossible to disguise, but which did not, however, protect her from a suspicion that she was concerned in the transaction, her knowledge of which this letter appeared intended to conceal.

The marquis immediately dispatched servants upon the fleetest horses of his stables, with directions to take different routs, and to scour every corner of the island in pursuit of the fugitives. When these exertions had somewhat quieted his mind, he began to consider by what means Julia could have effected her escape. She had been confined in a small room in a remote part of the castle, to which no person had been admitted but her own woman and Robert, the confidential servant of the marquis. Even Lisette had not been suffered to enter, unless accompanied by Robert, in whose room, since the night of the fatal discovery, the keys had been regularly deposited. Without them it was impossible she could have escaped: the windows of the apartment being barred and grated, and opening into an inner court, at a prodigious height from the ground. Besides, who could she depend upon for protection—or whither could she intend to fly for concealment?—The associates of her former elopement were utterly unable to assist her even with advice. Ferdinand himself a prisoner, had been deprived of any means of intercourse with her, and Hippolitus had been carried lifeless on board a vessel, which had immediately sailed for Italy.

Robert, to whom the keys had been entrusted, was severely interrogated by the marquis. He persisted in a simple and uniform declaration of his innocence; but as the marquis believed it impossible that Julia could have escaped without his knowledge, he was ordered into imprisonment till he should confess the fact.

The pride of the duke was severely wounded by this elopement, which proved the excess of Julia's aversion, and compleated the disgraceful circumstances of his rejection. The marquis had carefully concealed from him her prior attempt at elopement, and her consequent confinement; but the truth now burst from disguise, and stood revealed with bitter aggravation. The duke, fired with indignation at the duplicity of the marquis, poured forth his resentment in terms of proud and bitter invective; and the marquis, galled by recent disappointment, was in no mood to restrain the impetuosity of his nature. He retorted with acrimony; and the consequence would have been serious, had not the friends of each party interposed for their preservation. The disputants were at length reconciled; it was agreed to pursue Julia with united, and indefatigable search; and that whenever she should be found, the nuptials should be solemnized without further delay. With the character of the duke, this conduct was consistent. His passions, inflamed by disappointment, and strengthened by repulse, now defied the power of obstacle; and those considerations which would have operated with a more delicate mind to overcome its original inclination, served only to encrease the violence of his.

Madame de Menon, who loved Julia with maternal affection, was an interested observer of all that passed at the castle. The cruel fate to which the marquis destined his daughter she had severely lamented, yet she could hardly rejoice to find that this had been avoided by elopement. She trembled for the future safety of her pupil; and her tranquillity, which was thus first disturbed for the welfare of others, she was not soon suffered to recover.

The marchioness had long nourished a secret dislike to Madame de Menon, whose virtues were a silent reproof to her vices. The contrariety of their disposition created in the marchioness an aversion which would have amounted to contempt, had not that dignity of virtue which strongly characterized the manners of madame, compelled the former to fear what she wished to despise. Her conscience whispered her that the dislike was mutual; and she now rejoiced in the opportunity which seemed to offer itself of lowering the proud integrity of madame's character. Pretending, therefore, to believe that she had encouraged Ferdinand to disobey his father's commands, and had been accessary to the elopement, she accused her of these offences, and stimulated the marquis to reprehend her conduct. But the integrity of Madame de Menon was not to be questioned with impunity. Without deigning to answer the imputation, she desired to resign an office of which she was no longer considered worthy, and to quit the castle immediately. This the policy of the marquis would not suffer; and he was compelled to make such ample concessions to madame, as induced her for the present to continue at the castle.

The news of Julia's elopement at length reached the ears of Ferdinand, whose joy at this event was equalled only by his surprize. He lost, for a moment, the sense of his own situation, and thought only of the escape of Julia. But his sorrow soon returned with accumulated force when he recollected that Julia might then perhaps want that assistance which his confinement alone could prevent his affording her.

The servants, who had been sent in pursuit, returned to the castle without any satisfactory information. Week after week elapsed in fruitless search, yet the duke was strenuous in continuing the pursuit. Emissaries were dispatched to Naples, and to the several estates of the Count Vereza, but they returned without any satisfactory information. The count had not been heard of since he quitted Naples for Sicily.

During these enquiries a new subject of disturbance broke out in the castle of Mazzini. On the night so fatal to the hopes of Hippolitus and Julia, when the tumult was subsided, and all was still, a light was observed by a servant as he passed by the window of the great stair-case in the way to his chamber, to glimmer through the casement before noticed in the southern buildings. While he stood observing it, it vanished, and presently reappeared. The former mysterious circumstances relative to these buildings rushed upon his mind; and fired with wonder, he roused some of his fellow servants to come and behold this phenomenon.

As they gazed in silent terror, the light disappeared, and soon after, they saw a small door belonging to the south tower open, and a figure bearing a light issue forth, which gliding along the castle walls, was quickly lost to their view. Overcome with fear they hurried back to their chambers, and revolved all the late wonderful occurrences. They doubted not, that this was the figure formerly seen by the lady Julia. The sudden change of Madame de Menon's apartments had not passed unobserved by the servants, but they now no longer hesitated to what to attribute the removal. They collected each various and uncommon circumstance attendant on this part of the fabric; and, comparing them with the present, their superstitious fears were confirmed, and their terror heightened to such a degree, that many of them resolved to quit the service of the marquis.

The marquis surprized at this sudden desertion, enquired into its cause, and learned the truth. Shocked by this discovery, he yet resolved to prevent, if possible, the ill effects which might be expected from a circulation of the report. To this end it was necessary to quiet the minds of his people, and to prevent their quitting his service. Having severely reprehended them for the idle apprehension they encouraged, he told them that, to prove the fallacy of their surmises, he would lead them over that part of the castle which was the subject of their fears, and ordered them to attend him at the return of night in the north hall. Emilia and Madame de Menon, surprised at this procedure, awaited the issue in silent expectation.

The servants, in obedience to the commands of the marquis, assembled at night in the north hall. The air of desolation which reigned through the south buildings, and the circumstance of their having been for so many years shut up, would naturally tend to inspire awe; but to these people, who firmly believed them to be the haunt of an unquiet spirit, terror was the predominant sentiment.

The marquis now appeared with the keys of these buildings in his hands, and every heart thrilled with wild expectation. He ordered Robert to precede him with a torch, and the rest of the servants following, he passed on. A pair of iron gates were unlocked, and they proceeded through a court, whose pavement was wildly overgrown with long grass, to the great door of the south fabric. Here they met with some difficulty, for the lock, which had not been turned for many years, was rusted.

During this interval, the silence of expectation sealed the lips of all present. At length the lock yielded. That door which had not been passed for so many years, creaked heavily upon its hinges, and disclosed the hall of black marble which Ferdinand had formerly crossed. 'Now,' cried the marquis, in a tone of irony as he entered, 'expect to encounter the ghosts of which you tell me; but if you fail to conquer them, prepare to quit my service. The people who live with me shall at least have courage and ability sufficient to defend me from these spiritual attacks. All I apprehend is, that the enemy will not appear, and in this case your valour will go untried.'

No one dared to answer, but all followed, in silent fear, the marquis, who ascended the great stair-case, and entered the gallery. 'Unlock that door,' said he, pointing to one on the left, 'and we will soon unhouse these ghosts.' Robert applied the key, but his hand shook so violently that he could not turn it. 'Here is a fellow,' cried the marquis, 'fit to encounter a whole legion of spirits. Do you, Anthony, take the key, and try your valour.'

'Please you, my lord,' replied Anthony,* 'I never was a good one at unlocking a door in my life, but here is Gregory will do it.'—'No, my lord, an' please you,' said Gregory, 'here is Richard.'—'Stand off,' said the marquis, 'I will shame your cowardice, and do it myself.'

Saying this he turned the key, and was rushing on, but the door refused to yield; it shook under his hands, and seemed as if partially held by some person on the other side. The marquis was surprized, and made several efforts to move it, without effect. He then ordered his servants to burst it open, but, shrinking back with one accord, they cried, 'For God's sake, my lord, go no farther; we are satisfied here are no ghosts, only let us get back.'

'It is now then my turn to be satisfied,' replied the marquis, 'and till I am, not one of you shall stir. Open me that door.'—'My lord!'—'Nay,' said the marquis, assuming a look of stern authority—'dispute not my commands. I am not to be trifled with.'

They now stepped forward, and applied their strength to the door, when a loud and sudden noise burst from within, and resounded through the hollow chambers! The men started back in affright, and were rushing headlong down the stair-case, when the voice of the marquis arrested their flight. They returned, with hearts palpitating with terror. 'Observe what I say,' said the marquis, 'and behave like men. Yonder door,' pointing to one at some distance, 'will lead us through other rooms to this chamber—unlock it therefore, for I will know the cause of these sounds.' Shocked at this determination, the servants again supplicated the marquis to go no farther; and to be obeyed, he was obliged to exert all his authority. The door was opened, and discovered a long narrow passage, into which they descended by a few steps. It led to a gallery that terminated in a back stair-case, where several doors appeared, one of which the marquis unclosed. A spacious chamber appeared beyond, whose walls, decayed and discoloured by the damps, exhibited a melancholy proof of desertion.

They passed on through a long suite of lofty and noble apartments, which were in the same ruinous condition. At length they came to the chamber whence the noise had issued. 'Go first, Robert, with the light,' said the marquis, as they approached the door; 'this is the key.' Robert trembled—but obeyed, and the other servants followed in silence. They stopped a moment at the door to listen, but all was still within. The door was opened, and disclosed a large vaulted chamber, nearly resembling those they had passed, and on looking round, they discovered at once the cause of the alarm.—A part of the decayed roof was fallen in, and the stones and rubbish of the ruin falling against the gallery door, obstructed the passage. It was evident, too, whence the noise which occasioned their terror had arisen; the loose stones which were piled against the door being shook by the effort made to open it, had given way, and rolled to the floor.

After surveying the place, they returned to the back stairs, which they descended, and having pursued the several windings of a long passage, found themselves again in the marble hall. 'Now,' said the marquis, 'what think ye? What evil spirits infest these walls? Henceforth be cautious how ye credit the phantasms of idleness, for ye may not always meet with a master who will condescend to undeceive ye.'—They acknowledged the goodness of the marquis, and professing themselves perfectly conscious of the error of their former suspicions, desired they might search no farther. 'I chuse to leave nothing to your imagination,' replied the marquis, 'lest hereafter it should betray you into a similar error. Follow me, therefore; you shall see the whole of these buildings.' Saying this, he led them to the south tower. They remembered, that from a door of this tower the figure which caused their alarm had issued; and notwithstanding the late assertion of their suspicions being removed, fear still operated powerfully upon their minds, and they would willingly have been excused from farther research. 'Would any of you chuse to explore this tower?' said the marquis, pointing to the broken stair-case; 'for myself, I am mortal, and therefore fear to venture; but you, who hold communion with disembodied spirits, may partake something of their nature; if so, you may pass without apprehension where the ghost has probably passed before.' They shrunk at this reproof, and were silent.

The marquis turning to a door on his right hand, ordered it to be unlocked. It opened upon the country, and the servants knew it to be the same whence the figure had appeared. Having relocked it, 'Lift that trapdoor; we will desend into the vaults,' said the marquis. 'What trapdoor, my Lord?' said Robert, with encreased agitation; 'I see none.' The marquis pointed, and Robert, perceived a door, which lay almost concealed beneath the stones that had fallen from the stair-case above. He began to remove them, when the marquis suddenly turning—'I have already suffi-ciently indulged your folly,' said he, 'and am weary of this business. If you are capable of receiving conviction from truth, you must now be convinced that these buildings are not the haunt of a supernatural being; and if you are incapable, it would be entirely useless to proceed. You,

Robert, may therefore spare yourself the trouble of removing the rubbish; we will quit this part of the fabric.'

The servants joyfully obeyed, and the marquis locking the several doors, returned with the keys to the habitable part of the castle.

Every enquiry after Julia had hitherto proved fruitless; and the imperious nature of the marquis, heightened by the present vexation, became intolerably oppressive to all around him. As the hope of recovering Julia declined, his opinion that Emilia had assisted her to escape strengthened, and he inflicted upon her the severity of his unjust suspicions. She was ordered to confine herself to her apartment till her innocence should be cleared, or her sister discovered. From Madame de Menon she received a faithful sympathy, which was the sole relief of her oppressed heart. Her anxiety concerning Julia daily encreased, and was heightened into the most terrifying apprehensions for her safety. She knew of no person in whom her sister could confide, or of any place where she could find protection; the most deplorable evils were therefore to be expected.

One day, as she was sitting at the window of her apartment, engaged in melancholy reflection, she saw a man riding towards the castle on full speed. Her heart beat with fear and expectation; for his haste made her suspect he brought intelligence of Julia; and she could scarcely refrain from breaking through the command of the marquis, and rushing into the hall to learn something of his errand. She was right in her conjecture; the person she had seen was a spy of the marquis's, and came to inform him that the lady Julia was at that time concealed in a cottage of the forest of Marentino. The marquis, rejoiced at this intelligence, gave the man a liberal reward. He learned also, that she was accompanied by a young cavalier; which circumstance surprized him exceedingly; for he knew of no person except the Count de Vereza with whom she could have entrusted herself, and the count had fallen by his sword! He immediately ordered a party of his people to accompany the messenger to the forest of Marentino, and to suffer neither Julia nor the cavalier to escape them, on pain of death.

When the Duke de Luovo was informed of this discovery, he entreated and obtained permission of the marquis to join in the pursuit. He immediately set out on the expedition, armed, and followed by a number of his servants. He resolved to encounter all hazards, and to practice the most desperate extremes, rather than fail in the object of his enterprize. In a short time he overtook the marquis's people, and they proceeded together with all possible speed. The forest lay several leagues distant from the castle of Mazzini, and the day was closing when they entered upon the borders. The thick foliage of the trees spread a deeper shade around; and they were obliged to proceed with caution. Darkness had long fallen upon the earth when they reached the cottage, to which they were directed by a light that glimmered from afar among the trees. The duke left his people at some distance; and dismounted, and accompanied only by one servant, approached the cottage. When he reached it he stopped, and looking through the window, observed a man and woman in the habit of peasants seated at their supper. They were conversing with earnestness, and the duke, hoping to obtain farther intelligence of Julia, endeavoured to listen to their discourse. They were praising the beauty of a lady, whom the duke did not doubt to be Julia, and the woman spoke much in praise of the cavalier. 'He has a noble heart,' said she; 'and I am sure, by his look, belongs to some great family.'—'Nay,' replied her companion, 'the lady is as good as he. I have been at Palermo, and ought to know what great folks are, and if she is not one of them, never take my word again. Poor thing, how she does take on! It made my heart ache to see her.'

They were some time silent. The duke knocked at the door, and enquired of the man who opened it concerning the lady and cavalier then in his cottage. He was assured there were no other persons in the cottage than those he then saw. The duke persisted in affirming that the persons he enquired for were there concealed; which the man being as resolute in denying, he gave the signal, and his people approached, and surrounded the cottage. The peasants, terrified by this circumstance, confessed that a lady and cavalier, such as the duke described, had been for some time concealed in the cottage; but that they were now departed.

Suspicious of the truth of the latter assertion, the duke ordered his people to search the cottage, and that part of the forest contiguous to it. The search ended in disappointment. The duke, however, resolved to obtain all possible information concerning the fugitives; and assuming, therefore, a stern air, bade the peasant, on pain of instant death, discover all he knew of them.

The man replied, that on a very dark and stormy night, about a week before, two persons had come to the cottage, and desired shelter. That they were unattended; but seemed to be persons of consequence in disguise. That they paid very liberally for what they had; and that they departed from the cottage a few hours before the arrival of the duke.

The duke enquired concerning the course they had taken, and having received information, remounted his horse, and set forward in pursuit. The road lay for several leagues through the forest, and the darkness, and the probability of encountering banditti, made the journey dangerous. About the break of day they quitted the forest, and entered upon a wild and mountainous country, in which they travelled some miles without perceiving a hut, or a human being. No vestige of cultivation appeared, and no sounds reached them but those of their horses feet, and the roaring of the winds through the deep forests that overhung the mountains. The pursuit was uncertain, but the duke resolved to persevere.

They came at length to a cottage, where he repeated his enquiries, and learned to his satisfaction that two persons, such as he described, had stopped there for refreshment about two hours before. He found it now necessary to stop for the same purpose. Bread and milk, the only provisions of the place, were set before him, and his attendants would have been well contented, had there been sufficient of this homely fare to have satisfied their hunger.

Having dispatched an hasty meal, they again set forward in the way pointed out to them as the route of the fugitives. The country assumed a more civilized aspect. Corn, vineyards, olives, and groves of mulberry-trees adorned the hills. The vallies, luxuriant in shade, were frequently embellished by the windings of a lucid stream, and diversified by clusters of half-seen cottages. Here the rising turrets of a monastery appeared above the thick trees with which they were surrounded; and there the savage wilds the travellers had passed, formed a bold and picturesque background to the scene.

To the questions put by the duke to the several persons he met, he received answers that encouraged him to proceed. At noon he halted at a village to refresh himself and his people. He could gain no intelligence of Julia, and was perplexed which way to chuse; but determined at length to pursue the road he was then in, and accordingly again set forward. He travelled several miles without meeting any person who could give the necessary information, and began to despair of success. The lengthened shadows of the mountains, and the fading light gave signals of declining day; when having gained the summit of a high hill, he observed two persons travelling on horseback in the plains below. On one of them he distinguished the habiliments of a woman; and in her air he thought he discovered that of Julia. While he stood attentively surveying them, they looked towards the hill, when, as if urged by a sudden impulse of terror, they set off on full speed over the plains. The duke had no doubt that these were the persons he sought; and he, therefore, ordered some of his people to pursue them, and pushed his horse into a full gallop. Before he reached the plains, the fugitives, winding round an abrupt hill, were lost to his view. The duke continued his course, and his people, who were a considerable way before him, at length reached the hill, behind which the two persons had disappeared. No traces of them were to be seen, and they entered a narrow defile between two ranges of high and savage mountains; on the right of which a rapid stream rolled along, and broke with its deep resounding murmurs the solemn silence of the place. The shades of evening now fell thick, and the scene was soon enveloped in darkness; but to the duke, who was animated by a strong and impetuous passion, these were unimportant circumstances. Although he knew that the wilds of Sicily were frequently infested with banditti, his numbers made him fearless of attack. Not so his attendants, many of whom, as the darkness increased, testified emotions not very honourable to their courage: starting at every bush, and believing it concealed a murderer. They endeavoured to dissuade the duke from proceeding, expressing uncertainty of their being in the right route, and recommending the open plains. But the duke, whose eye had been vigilant to mark the flight of the fugitives, and who was not to be dissuaded from his purpose, quickly repressed their arguments. They continued their course without meeting a single person.

The moon now rose, and afforded them a shadowy imperfect view of the surrounding objects. The prospect was gloomy and vast, and not a human habitation met their eyes. They had now lost every trace of the fugitives, and found themselves bewildered in a wild and savage country. Their only remaining care was to extricate themselves from so forlorn a situation, and they listened at every step with anxious attention for some sound that might discover to them the haunts of men. They listened in vain; the stillness of night was undisturbed but by the wind, which broke at intervals in low and hollow murmurs from among the mountains.

As they proceeded with silent caution, they perceived a light break from among the rocks at some distance. The duke hesitated whether to approach, since it might probably proceed from a party of the banditti with which these mountains were said to be infested.* While he hesitated, it disappeared; but he had not advanced many steps when it returned. He now perceived it to issue from the mouth of a cavern, and cast a bright reflection upon the overhanging rocks and shrubs.

He dismounted, and followed by two of his people, leaving the rest at some distance, moved with slow and silent steps

towards the cave. As he drew near, he heard the sound of
many voices in high carousal. Suddenly the uproar ceased,
and the following words were sung by a clear and manly
voice:

SONG

Pour the rich libation high;
  The sparkling cup to Bacchus fill;
His joys shall dance in ev'ry eye,
  And chace the forms of future ill!

Quick the magic raptures steal
  O'er the fancy-kindling brain.
Warm the heart with social zeal,
  And song and laughter reign.

Then visions of pleasure shall float on our sight,
  While light bounding our spirits shall flow;
And the god shall impart a fine sense of delight
  Which in vain *sober* mortals would know.

The last verse was repeated in loud chorus. The duke
listened with astonishment! Such social merriment amid a
scene of such savage wildness, appeared more like enchantment than reality. He would not have hesitated to pronounce
this a party of banditti, had not the delicacy of expression
preserved in the song appeared unattainable by men of their
class.

He had now a full view of the cave; and the moment
which convinced him of his error served only to encrease
his surprize. He beheld, by the light of a fire, a party of
banditti seated within the deepest recess of the cave round
a rude kind of table formed in the rock. The table was
spread with provisions, and they were regaling themselves
with great eagerness and joy. The countenances of the men
exhibited a strange mixture of fierceness and sociality; and
the duke could almost have imagined he beheld in these
robbers a band of the early Romans before knowledge had
civilized, or luxury had softened them.* But he had not
much time for meditation; a sense of his danger bade him
fly while to fly was yet in his power. As he turned to depart,

he observed two saddle-horses grazing upon the herbage near the mouth of the cave. It instantly occurred to him that they belonged to Julia and her companion. He hesitated, and at length determined to linger awhile, and listen to the conversation of the robbers, hoping from thence to have his doubts resolved. They talked for some time in a strain of high conviviality, and recounted in exultation many of their exploits. They described also the behaviour of several people whom they had robbed, with highly ludicrous allusions, and with much rude humour, while the cave re-echoed with loud bursts of laughter and applause. They were thus engaged in tumultuous merriment, till one of them cursing the scanty plunder of their late adventure, but praising the beauty of a lady, they all lowered their voices together, and seemed as if debating upon a point uncommonly interesting to them. The passions of the duke were roused, and he became certain that it was Julia of whom they had spoken. In the first impulse of feeling he drew his sword; but recollecting the number of his adversaries, restrained his fury. He was turning from the cave with a design of summoning his people, when the light of the fire glittering upon the bright blade of his weapon, caught the eye of one of the banditti. He started from his seat, and his comrades instantly rising in consternation, discovered the duke. They rushed with loud vociferation towards the mouth of the cave. He endeavoured to escape to his people; but two of the banditti mounting the horses which were grazing near, quickly overtook and seized him. His dress and air proclaimed him to be a person of distinction; and, rejoicing in their prospect of plunder, they forced him towards the cave. Here their comrades awaited them; but what were the emotions of the duke, when he discovered in the person of the principal robber his own son! who, to escape the galling severity of his father, had fled from his castle some years before, and had not been heard of since.

He had placed himself at the head of a party of banditti, and, pleased with the liberty which till then he had never tasted, and with the power which his new situation afforded him, he became so much attached to this wild and lawless mode of life, that he determined never to quit it till death should dissolve those ties which now made his rank only oppressive. This event seemed at so great a distance, that he seldom allowed himself to think of it. Whenever it should happen, he had no doubt that he might either resume his rank without danger of discovery, or might justify his present conduct as a frolic which a few acts of generosity would easily excuse. He knew his power would then place him beyond the reach of censure, in a country where the people are accustomed to implicit subordination, and seldom dare to scrutinize the actions of the nobility.

His sensations, however, on discovering his father, were not very pleasing; but proclaiming the duke, he protected him from farther outrage.

With the duke, whose heart was a stranger to the softer affections, indignation usurped the place of parental feeling. His pride was the only passion affected by the discovery; and he had the rashness to express the indignation, which the conduct of his son had excited, in terms of unrestrained invective. The banditti, inflamed by the opprobium with which he loaded their order, threatened instant punishment to his temerity; and the authority of Riccardo could hardly restrain them within the limits of forbearance.

The menaces, and at length entreaties of the duke, to prevail with his son to abandon his present way of life, were equally ineffectual. Secure in his own power, Riccardo laughed at the first, and was insensible to the latter; and his father was compelled to relinquish the attempt. The duke, however, boldly and passionately accused him of having plundered and secreted a lady and cavalier, his friends, at the same time describing Julia, for whose libera-tion he offered large rewards. Riccardo denied the fact, which so much exasperated the duke, that he drew his sword with an intention of plunging it in the breast of his son. His arm was arrested by the surrounding banditti, who half unsheathed their swords, and stood suspended in an attitude of menace. The fate of the father now hung upon the voice of the son. Riccardo raised his arm, but instantly dropped it, and turned away. The banditti sheathed their weapons, and stepped back.

Riccardo solemnly swearing that he knew nothing of the persons described, the duke at length became convinced of the truth of the assertion, and departing from the cave, rejoined his people. All the impetuous passions of his nature were roused and inflamed by the discovery of his son in a situation so wretchedly disgraceful. Yet it was his pride rather than his virtue that was hurt; and when he wished him dead, it was rather to save himself from disgrace, than his son from the real indignity of vice. He had no means of reclaiming him; to have attempted it by force, would have been at this time the excess of temerity, for his attendants, though numerous, were undisciplined, and would have fallen certain victims to the power of a savage and dexterous banditti.

With thoughts agitated in fierce and agonizing conflict, he pursued his journey; and having lost all trace of Julia, sought only for an habitation which might shelter him from the night, and afford necessary refreshment for himself and his people. With this, however, there appeared little hope of meeting.

CHAPTER V

The night grew stormy. The hollow winds swept over the mountains, and blew bleak and cold around; the clouds were driven swiftly over the face of the moon, and the duke and his people were frequently involved in total darkness. They had travelled on silently and dejectedly for some hours, and were bewildered in the wilds, when they suddenly heard the bell of a monastery chiming for midnight-prayer. Their hearts revived at the sound, which they endeavoured to follow, but they had not gone far, when the gale wafted it away, and they were abandoned to the uncertain guide of their own conjectures.

They had pursued for some time the way which they judged led to the monastery, when the note of the bell returned upon the wind, and discovered to them that they had mistaken their route. After much wandering and difficulty they arrived, overcome with weariness, at the gates of a large and gloomy fabric. The bell had ceased, and all was still. By the moonlight, which through broken clouds now streamed upon the building, they became convinced it was the monastery they had sought, and the duke himself struck loudly upon the gate.

Several minutes elapsed, no person appeared, and he repeated the stroke. A step was presently heard within, the gate was unbarred, and a thin shivering figure presented itself. The duke solicited admission, but was refused, and reprimanded for disturbing the convent at the hour sacred to prayer. He then made known his rank, and bade the friar inform the Superior that he requested shelter from the night. The friar, suspicious of deceit, and apprehensive of robbers, refused with much firmness, and repeated that the convent was engaged in prayer; he had almost closed the gate, when the duke, whom hunger and fatigue made desperate, rushed by him, and passed into the court.

It was his intention to present himself to the Superior, and he had not proceeded far when the sound of laughter, and of many voices in loud and mirthful jollity, attracted his steps. It led him through several passages to a door, through the crevices of which light appeared. He paused a moment, and heard within a wild uproar of merriment and song. He was struck with astonishment, and could scarcely credit his senses!*

He unclosed the door, and beheld in a large room, well lighted, a company of friars, dressed in the habit of their order, placed round a table, which was profusely spread with wines and fruits. The Superior, whose habit distinguished him from his associates, appeared at the head of the table. He was lifting a large goblet of wine to his lips, and was roaring out, 'Profusion and confusion,' at the moment when the duke entered. His appearance caused a general alarm; that part of the company who were not too much intoxicated, arose from their seats; and the Superior, dropping the goblet from his hands, endeavoured to assume a look of austerity, which his rosy countenance belied. The duke received a reprimand, delivered in the lisping accents of intoxication, and embellished with frequent interjections of hiccup. He made known his quality, his distress, and solicited a night's lodging for himself and his people. When the Superior understood the distinction of his guest, his features relaxed into a smile of joyous welcome; and taking him by the hand, he placed him by his side.

The table was quickly covered with luxurious provisions, and orders were given that the duke's people should be admitted, and taken care of. He was regaled with a variety of the finest wines, and at length, highly elevated by monastic hospitality, he retired to the apartment allotted him, leaving the Superior in a condition which precluded all ceremony.

He departed in the morning, very well pleased with the accommodating principles of monastic religion. He had been told that the enjoyment of the good things of this life was the surest sign of our gratitude to Heaven; and it appeared, that within the walls of a Sicilian monastery, the precept and the practice were equally enforced.

He was now at a loss what course to chuse, for he had no clue to direct him towards the object of his pursuit; but hope still invigorated, and urged him to perseverance. He was not many leagues from the coast; and it occurred to him that the fugitives might make towards it with a design of escaping into Italy. He therefore determined to travel towards the sea and proceed along the shore.

At the house where he stopped to dine, he learned that two persons, such as he described, had halted there about an hour before his arrival, and had set off again in much seeming haste. They had taken the road towards the coast, whence it was obvious to the duke they designed to embark. He stayed not to finish the repast set before him, but instantly remounted to continue the pursuit.

To the enquiries he made of the persons he chanced to meet, favorable answers were returned for a time, but he was at length bewildered in uncertainity, and travelled for some hours in a direction which chance, rather than judgment, prompted him to take.

The falling evening again confused his prospects, and unsettled his hopes. The shades were deepened by thick and heavy clouds that enveloped the horizon, and the deep sounding air foretold a tempest. The thunder now rolled at a distance, and the accumulated clouds grew darker. The duke and his people were on a wild and dreary heath, round which they looked in vain for shelter, the view being terminated on all sides by the same desolate scene. They rode, however, as hard as their horses would carry them; and at length one of the attendants spied on the skirts of the waste a large mansion, towards which they immediately directed their course.

They were overtaken by the storm, and at the moment when they reached the building, a peal of thunder, which seemed to shake the pile, burst over their heads. They now found themselves in a large and ancient mansion, which seemed totally deserted, and was falling to decay. The edifice was distinguished by an air of magnificence, which ill accorded with the surrounding scenery, and which excited some degree of surprize in the mind of the duke, who, however, fully justified the owner in forsaking a spot which presented to the eye only views of rude and desolated nature.

The storm increased with much violence, and threatened to detain the duke a prisoner in his present habitation for the night. The hall, of which he and his people had taken possession, exhibited in every feature marks of ruin and desolation. The marble pavement was in many places broken, the walls were mouldering in decay, and round the high and shattered windows the long grass waved to the lonely gale. Curiosity led him to explore the recesses of the mansion. He quitted the hall, and entered upon a passage which conducted him to a remote part of the edifice. He wandered through the wild and spacious apartments in gloomy meditation, and often paused in wonder at the remains of magnificence which he beheld.

The mansion was irregular and vast, and he was bewildered in its intricacies. In endeavouring to find his way back, he only perplexed himself more, till at length he arrived at a door, which he believed led into the hall he first quitted. On opening it he discovered, by the faint light of the moon, a large place which he scarcely knew whether to think a cloister, a chapel, or a hall. It retired in long perspective, in arches, and terminated in a large iron gate, through which appeared the open country.

The lighting flashed thick and blue around, which, together with the thunder that seemed to rend the wide arch of heaven, and the melancholy aspect of the place, so awed the duke, that he involuntarily called to his people. His voice was answered only by the deep echoes which ran in murmurs through the place, and died away at a distance; and the moon now sinking behind a cloud, left him in total darkness.

He repeated the call more loudly, and at length heard the approach of footsteps. A few moments relieved him from his anxiety, for his people appeared. The storm was yet loud, and the heavy and sulphureous appearance of the atmosphere promised no speedy abatement of it. The duke endeavoured to reconcile himself to pass the night in his present situation, and ordered a fire to be lighted in the place he was in. This with much difficulty was accomplished. He then threw himself on the pavement before it, and tried to endure the abstinence which he had so ill observed in the monastery on the preceding night. But to his great joy his attendants, more provident than himself, had not scrupled to accept a comfortable quantity of provisions which had been offered them at the monastery; and which they now drew forth from a wallet. They were spread upon the pavement; and the duke, after refreshing himself, delivered up the remains to his people. Having ordered them to watch by turns at the gate, he wrapt his cloak round him, and resigned himself to repose.

The night passed without any disturbance. The morning arose fresh and bright; the Heavens exhibited a clear and unclouded concave; even the wild heath, refreshed by the late rains, smiled around, and sent up with the morning gale a stream of fragrance.

The duke quitted the mansion, re-animated by the cheerfulness of morn, and pursued his journey. He could gain no intelligence of the fugitives. About noon he found himself in a beautiful romantic country; and having reached the summit of some wild cliffs, he rested, to view the picturesque imagery of the scene below. A shadowy sequestered dell appeared buried deep among the rocks, and in the bottom was seen a lake, whose clear bosom reflected the impending cliffs, and the beautiful luxuriance of the overhanging shades.

But his attention was quickly called from the beauties of inanimate nature, to objects more interesting; for he observed two persons, whom he instantly recollected to be the same that he had formerly pursued over the plains. They were seated on the margin of the lake, under the shade of some high trees at the foot of the rocks, and seemed partaking of a repast which was spread upon the grass. Two horses were grazing near. In the lady the duke saw the very air and shape of Julia, and his heart bounded at the sight. They were seated with their backs to the cliffs upon which the duke stood, and he therefore surveyed them unobserved. They were now almost within his power, but the difficulty was how to descend the rocks, whose stupendous heights and craggy steeps seemed to render them impassable. He examined them with a scrutinizing eye, and at length espied, where the rock receded, a narrow winding sort of path. He dismounted, and some of his attendants doing the same, followed their lord down the cliffs, treading lightly, lest their steps should betray them. Immediately upon their reaching the bottom, they were perceived by the lady, who fled among the rocks, and was presently pursued by the duke's people. The cavalier had no time to escape, but drew his sword, and defended himself against the furious assault of the duke.

The combat was sustained with much vigour and dexterity on both sides for some minutes, when the duke received the point of his adversary's sword, and fell. The cavalier, endeavouring to escape, was seized by the duke's people, who now appeared with the fair fugitive; but what was the disappointment—the rage of the duke, when in the person of the lady he discovered a stranger! The astonishment was mutual, but the accompanying feelings were, in the different persons, of a very opposite nature. In the duke, astonishment was heightened by vexation, and embittered by disappointment:—in the lady, it was softened by the joy of unexpected deliverance.

This lady was the younger daughter of a Sicilian nobleman, whose avarice, or necessities, had devoted her to a convent. To avoid the threatened fate, she fled with the lover to whom her affections had long been engaged, and whose only fault, even in the eye of her father, was inferiority of birth. They were now on their way to the coast, whence they designed to pass over to Italy, where the church would confirm the bonds which their hearts had already formed. There the friends of the cavalier resided, and with them they expected to find a secure retreat.

The duke, who was not materially wounded, after the first transport of his rage had subsided, suffered them to depart. Relieved from their fears, they joyfully set forward, leaving their late pursuer to the anguish of defeat, and fruitless endeavour. He was remounted on his horse; and having dispatched two of his people in search of a house where he might obtain some relief, he proceeded slowly on his return to the castle of Mazzini.

It was not long ere he recollected a circumstance which, in the first tumult of his disappointment, had escaped him, but which so essentially affected the whole tenour of his hopes, as to make him again irresolute how to proceed. He considered that, although these were the fugitives he had pursued over the plains, they might not be the same who had been secreted in the cottage, and it was therefore possible that Julia might have been the person whom they had for some time followed from thence. This suggestion awakened his hopes, which were however quickly destroyed; for he remembered that the only persons who could have satisfied his doubts, were now gone beyond the power of recall. To pursue Julia, when no traces of her flight remained, was absurd; and he was, therefore, compelled to return to the marquis, as ignorant and more hopeless than he had left him. With much pain he reached the village which his emissaries had discovered, when fortunately he obtained some medical assistance. Here he was obliged by indisposition to rest. The anguish of his mind equalled that of his body. Those impetuous passions which so strongly marked his nature, were roused and exasperated to a degree that operated powerfully upon his constitution, and threatened him with the most alarming consequences. The effect of his wound was heightened by the agitation of his mind; and a fever, which quickly assumed a very serious aspect, co-operated to endanger his life.

CHAPTER VI

THE castle of Mazzini was still the scene of dissension and misery. The impatience and astonishment of the marquis being daily increased by the lengthened absence of the duke, he dispatched servants to the forest of Marentino, to enquire the occasion of this circumstance. They returned with intelligence that neither Julia, the duke, nor any of his people were there. He therefore concluded that his daughter had fled the cottage upon information of the approach of the duke, who, he believed, was still engaged in the pursuit. With respect to Ferdinand, who yet pined in sorrow and anxiety in his dungeon, the rigour of the marquis's conduct was unabated. He apprehended that his son, if liberated, would quickly discover the retreat of Julia, and by his advice and assistance confirm her in disobedience.

Ferdinand, in the stillness and solitude of his dungeon, brooded over the late calamity in gloomy ineffectual lamentation. The idea of Hippolitus—of Hippolitus murdered—arose to his imagination in busy intrusion, and subdued the strongest efforts of his fortitude. Julia too, his beloved sister—unprotected—unfriended—might, even at the moment he lamented her, be sinking under sufferings dreadful to humanity. The airy schemes he once formed of future felicity, resulting from the union of two persons so justly dear to him—with the gay visions of past happiness—floated upon his fancy, and the lustre they reflected served only to heighten, by contrast, the obscurity and gloom of his present views. He had, however, a new subject of astonishment, which often withdrew his thoughts from their accustomed object, and substituted a sensation less painful, though scarcely less powerful. One night as he lay ruminating on the past, in melancholy dejection, the stillness of the place was suddenly interrupted by a low and dismal sound. It returned at intervals in hollow sighings, and seemed to come from some person in deep distress. So much did fear operate upon his mind, that he was uncertain whether it arose from within or from without. He looked around his dungeon, but could distinguish no object through the impenetrable darkness. As he listened in deep amazement, the sound was repeated in moans more hollow. Terror now occupied his mind, and disturbed his reason; he started from his posture, and, determined to be satisfied whether any person beside himself was in the dungeon, groped, with arms extended, along the walls. The place was empty; but coming to a particular spot, the sound suddenly arose more distinctly to his ear. He called aloud, and asked who was there; but received no answer. Soon after all was still; and after listening for some time without hearing the sounds renewed, he laid himself down to sleep. On the following day he mentioned to the man who brought him food what he had heard, and enquired concerning the noise. The servant appeared very much terrified, but could give no information that might in the least account for the circumstance, till he mentioned the vicinity of the dungeon to the southern buildings. The dreadful relation formerly given by the marquis instantly recurred to the mind of Ferdinand, who did not hesitate to believe that the moans he heard came from the restless spirit of the murdered Della Campo. At this conviction, horror thrilled his nerves; but he remembered his oath, and was silent. His courage, however, yielded to the idea of passing another night alone in his prison, where, if the vengeful spirit of the murdered should appear, he might even die of the horror which its appearance would inspire.

The mind of Ferdinand was highly superior to the general influence of superstition; but, in the present instance, such strong correlative circumstances appeared, as compelled even incredulity to yield. He had himself heard strange and awful sounds in the forsaken southern buildings; he received from his father a dreadful secret relative to them—a secret in which his honor, nay even his life, was bound up. His father had also confessed, that he had himself there seen appearances which he could never after remember without horror, and which had occasioned him to quit that part of the castle. All these recollections presented to Ferdinand a chain of evidence too powerful to be resisted; and he could not doubt that the spirit of the dead had for once been permitted to revisit the earth, and to call down vengeance on the descendants of the murderer.

This conviction occasioned him a degree of horror, such as no apprehension of mortal powers could have excited; and he determined, if possible, to prevail on Peter to pass the hours of midnight with him in his dungeon. The strictness of Peter's fidelity yielded to the persuasions of Ferdinand, though no bribe could tempt him to incur the resentment of the marquis, by permitting an escape. Ferdinand passed the day in lingering anxious expectation, and the return of night brought Peter to the dungeon. His kindness exposed him to a danger which he had not foreseen; for when seated in the dungeon alone with his prisoner, how easily might that prisoner have conquered him and left him to pay his life to the fury of the marquis. He was preserved by the humanity of Ferdinand, who instantly perceived his advantage, but disdained to involve an innocent man in destruction, and spurned the suggestion from his mind.

Peter, whose friendship was stronger than his courage, trembled with apprehension as the hour drew nigh in which the groans had been heard on the preceding night. He recounted to Ferdinand a variety of terrific circumstances, which existed only in the heated imaginations of his fellow-servants, but which were still admitted by them as facts. Among the rest, he did not omit to mention the light and the figure which had been seen to issue from the south tower on the night of Julia's intended elopement; a circumstance which he embellished with innumerable aggravations of fear and wonder. He concluded with describing the general consternation it had caused, and the consequent behaviour of the marquis, who laughed at the fears of his people, yet condescended to quiet them by a formal review of the buildings whence their terror had originated. He related the adventure of the door which refused to yield, the sounds which arose from within, and the discovery of the fallen roof; but declared that neither he, nor any of his fellow servants, believed the noise or the obstruction proceeded from that, 'because, my lord,' continued he, 'the door seemed to be held only in one place; and as for the noise—O! Lord! I never shall forget what a noise it was!— it was a thousand times louder than what any stones could make.'

Ferdinand listened to this narrative in silent wonder! wonder not occasioned by the adventure described, but by the hardihood and rashness of the marquis, who had thus exposed to the inspection of his people, that dreadful spot which he knew from experience to be the haunt of an injured spirit; a spot which he had hitherto scrupulously concealed from human eye, and human curiosity; and which, for so many years, he had not dared even himself to enter. Peter went on, but was presently interrupted by a hollow moan, which seemed to come from beneath the ground. 'Blessed virgin!' exclaimed he: Ferdinand listened in awful expectation. A groan longer and more dreadful was repeated, when Peter started from his seat, and snatching up the lamp, rushed out of the dungeon. Ferdinand, who was left in total darkness, followed to the door, which the affrighted Peter had not stopped to fasten, but which had closed, and seemed held by a lock that could be opened only on the outside. The sensations of Ferdinand, thus compelled to remain in the dungeon, are not to be imagined. The horrors of the night, whatever they were to be, he was to endure alone. By degrees, however, he seemed to acquire the valour of despair. The sounds were repeated, at intervals, for near an hour, when silence returned, and remained undisturbed during the rest of the night. Ferdinand was alarmed by no appearance, and at length, overcome with anxiety and watching, he sunk to repose.

On the following morning Peter returned to the dungeon, scarcely knowing what to expect, yet expecting something very strange, perhaps the murder, perhaps the supernatural disappearance of his young lord. Full of these wild apprehensions, he dared not venture thither alone, but persuaded some of the servants, to whom he had communicated his terrors, to accompany him to the door. As they passed along he recollected, that in the terror of the preceding night he had forgot to fasten the door, and he now feared that his prisoner had made his escape without a miracle. He hurried to the door; and his surprize was extreme to find it fastened. It instantly struck him that this was the work of a supernatural power, when on calling aloud, he was answered by a voice from within. His absurd fear did not suffer him to recognize the voice of Ferdinand, neither did he suppose that Ferdinand had failed to escape, he, therefore, attributed the voice to the being he had heard on the preceding night; and starting back from the door, fled with his companions to the great hall. There the uproar occasioned by their entrance called together a number of persons, amongst whom was the marquis, who was soon informed of the cause of alarm, with a long history of the circumstances of the foregoing night. At this information, the marquis assumed a very stern look, and severely reprimanded Peter for his imprudence, at the same time reproaching the other servants with their undutifulness in thus disturbing his peace. He reminded them of the condescension he had practised to dissipate their former terrors, and of the result of their examination. He then assured them, that since indulgence had only encouraged intrusion, he would for the future be severe; and concluded with declaring, that the first man who should disturb him with a repetition of such ridiculous apprehensions, or should attempt to disturb the peace of the castle by circulating these idle notions, should be rigorously punished, and banished his dominions. They shrunk back at his reproof, and were silent. 'Bring a torch,' said the marquis, 'and shew me to the dungeon. I will once more condescend to confute you.'

They obeyed, and descended with the marquis, who, arriving at the dungeon, instantly threw open the door, and discovered to the astonished eyes of his attendants—Ferdi-nand!—He started with surprize at the entrance of his father thus attended. The marquis darted upon him a severe look, which he perfectly comprehended.—'Now,' cried he, turn-ing to his people, 'what do you see? My son, whom I myself placed here, and whose voice, which answered to your calls, you have transformed into unknown sounds. Speak, Ferdi-nand, and confirm what I say.' Ferdinand did so. 'What dreadful spectre appeared to you last night?' resumed the marquis, looking stedfastly upon him: 'gratify these fellows with a description of it, for they cannot exist without something of the marvellous.' 'None, my lord,' replied Ferdinand, who too well understood the manner of the marquis. ' 'Tis well,' cried the marquis, 'and this is the last time,' turning to his attendants, 'that your folly shall be treated with so much lenity.' He ceased to urge the subject, and forbore to ask Ferdinand even one question before his servants, concerning the nocturnal sounds described by Peter. He quitted the dungeon with eyes steadily bent in anger and suspicion upon Ferdinand. The marquis suspected that the fears of his son had inadvertently betrayed to Peter a part of the secret entrusted to him, and he artfully interrogated Peter with seeming carelessness, concerning the circumstances of the preceding night. From him he drew such answers as honorably acquitted Ferdinand of indiscre-tion, and relieved himself from tormenting apprehensions.

The following night passed quietly away; neither sound nor appearance disturbed the peace of Ferdinand. The mar-quis, on the next day, thought proper to soften the severity of his sufferings, and he was removed from his dungeon to a room strongly grated, but exposed to the light of day.

Meanwhile a circumstance occurred which increased the general discord, and threatened Emilia with the loss of her last remaining comfort—the advice and consolation of Ma-dame de Menon. The marchioness, whose passion for the Count de Vereza had at length yielded to absence, and the pressure of present circumstances, now bestowed her smiles upon a young Italian cavalier, a visitor at the castle, who possessed too much of the spirit of gallantry to permit a lady to languish in vain. The marquis, whose mind was occupied with other passions, was insensible to the misconduct of his wife, who at all times had the address to disguise her vices beneath the gloss of virtue and innocent freedom. The intrigue was discovered by madame, who, having one day left a book in the oak parlour, returned thither in search of it. As she opened the door of the apartment, she heard the voice of the cavalier in passionate exclamation; and on entering, discovered him rising in some confusion from the feet of the marchioness, who, darting at madame a look of severity, arose from her seat. Madame, shocked at what she had seen, instantly retired, and buried in her own bosom that secret, the discovery of which would most essentially have poisoned the peace of the marquis. The marchioness, who was a stranger to the generosity of sentiment which actuated Madame de Menon, doubted not that she would seize the moment of retaliation, and expose her conduct where most she dreaded it should be known. The consciousness of guilt tortured her with incessant fear of discovery, and from this period her whole attention was employed to dislodge from the castle the person to whom her character was committed. In this it was not difficult to succeed; for the delicacy of madame's feelings made her quick to perceive, and to withdraw from a treatment unsuitable to the natural dignity of her character. She therefore resolved to depart from the castle; but disdaining to take an advantage even over a successful enemy, she determined to be silent on that subject which would instantly have transferred the triumph from her adversary to herself. When the marquis, on hearing her determination to retire, earnestly enquired for the motive of her conduct, she forbore to acquaint him with the real one, and left him to incertitude and disappointment.

To Emilia this design occasioned a distress which almost subdued the resolution of madame. Her tears and intreaties spoke the artless energy of sorrow. In madame she lost her only friend; and she too well understood the value of that friend, to see her depart without feeling and expressing the deepest distress. From a strong attachment to the memory of the mother, madame had been induced to undertake the education of her daughters, whose engaging dispositions had perpetuated a kind of hereditary affection. Regard for Emilia and Julia had alone for some time detained her at the castle; but this was now succeeded by the influence of considerations too powerful to be resisted. As her income was small, it was her plan to retire to her native place, which was situated in a distant part of the island, and there take up her residence in a convent.

Emilia saw the time of madame's departure approach with increased distress. They left each other with a mutual sorrow, which did honour to their hearts. When her last friend was gone, Emilia wandered through the forsaken apartments, where she had been accustomed to converse with Julia, and to receive consolation and sympathy from her dear instructress, with a kind of anguish known only to those who have experienced a similar situation. Madame pursued her journey with a heavy heart. Separated from the objects of her fondest affections, and from the scenes and occupations for which long habit had formed claims upon her heart, she seemed without interest and without motive for exertion. The world appeared a wide and gloomy desert, where no heart welcomed her with kindness—no countenance brightened into smiles at her approach. It was many years since she quitted Calini—and in the interval, death had swept away the few friends she left there. The future presented a melancholy scene; but she had the retrospect of years spent in honorable endeavour and strict integrity, to cheer her heart and encouraged her hopes.

But her utmost endeavours were unable to express the anxiety with which the uncertain fate of Julia overwhelmed her. Wild and terrific images arose to her imagination. Fancy drew the scene;—she deepened the shades; and the terrific aspect of the objects she presented was heightened by the obscurity which involved them.*

[END OF VOL. I]

CHAPTER VII

TOWARDS the close of day Madame de Menon arrived at a small village situated among the mountains, where she purposed to pass the night. The evening was remarkably fine, and the romantic* beauty of the surrounding scenery invited her to walk. She followed the windings of a stream, which was lost at some distance amongst luxuriant groves of chesnut. The rich colouring of evening glowed through the dark foliage, which spreading a pensive gloom around, offered a scene congenial to the present temper of her mind, and she entered the shades. Her thoughts, affected by the surrounding objects, gradually sunk into a pleasing and complacent melancholy, and she was insensibly led on. She still followed the course of the stream to where the deep shades retired, and the scene again opening to day, yielded to her a view so various and sublime, that she paused in thrilling and delightful wonder. A group of wild and grotesque rocks rose in a semicircular form, and their fantastic shapes exhibited Nature in her most sublime and striking attitudes. Here her vast magnificence elevated the mind of the beholder to enthusiasm. Fancy caught the thrilling sensation, and at her touch the towering steeps became shaded with unreal glooms; the caves more darkly frowned— the projecting cliffs assumed a more terrific aspect, and the wild overhanging shrubs waved to the gale in deeper murmurs. The scene inspired madame with reverential awe, and her thoughts involuntarily rose, 'from Nature up to Nature's God.'* The last dying gleams of day tinted the rocks and shone upon the waters, which retired through a rugged channel and were lost afar among the receding cliffs. While she listened to their distant murmur, a voice of liquid and melodious sweetness arose from among the rocks; it sung an air, whose melancholy expression awakened all her attention, and captivated her heart. The tones swelled and died faintly away among the clear, yet languishing echoes which the rocks repeated with an effect like that of enchantment. Madame looked around in search of the sweet warbler, and observed at some distance a peasant girl seated on a small projection of the rock, overshadowed by drooping syca-mores. She moved slowly towards the spot, which she had almost reached, when the sound of her steps startled and silenced the syren, who, on perceiving a stranger, arose in an attitude to depart. The voice of madame arrested her, and she approached. Language cannot paint the sensation of madame, when in the disguise of a peasant girl, she distinguished the features of Julia, whose eyes lighted up with sudden recollection, and who sunk into her arms overcome with joy. When their first emotions were subsided, and Julia had received answers to her enquiries concerning Ferdinand and Emilia, she led madame to the place of her concealment. This was a solitary cottage, in a close valley surrounded by mountains, whose cliffs appeared wholly inaccessible to mortal foot. The deep solitude of the scene dissipated at once madame's wonder that Julia had so long remained undiscovered, and excited surprize how she had been able to explore a spot thus deeply sequestered; but madame observed with extreme concern, that the counten-ance of Julia no longer wore the smile of health and gaiety. Her fine features had received the impressions not only of melancholy, but of grief. Madame sighed as she gazed, and read too plainly the cause of the change. Julia understood that sigh, and answered it with her tears. She pressed the hand of madame in mournful silence to her lips, and her cheeks were suffused with a crimson glow. At length, re-covering herself, 'I have much, my dear madam, to tell,' said she, 'and much to explain, 'ere you will admit me again to that esteem of which I was once so justly proud. I had no resource from misery, but in flight; and of that I could not make you a confidant, without meanly involving you in its disgrace.'—'Say no more, my love, on the subject,' replied madame; 'with respect to myself, I admired your conduct, and felt severely for your situation. Rather let me hear by what means you effected your escape, and what has since be fallen you.'—Julia paused a moment, as if to stifle her rising emotion, and then commenced her narrative.

'You are already acquainted with the secret of that night, so fatal to my peace. I recall the remembrance of it with an anguish which I cannot conceal; and why should I wish its concealment, since I mourn for one, whose noble qualities justified all my admiration, and deserved more than my feeble praise can bestow; the idea of whom will be the last to linger in my mind till death shuts up this painful scene.' Her voice trembled, and she paused. After a few moments she resumed her tale. 'I will spare myself the pain of recurring to scenes with which you are not unacquainted, and proceed to those which more immediately attract your interest. Caterina, my faithful servant, you know, attended me in my confinement; to her kindness I owe my escape. She obtained from her lover, a servant in the castle, that assistance which gave me liberty. One night when Carlo, who had been appointed my guard, was asleep, Nicolo crept into his chamber, and stole from him the keys of my prison. He had previously procured a ladder of ropes. O! I can never forget my emotions, when in the dead hour of that night, which was meant to precede the day of my sacrifice, I heard the door of my prison unlock, and found myself half at liberty! My trembling limbs with difficulty supported me as I followed Caterina to the saloon, the windows of which being low and near to the terrace, suited our purpose. To the terrace we easily got, where Nicolo awaited us with the rope-ladder. He fastened it to the ground; and having climbed to the top of the parapet, quickly slided down on the other side. There he held it, while we ascended and descended; and I soon breathed the air of freedom again. But the apprehension of being retaken was still too powerful to permit a full enjoyment of my escape. It was my plan to proceed to the place of my faithful Caterina's nativity, where she had assured me I might find a safe asylum in the cottage of her parents, from whom, as they had never seen me, I might conceal my birth. This place, she said, was entirely unknown to the marquis, who had hired her at Naples only a few months before, without any enquiries concerning her family. She had informed me that the village was many leagues distant from the castle, but that she was very well acquainted with the road. At the foot of the walls we left Nicolo, who returned to the castle to prevent suspicion, but with an intention to leave it at a less dangerous time, and repair to Farrini to his good Caterina. I parted from him with many thanks, and gave him a small diamond cross, which, for that purpose, I had taken from the jewels sent to me for wedding ornaments.'

CHAPTER VIII

'ABOUT a quarter of a league from the walls we stopped, and I assumed the habit in which you now see me. My own dress was fastened to some heavy stones, and Caterina threw it into the stream, near the almond grove, whose murmurings you have so often admired. The fatigue and hardship I endured in this journey, performed almost wholly on foot, at any other time would have overcome me; but my mind was so occupied by the danger I was avoiding that these lesser evils were disregarded. We arrived in safety at the cottage, which stood at a little distance from the village of Ferrini, and were received by Caterina's parents with some surprise and more kindness. I soon perceived it would be useless, and even dangerous, to attempt to preserve the character I personated. In the eyes of Caterina's mother I read a degree of surprise and admiration which declared she believed me to be of superior rank; I, therefore, thought it more prudent to win her fidelity by entrusting her with my secret than, by endeavouring to conceal it, leave it to be discovered by her curiosity or discernment. Accordingly, I made known my quality and my distress, and received strong assurances of assistance and attachment. For further security, I removed to this sequestered spot. The cottage we are now in belongs to a sister of Caterina, upon whose faithfulness I have been hitherto fully justified in relying. But I am not even here secure from apprehension, since for several days past horsemen of a suspicious appearance have been observed near Marcy, which is only half a league from hence.'

Here Julia closed her narration, to which madame had listened with a mixture of surprise and pity, which her eyes sufficiently discovered. The last circumstance of the narrative seriously alarmed her. She acquainted Julia with the pursuit which the duke had undertaken; and she did not hesitate to believe it a party of his people whom Julia had described. Madame, therefore, earnestly advised her to quit her present situation, and to accompany her in disguise to the monastery of St Augustin, where she would find a secure retreat; because, even if her place of refuge should be discovered, the superior authority of the church would protect her. Julia accepted the proposal with much joy. As it was necessary that madame should sleep at the village where she had left her servants and horses, it was agreed that at break of day she should return to the cottage, where Julia would await her. Madame took an affectionate leave of Julia, whose heart, in spite of reason, sunk when she saw her depart, though but for the necessary interval of repose.

At the dawn of day madame arose. Her servants, who were hired for the journey, were strangers to Julia: from them, therefore, she had nothing to apprehend. She reached the cottage before sunrise, having left her people at some little distance. Her heart foreboded evil, when, on knocking at the door, no answer was returned. She knocked again, and still all was silent. Through the casement she could discover no object, amidst the grey obscurity of the dawn. She now opened the door, and, to her inexpressible surprise and distress, found the cottage empty. She proceeded to a small inner room, where lay a part of Julia's apparel. The bed had no appearance of having being slept in, and every moment served to heighten and confirm her apprehensions. While she pursued the search, she suddenly heard the trampling of feet at the cottage door, and presently after some people entered. Her fears for Julia now yielded to those for her own safety, and she was undetermined whether to discover herself, or remain in her present situation, when she was relieved from her irresolution by the appearance of Julia.

On the return of the good woman, who had accompanied madame to the village on the preceding night, Julia went to the cottage at Farrini. Her grateful heart would not suffer her to depart without taking leave of her faithful friends, thanking them for their kindness, and informing them of her future prospects. They had prevailed upon her to spend the few intervening hours at this cot, whence she had just risen to meet madame.

They now hastened to the spot where the horses were stationed, and commenced their journey. For some leagues they travelled in silence and thought, over a wild and picturesque country. The landscape was tinted with rich and variegated hues; and the autumnal lights, which streamed upon the hills, produced a spirited and beautiful effect upon the scenery. All the glories of the vintage rose to their view: the purple grapes flushed through the dark green of the surrounding foliage, and the prospect glowed with luxuriance.

They now descended into a deep valley, which appeared more like a scene of airy enchantment than reality. Along the bottom flowed a clear majestic stream, whose banks were adorned with thick groves of orange and citron trees. Julia surveyed the scene in silent complacency, but her eye quickly caught an object which changed with instantaneous shock the tone of her feelings. She observed a party of horsemen winding down the side of a hill behind her. Their uncommon speed alarmed her, and she pushed her horse into a gallop. On looking back Madame de Menon clearly perceived they were in pursuit. Soon after the men suddenly appeared from behind a dark grove within a small distance of them; and, upon their nearer approach, Julia, overcome with fatigue and fear, sunk breathless from her horse. She was saved from the ground by one of the pursuers, who caught her in his arms. Madame, with the rest of the party, were quickly overtaken; and as soon as Julia revived, they were bound, and reconducted to the hill from whence they had descended. Imagination only can paint the anguish of Julia's mind, when she saw herself thus delivered up to the power of her enemy. Madame, in the surrounding troop, discovered none of the marquis's people, and they were therefore evidently in the hands of the duke. After travelling for some hours, they quitted the main road, and turned into a narrow winding dell, overshadowed by high trees, which almost excluded the light. The gloom of the place inspired terrific images. Julia trembled as she entered; and her emotion was heightened, when she perceived at some distance, through the long perspective of the trees, a large ruinous mansion. The gloom of the surrounding shades partly concealed it from her view; but, as she drew near, each forlorn and decaying feature of the fabric was gradually disclosed, and struck upon her heart a horror such as she had never before experienced. The broken battlements, enwreathed with ivy, proclaimed the fallen grandeur of the place, while the shattered vacant window-frames exhibited its desolation, and the high grass that overgrew the threshold seemed to say how long it was since mortal foot had entered. The place appeared fit only for the purposes of violence and destruction: and the unfortunate captives, when they stopped at its gates, felt the full force of its horrors.

They were taken from their horses, and conveyed to an interior part of the building, which, if it had once been a chamber, no longer deserved the name. Here the guard said they were directed to detain them till the arrival of their lord, who had appointed this the place of rendezvous. He was expected to meet them in a few hours, and these were hours of indescribable torture to Julia and madame. From the furious passions of the duke, exasperated by frequent disappointment, Julia had every evil to apprehend; and the loneliness of the spot he had chosen, enabled him to perpetrate any designs, however violent. For the first time, she repented that she had left her father's house. Madame wept over her, but comfort she had none to give. The day closed—the duke did not appear, and the fate of Julia yet hung in perilous uncertainty. At length, from a window of the apartment she was in, she distinguished a glimmering of torches among the trees, and presently after the clattering of hoofs convinced her the duke was approaching. Her heart sunk at the sound; and throwing her arms round madame's neck, she resigned herself to despair. She was soon roused by some men, who came to announce the arrival of their lord. In a few moments the place, which had lately been so silent, echoed with tumult; and a sudden blaze of light illumining the fabric, served to exhibit more forcibly its striking horrors. Julia ran to the window; and, in a sort of court below, perceived a group of men dismounting from their horses. The torches shed a partial light; and while she anxiously looked round for the person of the duke, the whole party entered the mansion. She listened to a confused uproar of voices, which sounded from the room beneath, and soon after it sunk into a low murmur, as if some matter of importance was in agitation. For some moments she sat in lingering terror, when she heard footsteps advancing towards the chamber, and a sudden gleam of torchlight flashed upon the walls. 'Wretched girl! I have at least secured you!' said a cavalier, who now entered the room. He stopped as he perceived Julia; and turning to the men who stood without, 'Are these,' said he, 'the fugitives you have taken?'—'Yes, my lord.'—'Then you have deceived yourselves, and misled me; this is not my daughter.' These words struck the sudden light of truth and joy upon the heart of Julia, whom terror had before rendered almost lifeless; and who had not perceived that the person entering was a stranger. Madame now stepped forward, and an explanation ensued, when it appeared that the stranger was the Marquis Murani, the father of the fair fugitive whom the duke had before mistaken for Julia.

The appearance and the evident flight of Julia had deceived the banditti employed by this nobleman, into a belief that she was the object of their search, and had occasioned her this unnecessary distress. But the joy she now felt, on finding herself thus unexpectedly at liberty, surpassed, if possible, her preceding terrors. The marquis made madame and Julia all the reparation in his power, by offering immediately to reconduct them to the main road, and to guard them to some place of safety for the night. This offer was eagerly and thankfully accepted; and though faint from distress, fatigue, and want of sustenance, they joyfully remounted their horses, and by torchlight quitted the mansion. After some hours travelling they arrived at a small town, where they procured the accommodation so necessary to their support and repose. Here their guides quitted them to continue their search.

They arose with the dawn, and continued their journey, continually terrified with the apprehension of encountering the duke's people. At noon they arrived at Azulia, from whence the monastery, or abbey of St Augustin, was distant only a few miles. Madame wrote to the *Padre Abate*, to whom she was somewhat related, and soon after received an answer very favourable to her wishes. The same evening they repaired to the abbey; where Julia, once more relieved from the fear of pursuit, offered up a prayer of gratitude to heaven, and endeavoured to calm her sorrows by devotion. She was received by the abbot with a sort of paternal affection, and by the nuns with officious kindness. Comforted by these circumstances, and by the tranquil appearance of every thing around her, she retired to rest, and passed the night in peaceful slumbers.

In her present situation she found much novelty to amuse, and much serious matter to interest her mind. Entendered by distress, she easily yielded to the pensive manners of her companions and to the serene uniformity of a monastic life. She loved to wander through the lonely cloisters, and high-arched aisles, whose long perspectives retired in simple grandeur, diffusing a holy calm around. She found much pleasure in the conversation of the nuns, many of whom were uncommonly amiable, and the dignified sweetness of whose manners formed a charm irresistibly attractive. The soft melancholy impressed upon their countenances, pourtrayed the situation of their minds, and excited in Julia a very interesting mixture of pity and esteem. The affectionate appellation of sister, and all that endearing tenderness which they so well know how to display, and of which they so well understand the effect, they bestowed on Julia, in the hope of winning her to become one of their order.

Soothed by the presence of madame, the assiduity of the nuns, and by the stillness and sanctity of the place, her mind gradually recovered a degree of complacency to which it had long been a stranger. But notwithstanding all her efforts, the idea of Hippolitus would at intervals return upon her memory with a force that at once subdued her fortitude, and sunk her in a temporary despair.

Among the holy sisters, Julia distinguished one, the singular fervor of whose devotion, and the pensive air of whose countenance, softened by the languor of illness, attracted her curiosity, and excited a strong degree of pity. The nun, by a sort of sympathy, seemed particularly inclined towards Julia, which she discovered by innumerable acts of kindness, such as the heart can quickly understand and acknowledge, although description can never reach them. In conversation with her, Julia endeavoured, as far as delicacy would permit, to prompt an explanation of that more than common dejection which shaded those features, where beauty, touched by resignation and sublimed by religion, shone forth with mild and lambent lustre.

The Duke de Luovo, after having been detained for some weeks by the fever which his wounds had produced, and his irritated passions had much prolonged, arrived at the castle of Mazzini.

When the marquis saw him return, and recollected the futility of those exertions, by which he had boastingly promised to recover Julia, the violence of his nature spurned the disguise of art, and burst forth in contemptuous impeachment of the valour and discernment of the duke, who soon retorted with equal fury. The consequence might have been fatal, had not the ambition of the marquis subdued the sudden irritation of his inferior passions, and induced him to soften the severity of his accusations, by subsequent concessions. The duke, whose passion for Julia was heightened by the difficulty which opposed it, admitted such concessions as in other circumstances he would have rejected; and thus each, conquered by the predominant passion of the moment, submitted to be the slave of his adversary.

Emilia was at length released from the confinement she had so unjustly suffered. She had now the use of her old apartments, where, solitary and dejected, her hours moved

heavily along, embittered by incessant anxiety for Julia, and
by regret for the lost society of madame. The marchioness,
whose pleasures suffered a temporary suspense during the
present confusion at the castle, exercised the ill-humoured
caprice, which disappointment and lassitude inspired, upon
her remaining subject. Emilia was condemned to suffer, and
to endure without the privilege of complaining. In reviewing
the events of the last few weeks, she saw those most dear
to her banished, or imprisoned by the secret influence of a
woman, every feature of whose character was exactly opposite to that of the amiable mother she had been appointed
to succeed.

The search after Julia still continued, and was still unsuccessful. The astonishment of the marquis increased with
his disappointments; for where could Julia, ignorant of the
country, and destitute of friends, have possibly found an
asylum? He swore with a terrible oath to revenge on her
head, whenever she should be found, the trouble and vexation she now caused him. But he agreed with the duke to
relinquish for a while the search; till Julia, gaining confidence from the observation of this circumstance, might
gradually suppose herself secure from molestation, and thus
be induced to emerge from concealment.

CHAPTER IX

MEANWHILE Julia, sheltered in the obscure recesses of St Augustin, endeavoured to attain a degree of that tranquillity which so strikingly characterized the scenes around her. The abbey of St Augustin was a large magnificent mass of Gothic architecture, whose gloomy battlements, and majestic towers arose in proud sublimity from amid the darkness of the surrounding shades. It was founded in the twelfth century, and stood a proud monument of monkish superstition and princely magnificence. In the times when Italy was agitated by internal commotions, and persecuted by foreign invaders, this edifice afforded an asylum to many noble Italian emigrants, who here consecrated the rest of their days to religion. At their death they enriched the monastery with the treasures which it had enabled them to secure.

The view of this building revived in the mind of the beholder the memory of past ages. The manners and characters which distinguished them arose to his fancy, and through the long lapse of years he discriminated those customs and manners which formed so striking a contrast to the modes of his own times. The rude manners, the boisterous passions, the daring ambition, and the gross indulgences which formerly characterized the priest, the nobleman, and the sovereign, had now begun to yield to learning—the charms of refined conversation—political intrigue and private artifices. Thus do the scenes of life vary with the predominant passions of mankind, and with the progress of civilization. The dark clouds of prejudice break away before the sun of science, and gradually dissolving, leave the brightening hemisphere to the influence of his beams. But through the present scene appeared only a few scattered rays, which served to shew more forcibly the vast and heavy masses that concealed the form of truth. Here prejudice, not reason, suspended the influence of the passions; and scholastic learning, mysterious philosophy, and crafty sanctity supplied the place of wisdom, simplicity, and pure devotion.

At the abbey, solitude and stillness conspired with the solemn aspect of the pile to impress the mind with religious awe. The dim glass of the high-arched windows, stained with the colouring of monkish fictions, and shaded by the thick trees that environed the edifice, spread around a sacred gloom, which inspired the beholder with congenial feelings.

As Julia mused through the walks, and surveyed this vast monument of barbarous superstition, it brought to her recollection an ode which she often repeated with melancholy pleasure, as the composition of Hippolitus.

SUPERSTITION
AN ODE*

High mid Alverna's* awful steeps,
    Eternal shades, and silence dwell.
Save, when the gale resounding sweeps,
    Sad strains are faintly heard to swell:

Enthron'd amid the wild impending rocks,
    Involved in clouds, and brooding future woe,
The demon Superstition Nature shocks,
    And waves her sceptre o'er the world below.

Around her throne, amid the mingling glooms,
    Wild—hideous forms are slowly seen to glide,
She bids them fly to shade earth's brightest blooms,
    And spread the blast of Desolation wide.

See! in the darkened air their fiery course!
    The sweeping ruin settles o'er the land,
Terror leads on their steps with madd'ning force,
    And Death and Vengeance close the ghastly band!

      Mark the purple streams that flow!
      Mark the deep empassioned woe!
      Frantic Fury's dying groan!
      Virtue's sigh, and Sorrow's moan!

Wide—wide the phantoms swell the loaded air
With shrieks of anguish—madness and despair!

Cease your ruin! spectres dire!
  Cease your wild terrific sway!
Turn your steps—and check your ire,
  Yield to peace the mourning day!

She wept to the memory of times past, and there was a romantic sadness in her feelings, luxurious and indefinable. Madame behaved to Julia with the tenderest attention, and endeavoured to withdraw her thoughts from their mournful subject by promoting that taste for literature and music, which was so suitable to the powers of her mind.

But an object seriously interesting now obtained that regard, which those of mere amusement failed to attract. Her favorite nun, for whom her love and esteem daily increased, seemed declining under the pressure of a secret grief. Julia was deeply affected with her situation, and though she was not empowered to administer consolation to her sorrows, she endeavoured to mitigate the sufferings of illness. She nursed her with unremitting care, and seemed to seize with avidity the temporary opportunity of escaping from herself. The nun appeared perfectly reconciled to her fate, and exhibited during her illness so much sweetness, patience, and resignation as affected all around her with pity and love. Her angelic mildness, and steady fortitude characterized the beatification of a saint, rather than the death of a mortal. Julia watched every turn of her disorder with the utmost solicitude, and her care was at length rewarded by the amendment of Cornelia. Her health gradually improved, and she attributed this circumstance to the assiduity and tenderness of her young friend, to whom her heart now expanded in warm and unreserved affection. At length Julia ventured to solicit what she had so long and so earnestly wished for, and Cornelia unfolded the history of her sorrows.

'Of the life which your care has prolonged,' said she, 'it is but just that you should know the events; though those events are neither new, or striking, and possess little power of interesting persons unconnected with them. To me they have, however, been unexpectedly dreadful in effect, and my heart assures me, that to you they will not be indifferent.

'I am the unfortunate descendant of an ancient and illustrious Italian family. In early childhood I was deprived of a mother's care, but the tenderness of my surviving parent made her loss, as to my welfare, almost unfelt. Suffer me here to do justice to the character of my noble father. He united in an eminent degree the mild virtues of social life, with the firm unbending qualities of the noble Romans, his ancestors, from whom he was proud to trace his descent. Their merit, indeed, continually dwelt on his tongue, and their actions he was always endeavouring to imitate, as far as was consistent with the character of his times, and with the limited sphere in which he moved. The recollection of his virtue elevates my mind, and fills my heart with a noble pride, which even the cold walls of a monastery have not been able to subdue.

'My father's fortune was unsuitable to his rank. That his son might hereafter be enabled to support the dignity of his family, it was necessary for me to assume the veil. Alas! that heart was unfit to be offered at an heavenly shrine, which was already devoted to an earthly object. My affections had long been engaged by the younger son of a neighbouring nobleman, whose character and accomplishments attracted my early love, and confirmed my latest esteem. Our families were intimate, and our youthful intercourse occasioned an attachment which strengthened and expanded with our years. He solicited me of my father, but there appeared an insuperable barrier to our union. The family of my lover laboured under a circumstance of similar distress with that of my own—it was noble—but poor! My father, who was ignorant of the strength of my affection, and who considered a marriage formed in poverty as destructive to happiness, prohibited his suit.

'Touched with chagrin and disappointment, he immediately entered into the service of his Neapolitan majesty, and sought in the tumultuous scenes of glory, a refuge from the pangs of disappointed passion.

'To me, whose hours moved in one round of full uniformity—who had no pursuit to interest—no variety to animate my drooping spirits—to me the effort of forgetfulness was ineffectual. The loved idea of Angelo still rose upon my fancy, and its powers of captivation, heightened by absence, and, perhaps even by despair, pursued me with incessant grief. I concealed in silence the anguish that preyed upon my heart, and resigned myself a willing victim to monastic austerity. But I was now threatened with a new evil, terrible and unexpected. I was so unfortunate as to attract the admiration of the Marquis Marinelli, and he applied to my father. He was illustrious at once in birth and fortune, and his visits could only be unwelcome to me. Dreadful was the moment in which my father disclosed to me the proposal. My distress, which I vainly endeavoured to command, discovered the exact situation of my heart, and my father was affected.

'After a long and awful pause, he generously released me from my sufferings by leaving it to my choice to accept the marquis, or to assume the veil. I fell at his feet, overcome by the noble disinterestedness of his conduct, and instantly accepted the latter.

'This affair removed entirely the disguise with which I had hitherto guarded my heart;—my brother—my generous brother! learned the true state of its affections. He saw the grief which prayed upon my health; he observed it to my father, and he nobly—oh how nobly! to restore my happiness, desired to resign a part of the estate which had already descended to him in right of his mother. Alas! Hippolitus,' continued Cornelia, deeply sighing, 'thy virtues deserved a better fate.'

'Hippolitus!' said Julia, in a tremulous accent, 'Hippolitus, Count de Vereza!'—'The same,' replied the nun, in a tone of surprize. Julia was speechless; tears, however, came to her relief. The astonishment of Cornelia for some moment surpassed expression; at length a gleam of recollection crossed her mind, and she too well understood the scene before her. Julia, after some time revived, when Cornelia tenderly approaching her, 'Do I then embrace my sister!' said she. 'United in sentiment, are we also united in misfortune?' Julia answered with her sighs, and their tears flowed in mournful sympathy together. At length Cornelia resumed her narrative.

'My father, struck with the conduct of Hippolitus, paused upon the offer. The alteration in my health was too obvious to escape his notice; the conflict between pride and parental tenderness, held him for some time in indecision, but the latter finally subdued every opposing feeling, and he yielded his consent to my marriage with Angelo. The sudden transition from grief to joy was almost too much for my feeble frame; judge then what must have been the effect of the dreadful reverse, when the news arrived that Angelo had fallen in a foreign engagement! Let me obliterate, if possible, the impression of sensations so dreadful. The sufferings of my brother, whose generous heart could so finely feel for another's woe, were on this occasion inferior only to my own.

'After the first excess of my grief was subsided, I desired to retire from a world which had tempted me only with illusive visions of happiness, and to remove from those scenes which prompted recollection, and perpetuated my distress. My father applauded my resolution, and I immediately was admitted a noviciate* into this monastery, with the Superior of which my father had in his youth been acquainted.

'At the expiration of the year I received the veil. Oh! I well remember with what perfect resignation, with what comfortable complacency I took those vows which bound me to a life of retirement, and religious rest.

'The high importance of the moment, the solemnity of the ceremony, the sacred glooms which surrounded me, and the chilling silence that prevailed when I uttered the irrevocable vow—all conspired to impress my imagination, and to raise my views to heaven. When I knelt at the altar, the sacred flame of pure devotion glowed in my heart, and elevated my soul to sublimity. The world and all its recollections faded from my mind, and left it to the influence of a serene and holy enthusiasm which no words can describe.

'Soon after my noviciation, I had the misfortune to lose my dear father. In the tranquillity of this monastery, however, in the soothing kindness of my companions, and in devotional exercises, my sorrows found relief, and the sting of grief was blunted. My repose was of short continuance. A circumstance occurred that renewed the misery, which can now never quit me but in the grave, to which I look with no fearful apprehension, but as a refuge from calamity, trusting that the power who has seen good to afflict me, will pardon the imperfectness of my devotion, and the too frequent wandering of my thoughts to the object once so dear to me.'

As she spoke she raised her eyes, which beamed with truth and meek assurance to heaven; and the fine devotional suffusion of her countenance seemed to characterize the beauty of an inspired saint.

'One day, Oh! never shall I forget it, I went as usual to the confessional to acknowledge my sins. I knelt before the father with eyes bent towards the earth, and in a low voice proceeded to confess. I had but one crime to deplore, and that was the too tender remembrance of him for whom I mourned, and whose idea, impressed upon my heart, made it a blemished offering to God.

'I was interrupted in my confession by a sound of deep sobs, and rising my eyes, Oh God, what were my sensations, when in the features of the holy father I discovered Angelo! His image faded like a vision from my sight, and I sunk at his feet. On recovering I found myself on my matrass, attended by a sister, who I discovered by her conversation had no suspicion of the occasion of my disorder. Indisposition confined me to my bed for several days; when I recovered, I saw Angelo no more, and could almost have doubted my senses, and believed that an illusion had crossed my sight, till one day I found in my cell a written paper. I distinguished at the first glance the handwriting of Angelo, that well-known hand which had so often awakened me to

other emotions. I trembled at the sight; my beating heart
acknowledged the beloved characters; a cold tremor shook
my frame, and half breathless I seized the paper. But
recollecting myself, I paused—I hesitated: duty at length
yielded to the strong temptation, and I read the lines! Oh!
those lines prompted by despair, and bathed in my tears!
every word they offered gave a new pang to my heart, and
swelled its anguish almost beyond endurance. I learned that
Angelo, severely wounded in a foreign engagement, had been
left for dead upon the field; that his life was saved by the
humanity of a common soldier of the enemy, who perceiving
signs of existence, conveyed him to a house. Assistance was
soon procured, but his wounds exhibited the most alarming
symptoms. During several months he languished between
life and death, till at length his youth and constitution
surmounted the conflict, and he returned to Naples. Here
he saw my brother, whose distress and astonishment at
beholding him occasioned a relation of past circumstances,
and of the vows I had taken in consequence of the report
of his death. It is unnecessary to mention the immediate
effect of this narration; the final one exhibited a very
singular proof of his attachment and despair;—he devoted
himself to a monastic life, and chose this abbey for the place
of his residence, because it contained the object most dear
to his affections. His letter informed me that he had purposely avoided discovering himself, endeavouring to be contented with the opportunities which occurred of silently
observing me, till chance had occasioned the foregoing
interview.—But that since its effects had been so mutually
painful, he would relieve me from the apprehension of a
similar distress, by assuring me, that I should see him no
more. He was faithful to his promise; from that day I have
never seen him, and am even ignorant whether he yet
inhabits this asylum; the efforts of religious fortitude, and
the just fear of exciting curiosity, having withheld me from
enquiry. But the moment of our last interview has been
equally fatal to my peace and to my health, and I trust I
shall, ere very long, be released from the agonizing ineffectual

struggles occasioned by the consciousness of sacred vows imperfectly performed, and by earthly affections not wholly subdued.'

Cornelia ceased, and Julia, who had listened to the narrative in deep attention, at once admired, loved, and pitied her. As the sister of Hippolitus, her heart expanded towards her, and it was now inviolably attached by the fine ties of sympathetic sorrow. Similarity of sentiment and suffering united them in the firmest bonds of friendship; and thus, from reciprocation of thought and feeling, flowed a pure and sweet consolation.

Julia loved to indulge in the mournful pleasure of conversing of Hippolitus, and when thus engaged, the hours crept unheeded by. A thousand questions she repeated concerning him, but to those most interesting to her, she received no consolatory answer. Cornelia, who had heard of the fatal transaction at the castle of Mazzini, deplored with her its too certain consequence.

CHAPTER X

JULIA accustomed herself to walk in the fine evenings under the shade of the high trees that environed the abbey. The dewy coolness of the air refreshed her. The innumerable roseate tints which the parting sun-beams reflected on the rocks above, and the fine vermil* glow diffused over the romantic scene beneath, softly fading from the eye, as the nightshades fell, excited sensations of a sweet and tranquil nature, and soothed her into a temporary forgetfulness of her sorrows.

The deep solitude of the place subdued her apprehension, and one evening she ventured with Madame de Menon to lengthen her walk. They returned to the abbey without having seen a human being, except a friar of the monastery, who had been to a neighbouring town to order provision. On the following evening they repeated their walk; and, engaged in conversation, rambled to a considerable distance from the abbey. The distant bell of the monastery sounding for vespers, reminded them of the hour, and looking round, they perceived the extremity of the wood. They were returning towards the abbey, when struck by the appearance of some majestic columns which were distinguishable between the trees, they paused. Curiosity tempted them to examine to what edifice pillars of such magnificent architecture could belong, in a scene so rude, and they went on.

There appeared on a point of rock impending over the valley the reliques of a palace, whose beauty time had impaired only to heighten its sublimity. An arch of singular magnificence remained almost entire, beyond which appeared wild cliffs retiring in grand perspective. The sun, which was now setting, threw a trembling lustre upon the ruins, and gave a finishing effect to the scene. They gazed in mute wonder upon the view; but the fast fading light, and the dewy chillness of the air, warned them to return.

As Julia gave a last look to the scene, she perceived two men leaning upon a part of the ruin at some distance, in earnest conversation. As they spoke, their looks were so attentively bent on her, that she could have no doubt she was the subject of their discourse. Alarmed at this circumstance, madame and Julia immediately retreated towards the abbey. They walked swiftly through the woods, whose shades, deepened by the gloom of evening, prevented their distinguishing whether they were pursued. They were surprized to observe the distance to which they had strayed from the monastery, whose dark towers were now obscurely seen rising among the trees that closed the perspective. They had almost reached the gates, when on looking back, they perceived the same men slowly advancing, without any appearance of pursuit, but clearly as if observing the place of their retreat.

This incident occasioned Julia much alarm. She could not but believe that the men whom she had seen were spies of the marquis;—if so, her asylum was discovered, and she had every thing to apprehend. Madame now judged it necessary to the safety of Julia, that the *Abate* should be informed of her story, and of the sanctuary she had sought in his monastery, and also that he should be solicited to protect her from parental tyranny. This was a hazardous, but a necessary step, to provide against the certain danger which must ensue, should the marquis, if he demanded his daughter of the *Abate*, be the first to acquaint him with her story. If she acted otherwise, she feared that the *Abate*, in whose generosity she had not confided, and whose pity she had not solicited, would, in the pride of his resentment, deliver her up, and thus would she become a certain victim to the Duke de Luovo.

Julia approved of this communication, though she trembled for the event; and requested madame to plead her cause with the *Abate*. On the following morning, therefore, madame solicited a private audience of the *Abate*; she obtained permission to see him, and Julia, in trembling anxiety, watched her to the door of his apartment. This conference was long, and every moment seemed an hour to Julia, who, in fearful expectation, awaited with Cornelia the sentence which would decide her destiny. She was now the constant companion of Cornelia, whose declining health interested her pity, and strengthened her attachment.

Meanwhile madame developed to the *Abate* the distressful story of Julia. She praised her virtues, commended her accomplishments, and deplored her situation. She described the characters of the marquis and the duke, and concluded with pathetically representing, that Julia had sought in this monastery, a last asylum from injustice and misery, and with entreating that the *Abate* would grant her his pity and protection.

The *Abate* during this discourse preserved a sullen silence; his eyes were bent to the ground, and his aspect was thoughful and solemn. When madame ceased to speak, a pause of profound silence ensued, and she sat in anxious expectation. She endeavoured to anticipate in his countenance the answer preparing, but she derived no comfort from thence. At length raising his head, and awakening from his deep reverie, he told her that her request required deliberation, and that the protection she solicited for Julia, might involve him in serious consequences, since, from a character so determined as the marquis's, much violence might reasonably be expected. 'Should his daughter be refused him,' concluded the *Abate*, 'he may even dare to violate the sanctuary.'

Madame, shocked by the stern indifference of this reply, was a moment silent. The *Abate* went on. 'Whatever I shall determine upon, the young lady has reason to rejoice that she is admitted into this holy house; for I will even now venture to assure her, that if the marquis fails to demand her, she shall be permitted to remain in this sanctuary unmolested. You, Madam, will be sensible of this indulgence, and of the value of the sacrifice I make in granting it; for, in thus concealing a child from her parent, I encourage her in disobedience, and consequently sacrifice my sense of duty, to what may be justly called a weak humanity.'

Madame listened to this pompous declamation in silent sorrow and indignation. She made another effort to interest the *Abate* in favor of Julia, but he preserved his stern inflexibility, and repeating that he would deliberate upon the matter, and acquaint her with the result, he arose with great solemnity, and quitted the room.

She now half repented of the confidence she had reposed in him, and of the pity she had solicited, since he discovered a mind incapable of understanding the first, and a temper inaccessible to the influence of the latter. With an heavy heart she returned to Julia, who read in her countenance, at the moment she entered the room, news of no happy import. When madame related the particulars of the conference, Julia presaged from it only misery, and giving herself up for lost—she burst into tears. She severely deplored the confidence she had been induced to yield; for she now saw herself in the power of a man, stern and unfeeling in his nature: and from whom, if he thought it fit to betray her, she had no means of escaping. But she concealed the anguish of her heart; and to console madame, affected to hope where she could only despair.

Several days elapsed, and no answer was returned from the *Abate*. Julia too well understood this silence.

One morning Cornelia entering her room with a disturbed and impatient air, informed her that some emissaries from the marquis were then in the monastery, having enquired at the gate for the *Abate*, with whom, they said, they had business of importance to transact. The *Abate* had granted them immediate audience, and they were now in close conference.

At this intelligence the spirits of Julia forsook her; she trembled, grew pale, and stood fixed in mute despair. Madame, though scarcely less distressed, retained a presence of mind. She understood too justly the character of the Superior to doubt that he would hesitate in delivering Julia to the hands of the marquis. On this moment, therefore, turned the crisis of her fate!—this moment she might escape—the next she was a prisoner. She therefore advised

Julia to seize the instant, and fly from the monastery before the conference was concluded, when the gates would most probably be closed upon her, assuring her, at the same time, she would accompany her in flight.

The generous conduct of madame called tears of gratitude into the eyes of Julia, who now awoke from the state of stupefaction which distress had caused. But before she could thank her faithful friend, a nun entered the room with a summons for madame to attend the *Abate* immediately. The distress which this message occasioned can not easily be conceived. Madame advised Julia to escape while she detained the *Abate* in conversation, as it was not probable that he had yet issued orders for her detention. Leaving her to this attempt, with an assurance of following her from the abbey as soon as possible, madame obeyed the summons. The coolness of her fortitude forsook her as she approached the *Abate*'s apartment, and she became less certain as to the occasion of this summons.

The *Abate* was alone. His countenance was pale with anger, and he was pacing the room with slow but agitated steps. The stern authority of his look startled her. 'Read this letter,' said he, stretching forth his hand which held a letter, 'and tell me what that mortal deserves, who dares insult our holy order, and set our sacred prerogative at defiance.' Madame distinguished the handwriting of the marquis, and the words of the Superior threw her into the utmost astonishment. She took the letter. It was dictated by that spirit of proud vindictive rage, which so strongly marked the character of the marquis. Having discovered the retreat of Julia, and believing the monastery afforded her a willing sanctuary from his pursuit, he accused the *Abate* of encouraging his child in open rebellion to his will. He loaded him and his sacred order with opprobrium, and threatened, if she was not immediately resigned to the emissaries in waiting, he would in person lead on a force which should compel the church to yield to the superior authority of the father.

The spirit of the *Abate* was roused by this menace; and Julia obtained from his pride, that protection which neither his principle or his humanity would have granted. 'The man shall tremble,' cried he, 'who dares defy our power, or question our sacred authority. The lady Julia is safe. I will protect her from this proud invader of our rights, and teach him at least to venerate the power he cannot conquer. I have dispatched his emissaries with my answer.'

These words struck sudden joy upon the heart of Madame de Menon, but she instantly recollected, that ere this time Julia had quitted the abbey, and thus the very precaution which was meant to ensure her safety, had probably precipitated her into the hand of her enemy. This thought changed her joy to anguish; and she was hurrying from the apartment in a sort of wild hope, that Julia might not yet be gone, when the stern voice of the *Abate* arrested her. 'Is it thus,' cried he, 'that you receive the knowledge of our generous resolution to protect your friend? Does such condescending kindness merit no thanks—demand no gratitude?' Madame returned in an agony of fear, lest one moment of delay might prove fatal to Julia, if haply she had not yet quitted the monastery. She was conscious of her deficiency in apparent gratitude, and of the strange appearance of her abrupt departure from the *Abate*, for which it was impossible to apologize, without betraying the secret, which would kindle all his resentment. Yet some atonement his present anger demanded, and these circumstances caused her a very painful embarrassment. She formed a hasty excuse; and expressing her sense of his goodness, again attempted to retire, when the *Abate* frowning in deep resentment, his features inflamed with pride, arose from his seat. 'Stay,' said he; 'whence this impatience to fly from the presence of a benefactor?—If my generosity fails to excite gratitude, my resentment shall not fail to inspire awe.— Since the lady Julia is insensible of my condescension, she is unworthy of my protection, and I will resign her to the tyrant who demands her.'

To this speech, in which the offended pride of the *Abate* overcoming all sense of justice, accused and threatened to punish Julia for the fault of her friend, madame listened in dreadful impatience. Every word that detained her struck torture to her heart, but the concluding sentence occasioned new terror, and she started at its purpose. She fell at the feet of the *Abate* in an agony of grief. 'Holy father,' said she, 'punish not Julia for the offence which I only have committed; her heart will bless her generous protector, and for myself, suffer me to assure you that I am fully sensible of your goodness.'

'If this is true,' said the *Abate*, 'arise, and bid the lady Julia attend me.' This command increased the confusion of madame, who had no doubt that her detention had proved fatal to Julia. At length she was suffered to depart, and to her infinite joy found Julia in her own room. Her intention of escaping had yielded, immediately after the departure of madame, to the fear of being discovered by the marquis's people. This fear had been confirmed by the report of Cornelia, who informed her, that at that time several horse-men were waiting at the gates for the return of their companions. This was a dreadful circumstance to Julia, who perceived it was utterly impossible to quit the monastery, without rushing upon certain destruction. She was lament-ing her destiny, when madame recited the particulars of the late interview, and delivered the summons of the *Abate*.

They had now to dread the effect of that tender anxiety, which had excited his resentment; and Julia, suddenly elated to joy by his first determination, was as suddenly sunk to despair by his last. She trembled with apprehension of the coming interview, though each moment of delay which her fear solicited, would, by heightening the resentment of the *Abate*, only increase the danger she dreaded.

At length, by a strong effort, she reanimated her spirits, and went to the *Abate's* closet to receive her sentence. He was seated in his chair, and his frowning aspect chilled her heart. 'Daughter,' said he, 'you have been guilty of heinous crimes. You have dared to dispute—nay openly to rebel, against the lawful authority of your father. You have dis-obeyed the will of him whose prerogative yields only to ours. You have questioned his right upon a point of all others the most decided—the right of a father to dispose of his child in marriage. You have even fled from his protection—and you have dared—insidiously, and meanly have dared, to screen your disobedience beneath this sacred roof. You have prophaned our sanctuary with your crime. You have brought insult upon our sacred order, and have caused bold and impious defiance of our high prerogative. What punishment is adequate to guilt like this?'

The father paused—his eyes sternly fixed on Julia, who, pale and trembling, could scarcely support herself, and who had no power to reply. 'I will be merciful, and not just,' resumed he,—'I will soften the punishment you deserve, and will only deliver you to your father.' At these dreadful words, Julia bursting into tears, sunk at the feet of the *Abate*, to whom she raised her eyes in supplicating expression, but was unable to speak. He suffered her to remain in this posture. 'Your duplicity,' he resumed, 'is not the least of your offences.—Had you relied upon our generosity for forgiveness and protection, an indulgence might have been granted;—but under the disguise of virtue you concealed your crimes, and your necessities were hid beneath the mask of devotion.'

These false aspersions roused in Julia the spirit of indignant virtue; she arose from her knees with an air of dignity, that struck even the *Abate*. 'Holy father,' said she, 'my heart abhors the crime you mention, and disclaims all union with it. Whatever are my offences, from the sin of hypocrisy I am at least free; and you will pardon me if I remind you, that my confidence has already been such, as fully justifies my claim to the protection I solicit. When I sheltered myself within these walls, it was to be presumed that they would protect me from injustice; and with what other term than injustice would you, Sir, distinguish the conduct of the marquis, if the fear of his power did not overcome the dictates of truth?'

The *Abate* felt the full force of this reproof; but disdaining to appear sensible to it, restrained his resentment. His wounded pride thus exasperated, and all the malignant passions of his nature thus called into action, he was prompted to that cruel surrender which he had never before seriously intended. The offence which Madame de Menon had unintentionally given his haughty spirit urged him to retaliate in punishment. He had, therefore, pleased himself with exciting a terror which he never meant to confirm, and he resolved to be further solicited for that protection which he had already determined to grant. But this reproof of Julia touched him where he was most conscious of defect; and the temporary triumph which he imagined it afforded her, kindled his resentment into flame. He mused in his chair, in a fixed attitude.—She saw in his countenance the deep workings of his mind—she revolved the fate preparing for her, and stood in trembling anxiety to receive her sentence. The *Abate* considered each aggravating circumstance of the marquis's menace, and each sentence of Julia's speech; and his mind experienced that vice is not only inconsistent with virtue, but with itself—for to gratify his malignity, he now discovered that it would be necessary to sacrifice his pride— since it would be impossible to punish the object of the first without denying himself the gratification of the latter. This reflection suspended his mind in a state of torture, and he sat wrapt in gloomy silence.

The spirit which lately animated Julia had vanished with her words—each moment of silence increased her apprehension; the deep brooding of his thoughts confirmed her in the apprehension of evil, and with all the artless eloquence of sorrow she endeavoured to soften him to pity. He listened to her pleadings in sullen stillness. But each instant now cooled the fervour of his resentment to her, and increased his desire of opposing the marquis. At length the predominant feature of his character resumed its original influence, and overcame the workings of subordinate passion. Proud of his religious authority, he determined never to yield the prerogative of the church to that of the father, and resolved to oppose the violence of the marquis with equal force.

He therefore condescended to relieve Julia from her terrors, by assuring her of his protection; but he did this in a manner so ungracious, as almost to destroy the gratitude which the promise demanded. She hastened with the joyful intelligence to Madame de Menon, who wept over her tears of thankfulness.

CHAPTER XI

NEAR a fortnight had elapsed without producing any appearance of hostility from the marquis, when one night, long after the hour of repose, Julia was awakened by the bell of the monastery. She knew it was not the hour customary for prayer, and she listened to the sounds, which rolled through the deep silence of the fabric, with strong surprise and terror. Presently she heard the doors of several cells creak on their hinges, and the sound of quick footsteps in the passages—and through the crevices of her door she distinguished passing lights. The whispering noise of steps increased, and every person of the monastery seemed to have awakened. Her terror heightened; it occurred to her that the marquis had surrounded the abbey with his people, in the design of forcing her from her retreat; and she arose in haste, with an intention of going to the chamber of Madame de Menon, when she heard a gentle tap at the door. Her enquiry of who was there, was answered in the voice of madame, and her fears were quickly dissipated, for she learned the bell was a summons to attend a dying nun, who was going to the high altar, there to receive extreme unction.

She quitted the chamber with madame. In her way to the church, the gleam of tapers on the walls, and the glimpse which her eye often caught of the friars in their long black habits, descending silently through the narrow winding passages, with the solemn toll of the bell, conspired to kindle imagination, and to impress her heart with sacred awe. But the church exhibited a scene of solemnity, such as she had never before witnessed. Its gloomy aisles were imperfectly seen by the rays of tapers from the high altar, which shed a solitary gleam over the remote parts of the fabric, and produced large masses of light and shade, striking and sublime in their effect.

While she gazed, she heard a distant chanting rise through the aisles; the sounds swelled in low murmurs on the ear, and drew nearer and nearer, till a sudden blaze of light issued from one of the portals, and the procession entered. The organ instantly sounded a high and solemn peal, and the voices rising altogether swelled the sacred strain. In front appeared the *Padre Abate*, with slow and measured steps, bearing the holy cross. Immediately followed a litter, on which lay the dying person covered with a white veil, borne along and surrounded by nuns veiled in white, each carrying in her hand a lighted taper. Last came the friars,* two and two, cloathed in black, and each bearing a light.

When they reached the high altar, the bier was rested, and in a few moments the anthem ceased. The *Abate* now approached to perform the unction; the veil of the dying nun was lifted—and Julia discovered her beloved Cornelia! Her countenance was already impressed with the image of death, but her eyes brightened with a faint gleam of recollection, when they fixed upon Julia, who felt a cold thrill run through her frame, and leaned for support on madame. Julia now for the first time distinguished the unhappy lover of Cornelia, on whose features was depictured the anguish of his heart, and who hung pale and silent over the bier. The ceremony being finished, the anthem struck up; the bier was lifted, when Cornelia faintly moved her hand, and it was again rested upon the steps of the altar. In a few minutes the music ceased, when lifting her heavy eyes to her lover, with an expression of ineffable tenderness and grief, she attempted to speak, but the sounds died on her closing lips. A faint smile passed over her countenance, and was succeeded by a fine devotional glow; she folded her hands upon her bosom, and with a look of meek resignation, raising towards heaven her eyes, in which now sunk the last sparkles of expiring life—her soul departed in a short deep sigh.

Her lover sinking back, endeavoured to conceal his emotions, but the deep sobs which agitated his breast betrayed his anguish, and the tears of every spectator bedewed the sacred spot where beauty, sense, and innocence expired.

The organ now swelled in mournful harmony; and the voices of the assembly chanted in choral strain, a low and solemn requiem to the spirit of the departed.

Madame hurried Julia, who was almost as lifeless as her departed friend, from the church. A death so sudden heightened the grief which separation would otherwise have occasioned. It was the nature of Cornelia's disorder to wear a changeful but flattering aspect. Though she had long been declining, her decay was so gradual and imperceptible as to lull the apprehensions of her friends into security. It was otherwise with herself; she was conscious of the change, but forbore to afflict them with the knowledge of the truth. The hour of her dissolution was sudden, even to herself; but it was composed, and even happy. In the death of Cornelia, Julia seemed to mourn again that of Hippolitus. Her decease appeared to dissolve the last tie which connected her with his memory.

In one of the friars of the convent, madame was surprized to find the father who had confessed the dying Vincent. His appearance revived the remembrance of the scene she had witnessed at the castle of Mazzini; and the last words of Vincent, combined with the circumstances which had since occurred, renewed all her curiosity and astonishment. But his appearance excited more sensations than those of wonder. She dreaded lest he should be corrupted by the marquis, to whom he was known, and thus be induced to use his interest with the *Abate* for the restoration of Julia.

From the walls of the monastery, Julia now never ventured to stray. In the gloom of evening she sometimes stole into the cloisters, and often lingered at the grave of Cornelia, where she wept for Hippolitus, as well as for her friend. One evening, during vespers, the bell of the convent was suddenly rang out; the *Abate*, whose countenance expressed at once astonishment and displeasure, suspended the service, and quitted the altar. The whole congregation repaired to the hall, where they learned that a friar, retiring to the convent, had seen a troop of armed men advancing through the wood; and not doubting they were the people of the marquis, and were approaching with hostile intention, had thought it necessary to give the alarm. The *Abate* ascended a turret, and thence discovered through the trees a glittering of arms, and in the succeeding moment a band of men issued from a dark part of the wood, into a long avenue which immediately fronted the spot where he stood. The clattering of hoofs was now distinctly heard; and Julia, sinking with terror, distinguished the marquis heading the troops, which, soon after separating in two divisions, surrounded the monastery. The gates were immediately secured; and the *Abate*, descending from the turret, assembled the friars in the hall, where his voice was soon heard above every other part of the tumult. The terror of Julia made her utterly forgetful of the *Padre*'s promise, and she wished to fly for conceal-ment to the deep caverns belonging to the monastery, which wound under the woods. Madame, whose penetration fur-nished her with a just knowledge of the *Abate*'s character, founded her security on his pride. She therefore dissuaded Julia from attempting to tamper with the honesty of a servant who had the keys of the vaults, and advised her to rely entirely on the effect of the *Abate*'s resentment towards the marquis. While madame endeavoured to soothe her to composure, a message from the *Abate* required her imme-diate attendance. She obeyed, and he bade her follow him to a room which was directly over the gates of the monas-tery. From thence she saw her father, accompanied by the Duke de Luovo; and as her spirits died away at the sight, the marquis called furiously to the *Abate* to deliver her instantly into his hands, threatening, if she was detained, to force the gates of the monastery. At this threat the coun-tenance of the *Abate* grew dark: and leading Julia forcibly to the window, from which she had shrunk back, 'Impious menacer!' said he, 'eternal vengeance be upon thee! From this moment we expel thee from all the rights and com-munities of our church. Arrogant and daring as you are, your threats I defy—Look here,' said he, pointing to Julia, 'and learn that you are in my power; for if you dare to violate these sacred walls, I will proclaim aloud, in the face of day, a secret which shall make your heart's blood run cold; a secret which involves your honour, nay, your very existence. Now triumph and exult in impious menace!' The marquis started involuntarily at this speech, and his features underwent a sudden change, but he endeavoured to recover himself, and to conceal his confusion. He hesitated for a few moments, uncertain how to act—to desist from violence was to confess himself conscious of the threatened secret; yet he dreaded to inflame the resentment of the *Abate*, whose menaces his own heart too surely seconded. At length—'All that you have uttered,' said he, 'I despise as the dastardly subterfuge of monkish cunning. Your new insults add to the desire of recovering my daughter, that of punishing you. I would proceed to instant violence, but that would now be an imperfect revenge. I shall, therefore, withdraw my forces, and appeal to a higher power. Thus shall you be compelled at once to restore my daughter and retract your scandalous impeachment of my honor.' Saying this, he turned his horse from the gates, and his people following him, quickly withdrew, leaving the *Abate* exulting in conquest, and Julia lost in astonishment and doubtful joy. When she recounted to madame the particulars of the conference, she dwelt with emphasis on the threats of the *Abate*; but madame, though her amazement was heightened at every word, very well understood how the secret, whatever it was, had been obtained. The confessor of Vincent she had already observed in the monastery, and there was no doubt that he had disclosed whatever could be collected from the dying words of Vincent. She knew, also, that the secret would never be published, unless as a punishment for immediate violence, it being one of the first principles of monastic duty, to observe a religious secrecy upon all matters entrusted to them in confession.

When the first tumult of Julia's emotions subsided, the joy which the sudden departure of the marquis occasioned yielded to apprehension. He had threatened to appeal to a higher power, who would compel the *Abate* to surrender her. This menace excited a just terror, and there remained no means of avoiding the tyranny of the marquis but by quitting the monastery. She therefore requested an audience of the *Abate*; and having represented the danger of her present situation, she intreated his permission to depart in quest of a safer retreat. The *Abate*, who well knew the marquis was wholly in his power, smiled at the repetition of his menaces, and denied her request, under pretence of his having now become responsible for her to the church. He bade her be comforted, and promised her his protection; but his assurances were given in so distant and haughty a manner, that Julia left him with fears rather increased than subdued. In crossing the hall, she observed a man hastily enter it, from an opposite door. He was not in the habit of the order, but was muffled up in a cloak, and seemed to wish concealment. As she passed he raised his head, and Julia discovered—her father! He darted at her a look of vengeance; but before she had time even to think, as if suddenly recollecting himself, he covered his face, and rushed by her. Her trembling frame could scarcely support her to the apartment of madame, where she sunk speechless upon a chair, and the terror of her look alone spoke the agony of her mind. When she was somewhat recovered, she related what she had seen, and her conversation with the *Abate*. But madame was lost in equal perplexity with herself, when she attempted to account for the marquis's appearance. Why, after his late daring menace, should he come secretly to visit the *Abate*, by whose connivance alone he could have gained admission to the monastery? And what could have influenced the *Abate* to such a conduct? These circumstances, though equally inexplicable, united to confirm a fear of treachery and surrender. To escape from the abbey was now inpracticable, for the gates were constantly guarded; and even was it possible to pass them, certain detection awaited Julia without from the marquis's people, who were stationed in the woods. Thus encompassed with danger, she could only await in the monastery the issue of her destiny.

While she was lamenting with madame her unhappy fate, she was summoned once more to attend the *Abate*. At this moment her spirits entirely forsook her; the crisis of her fate seemed arrived; for she did not doubt that the *Abate* intended to surrender her to the marquis, with whom she supposed he had negotiated the terms of accommodation. It was some time before she could recover composure sufficient to obey the summons; and when she did, every step that bore her towards the *Abate*'s room increased her dread. She paused a moment at the door, 'ere she had courage to open it; the idea of her father's immediate resentment arose to her mind, and she was upon the point of retreating to her chamber, when a sudden step within, near the door, destroyed her hesitation, and she entered the closet. The marquis was not there, and her spirits revived. The flush of triumph was diffused over the features of the *Abate*, though a shade of unappeased resentment yet remained visible. 'Daughter,' said he, 'the intelligence we have to communicate may rejoice you. Your safety now depends solely on yourself. I give your fate into your own hands, and its issue be upon your head.' He paused, and she was suspended in wondering expectation of the coming sentence. 'I here solemnly assure you of my protection, but it is upon one condition only—that you renounce the world, and dedicate your days to God.' Julia listened with a mixture of grief and astonishment. 'Without this concession on your part, I possess not the power, had I even the inclination, to protect you. If you assume the veil, you are safe within the pale of the church from temporal violence. If you neglect or refuse to do this, the marquis may apply to a power from whom I have no appeal, and I shall be compelled at last to resign you.

'But to ensure your safety, should the veil be your choice, we will procure a dispensation from the usual forms of noviciation, and a few days shall confirm your vows.' He ceased to speak; but Julia, agitated with the most cruel distress, knew not what to reply. 'We grant you three days to decide upon this matter,' continued he, 'at the expiration of which, the veil, or the Duke de Luovo, awaits you.' Julia quitted the closet in mute despair, and repaired to madame, who could now scarcely offer her the humble benefit of consolation.

Meanwhile the *Abate* exulted in successful vengeance, and the marquis smarted beneath the stings of disappointment. The menace of the former was too seriously alarming to suffer the marquis to prosecute violent measures; and he had therefore resolved, by opposing avarice to pride, to soothe the power which he could not subdue. But he was unwilling to entrust the *Abate* with a proof of his compliance and his fears by offering a bribe in a letter, and preferred the more humiliating, but safer method, of a private interview. His magnificent offers created a temporary hesitation in the mind of the *Abate*, who, secure of his advantage, shewed at first no disposition to be reconciled, and suffered the marquis to depart in anxious uncertainty. After maturely deliberating upon the proposals, the pride of the *Abate* surmounted his avarice, and he determined to prevail upon Julia effectually to destroy the hopes of the marquis, by consecrating her life to religion. Julia passed the night and the next day in a state of mental torture exceeding all description. The gates of the monastery beset with guards, and the woods surrounded by the marquis's people, made escape impossible. From a marriage with the duke, whose late conduct had confirmed the odious idea which his character had formerly impressed, her heart recoiled in horror, and to be immured for life within the walls of a convent, was a fate little less dreadful. Yet such was the effect of that sacred love she bore the memory of Hippolitus, and such her aversion to the duke, that she soon resolved to adopt the veil. On the following evening she informed the *Abate* of her determination. His heart swelled with secret joy; and even the natural severity of his manner relaxed at the intelligence. He assured her of his approbation and protection, with a degree of kindness which he had never before manifested, and told her the ceremony should be performed on the second day from the present. Her emotion

scarcely suffered her to hear his last words. Now that her
fate was fixed beyond recall, she almost repented of her
choice. Her fancy attached to it a horror not its own; and
that evil, which, when offered to her decision, she had
accepted with little hesitation, she now paused upon in
dubious regret; so apt we are to imagine that the calamity
most certain, is also the most intolerable!

When the marquis read the answer of the *Abate*, all the
baleful passions of his nature were roused and inflamed to
a degree which bordered upon distraction. In the first impulse
of his rage, he would have forced the gates of the monastery,
and defied the utmost malice of his enemy. But a moment's
reflection revived his fear of the threatened secret, and he saw
that he was still in the power of the Superior.

The *Abate* procured the necessary dispensation, and preparations were immediately began for the approaching ceremony. Julia watched the departure of those moments which
led to her fate with the calm fortitude of despair. She had
no means of escaping from the coming evil, without expos-
ing herself to a worse; she surveyed it therefore with a
steady eye, and no longer shrunk from its approach.

On the morning preceding the day of her consecration,
she was informed that a stranger enquired for her at the
grate. Her mind had been so long accustomed to the vicissitudes of apprehension, that fear was the emotion which now
occurred; she suspected, yet scarcely knew why, that the
marquis was below, and hesitated whether to descend. A
little reflection determined her, and she went to the parlour—where, to her equal joy and surprise, she beheld—
Ferdinand!

During the absence of the marquis from his castle, Ferdinand, who had been informed of the discovery of Julia,
effected his escape from imprisonment, and had hastened to
the monastery in the design of rescuing her. He had passed
the woods in disguise, with much difficulty eluding the
observation of the marquis's people, who were yet dispersed
round the abbey. To the monastery, as he came alone, he
had been admitted without difficulty.

When he learned the conditions of the *Abate*'s protection, and that the following day was appointed for the consecration of Julia, he was shocked, and paused in deliberation. A period so short as was this interval, afforded little opportunity for contrivance, and less for hesitation. The night of the present day was the only time that remained for the attempt and execution of a plan of escape, which if it then failed of success, Julia would not only be condemned for life to the walls of a monastery, but would be subjected to whatever punishment the severity of the *Abate*, exasperated by the detection, should think fit to inflict. The danger was desperate, but the occasion was desperate also.

The nobly disinterested conduct of her brother, struck Julia with gratitude and admiration; but despair of success made her now hesitate whether she should accept his offer. She considered that his generosity would most probably involve him in destruction with herself; and she paused in deep deliberation, when Ferdinand informed her of a circumstance which, till now, he had purposely concealed, and which at once dissolved every doubt and every fear. 'Hippolitus,' said Ferdinand, 'yet lives.'—'Lives!' repeated Julia faintly,—'lives, Oh! tell me where—how.'—Her breath refused to aid her, and she sunk in her chair overcome with the strong and various sensations that pressed upon her heart. Ferdinand, whom the grate withheld from assisting her, observed her situation with extreme distress. When she recovered, he informed her that a servant of Hippolitus, sent no doubt by his lord to enquire concerning Julia, had been lately seen by one of the marquis's people in the neighbourhood of the castle. From him it was known that the Count de Vereza was living, but that his life had been despaired of; and he was still confined, by dangerous wounds, in an obscure town on the coast of Italy. The man had steadily refused to mention the place of his lord's abode. Learning that the marquis was then at the abbey of St Augustin, whither he pursued his daughter, the man disappeared from Mazzini, and had not since been heard of.

It was enough for Julia to know that Hippolitus lived; her fears of detection, and her scruples concerning Ferdinand, instantly vanished; she thought only of escape—and the means which had lately appeared so formidable—so difficult in contrivance, and so dangerous in execution, now seemed easy, certain, and almost accomplished.

They consulted on the plan to be adopted, and agreed, that in attempting to bribe a servant of the monastery to their interest, they should incur a danger too imminent, yet it appeared scarcely practicable to succeed in their scheme without risquing this. After much consideration, they determined to entrust their secret to no person but to madame. Ferdinand was to contrive to conceal himself till the dead of night in the church, between which and the monastery were several doors of communication. When the inhabitants of the abbey were sunk in repose, Julia might without difficulty pass to the church, where Ferdinand awaiting her, they might perhaps escape either through an outer door of the fabric, or through a window, for which latter attempt Ferdinand was to provide ropes.

A couple of horses were to be stationed among the rocks beyond the woods, to convey the fugitives to a sea-port, whence they could easily pass over to Italy. Having arranged this plan, they separated in the anxious hope of meeting on the ensuing night.

Madame warmly sympathized with Julia in her present expectations, and was now somewhat relieved from the pressure of that self-reproach, with which the consideration of having withdrawn her young friend from a secure asylum, had long tormented her. In learning that Hippolitus lived, Julia experienced a sudden renovation of life and spirits. From the languid stupefaction which despair had occasioned she revived as from a dream, and her sensations resembled those of a person suddenly awakened from a frightful vision, whose thoughts are yet obscured in the fear and uncertainty which the passing images have impressed on his fancy. She emerged from despair; joy illumined her countenance; yet she doubted the reality of the scene which now opened to her view. The hours rolled heavily along till the evening, when expectation gave way to fear, for she was once more summoned by the *Abate*. He sent for her to administer the usual necessary exhortation on the approaching solemnity; and having detained her a considerable time in tedious and severe discourse, dismissed her with a formal benediction.

CHAPTER XII

THE evening now sunk in darkness, and the hour was fast approaching which would decide the fate of Julia. Trembling anxiety subdued every other sensation; and as the minutes passed, her fears increased. At length she heard the gates of the monastery fastened for the night; the bell rang the signal for repose; and the passing footsteps of the nuns told her they were hastening to obey it. After some time, all was silent. Julia did not yet dare to venture forth; she employed the present interval in interesting and affectionate conversation with Madame de Menon, to whom, notwithstanding her situation, her heart bade a sorrowful adieu.

The clock struck twelve, when she arose to depart. Having embraced her faithful friend with tears of mingled grief and anxiety, she took a lamp in her hand, and with cautious, fearful steps, descended through the long winding passages to a private door, which opened into the church of the monastery. The church was gloomy and desolate; and the feeble rays of the lamp she bore, gave only light enough to discover its chilling grandeur. As she passed silently along the aisles, she cast a look of anxious examination around— but Ferdinand was no where to be seen. She paused in timid hesitation, fearful to penetrate the gloomy obscurity which lay before her, yet dreading to return.

As she stood examining the place, vainly looking for Ferdinand, yet fearing to call, lest her voice should betray her, a hollow groan arose from a part of the church very near her. It chilled her heart, and she remained fixed to the spot. She turned her eyes a little to the left, and saw light appear through the chinks of a sepulchre at some distance. The groan was repeated—a low murmuring succeeded, and while she yet gazed, an old man issued from the vault with a lighted taper in his hand. Terror now subdued her, and she utterred an involuntary shriek. In the succeeding moment, a noise was heard in a remote part of the fabric; and Ferdinand rushing forth from his concealment, ran to her assistance. The old man, who appeared to be a friar, and who had been doing penance at the monument of a saint, now approached. His countenance expressed a degree of surprise and terror almost equal to that of Julia's, who knew him to be the confessor of Vincent. Ferdinand seized the father; and laying his hand upon his sword, threatened him with death if he did not instantly swear to conceal for ever his knowledge of what he then saw, and also assist them to escape from the abbey.

'Ungracious boy!' replied the father, in a calm voice, 'desist from this language, nor add to the follies of youth the crime of murdering, or terrifying a defenceless old man. Your violence would urge me to become your enemy, did not previous inclination tempt me to be your friend. I pity the distresses of the lady Julia, to whom I am no stranger, and will cheerfully give her all the assistance in my power.'

At these words Julia revived, and Ferdinand, reproved by the generosity of the father, and conscious of his own inferiority, shrunk back. 'I have no words to thank you,' said he, 'or to entreat your pardon for the impetuosity of my conduct; your knowledge of my situation must plead my excuse.'—'It does,' replied the father, 'but we have no time to lose;—follow me.'

They followed him through the church to the cloisters, at the extremity of which was a small door, which the friar unlocked. It opened upon the woods.

'This path,' said he, 'leads thro' an intricate part of the woods, to the rocks that rise on the right of the abbey; in their recesses you may secrete yourselves till you are prepared for a longer journey. But extinguish your light; it may betray you to the marquis's people, who are dispersed about this spot. Farewell! my children, and God's blessing be upon ye.'

Julia's tears declared her gratitude; she had no time for words. They stepped into the path, and the father closed the door. They were now liberated from the monastery, but

danger awaited them without, which it required all their
caution to avoid. Ferdinand knew the path which the friar
had pointed out to be the same that led to the rocks where
his horses were stationed, and he pursued it with quick and
silent steps. Julia, whose fears conspired with the gloom of
night to magnify and transform every object around her,
imagined at each step that she took, she perceived the
figures of men, and fancied every whisper of the breeze the
sound of pursuit.

They proceeded swiftly, till Julia, breathless and exhausted, could go no farther. They had not rested many
minutes, when they heard a rustling among the bushes at
some distance, and soon after distinguished a low sound of
voices. Ferdinand and Julia instantly renewed their flight,
and thought they still heard voices advance upon the wind.
This thought was soon confirmed, for the sounds now
gained fast upon them, and they distinguished words which
served only to heighten their apprehensions, when they
reached the extremity of the woods. The moon, which was
now up, suddenly emerging from a dark cloud, discovered
to them several man in pursuit; and also shewed to the
pursuers the course of the fugitives. They endeavoured to
gain the rocks where the horses were concealed, and which
now appeared in view. These they reached when the pursuers had almost overtaken them—but their horses were
gone! Their only remaining chance of escape was to fly into
the deep recesses of the rock. They, therefore, entered a
winding cave, from whence branched several subterraneous
avenues, at the extremity of one of which they stopped. The
voices of men now vibrated in tremendous echoes through
the various and secret caverns of the place,* and the sound
of footsteps seemed fast approaching. Julia trembled with
terror, and Ferdinand drew his sword, determined to protect
her to the last. A confused volley of voices now sounded up
that part of the cave were Ferdinand and Julia lay concealed.
In a few moments the steps of the pursuers suddenly took
a different direction, and the sounds sunk gradually away,
and were heard no more. Ferdinand listened attentively for

a considerable time, but the stillness of the place remained undisturbed. It was now evident that the men had quitted the rock, and he ventured forth to the mouth of the cave. He surveyed the wilds around, as far as his eye could penetrate, and distinguished no human being; but in the pauses of the wind he still thought he heard a sound of distant voices. As he listened in anxious silence, his eye caught the appearance of a shadow, which moved upon the ground near where he stood. He started back within the cave, but in a few minutes again ventured forth. The shadow remained stationary, but having watched it for some time, Ferdinand saw it glide along till it disappeared behind a point of rock. He had now no doubt that the cave was watched, and that it was one of his late pursuers whose shade he had seen. He returned, therefore, to Julia, and remained near an hour hid in the deepest recess of the rock; when, no sound having interrupted the profound silence of the place, he at length once more ventured to the mouth of the cave. Again he threw a fearful look around, but discerned no human form. The soft moon-beam slept upon the dewy landscape, and the solemn stillness of midnight wrapt the world. Fear heightened to the fugitives the sublimity of the hour. Ferdinand now led Julia forth, and they passed silently along the shelving foot of the rocks.

They continued their way without farther interruption; and among the cliffs, at some distance from the cave, discovered, to their inexpressible joy, their horses, who having broken their fastenings, had strayed thither, and had now laid themselves down to rest. Ferdinand and Julia immediately mounted; and descending to the plains, took the road that led to a small sea-port at some leagues distant, whence they could embark for Italy.

They travelled for some hours through gloomy forests of beech and chesnut; and their way was only faintly illumi-nated by the moon, which shed a trembling lustre through the dark foliage, and which was seen but at intervals, as the passing clouds yielded to the power of her rays. They reached at length the skirts of the forest. The grey dawn now appeared, and the chill morning air bit shrewdly. It was with inexpressible joy that Julia observed the kindling atmosphere; and soon after the rays of the rising sun touching the tops of the mountains, whose sides were yet involved in dark vapours.

Her fears dissipated with the darkness.—The sun now appeared amid clouds of inconceivable splendour; and unveiled a scene which in other circumstances Julia would have contemplated with rapture. From the side of the hill, down which they were winding, a vale appeared, from whence arose wild and lofty mountains, whose steeps were cloathed with hanging woods, except where here and there a precipice projected its bold and rugged front. Here, a few half-withered trees hung from the crevices of the rock, and gave a picturesque wildness to the object; there, clusters of half-seen cottages, rising from among tufted groves, embellished the green margin of a stream which meandered in the bottom, and bore its waves to the blue and distant main.

The freshness of morning breathed over the scene, and vivified each colour of the landscape. The bright dewdrops hung trembling from the branches of the trees, which at intervals overshadowed the road; and the sprightly music of the birds saluted the rising day. Notwithstanding her anxiety the scene diffused a soft complacency over the mind of Julia.

About noon they reached the port, where Ferdinand was fortunate enough to obtain a small vessel; but the wind was unfavourable, and it was past midnight before it was possible for them to embark.

When the dawn appeared, Julia returned to the deck; and viewed with a sigh of unaccountable regret, the receding coast of Sicily. But she observed, with high admiration, the light gradually spreading through the atmosphere, darting a feeble ray over the surface of the waters, which rolled in solemn soundings upon the distant shores. Fiery beams now marked the clouds, and the east glowed with increasing radiance, till the sun rose at once above the waves, and illuminating them with a flood of splendour, diffused gaiety and gladness around. The bold concave of the heavens, uniting with the vast expanse of the ocean, formed, a *coup d'œil*,* striking and sublime. The magnificence of the scenery inspired Julia with delight; and her heart dilating with high enthusiasm, she forgot the sorrows which had oppressed her.

The breeze wafted the ship gently along for some hours, when it gradually sunk into a calm. The glassy surface of the waters was not curled by the lightest air, and the vessel floated heavily on the bosom of the deep. Sicily was yet in view, and the present delay agitated Julia with wild apprehension. Towards the close of day a light breeze sprang up, but it blew from Italy, and a train of dark vapours emerged from the verge of the horizon, which gradually accumulating, the heavens became entirely overcast. The evening shut in suddenly; the rising wind, the heavy clouds that loaded the atmosphere, and the thunder which murmured afar off terrified Julia, and threatened a violent storm.

The tempest came on, and the captain vainly sounded for anchorage: it was deep sea, and the vessel drove furiously before the wind. The darkness was interrupted only at intervals, by the broad expanse of vivid lightnings, which quivered upon the waters, and disclosing the horrible gaspings of the waves, served to render the succeeding darkness more awful. The thunder, which burst in tremendous crashes above, the loud roar of the waves below, the noise of the sailors, and the sudden cracks and groanings of the vessel conspired to heighten the tremendous sublimity of the scene.

> Far on the rocky shores the surges sound,*
> The lashing whirlwinds cleave the vast profound;
> While high in air, amid the rising storm,
> Driving the blast, sits Danger's black'ning form.

Julia lay fainting with terror and sickness in the cabin, and Ferdinand, though almost hopeless himself, was endeavouring to support her, when a loud and dreadful crash was heard from above. It seemed as if the whole vessel had parted. The voices of the sailors now rose together, and all was confusion and uproar. Ferdinand ran up to the deck, and learned that part of the main mast, borne away by the wind, had fallen upon the deck, whence it had rolled overboard.

It was now past midnight, and the storm continued with unabated fury. For four hours the vessel had been driven before the blast; and the captain now declared it was impossible she could weather the tempest much longer, ordered the long boat to be in readiness. His orders were scarcely executed, when the ship bulged upon a reef of rocks, and the impetuous waves rushed into the vessel:—a general groan ensued. Ferdinand flew to save his sister, whom he carried to the boat, which was nearly filled by the captain and most of the crew. The sea ran so high that it appeared impracticable to reach the shore: but the boat had not moved many yards, when the ship went to pieces. The captain now perceived, by the flashes of lightning, a high rocky coast at about the distance of half a mile. The men struggled hard at the oars; but almost as often as they gained the summit of a wave, it dashed them back again, and made their labour of little avail.

After much difficulty and fatigue they reached the coast, where a new danger presented itself. They beheld a wild rocky shore, whose cliffs appeared inaccessible, and which seemed to afford little possibility of landing. A landing, however, was at last affected; and the sailors, after much search, discovered a kind of pathway cut in the rock, which they all ascended in safety.

The dawn now faintly glimmered, and they surveyed the coast, but could discover no human habitation. They imagined they were on the shores of Sicily, but possessed no means of confirming this conjecture. Terror, sickness, and fatigue had subdued the strength and spirits of Julia, and she was obliged to rest upon the rocks.

The storm now suddenly subsided, and the total calm which succeeded to the wild tumult of the winds and waves, produced a striking and sublime effect. The air was hushed in a deathlike stillness, but the waves were yet violently agitated; and by the increasing light, parts of the wreck were seen floating wide upon the face of the deep. Some sailors, who had missed the boat, were also discovered clinging to pieces of the vessel, and making towards the shore. On observing this, their shipmates immediately descended to the boat; and, putting off to sea, rescued them from their perilous situation. When Julia was somewhat reanimated, they proceeded up the country in search of a dwelling.

They had travelled near half a league, when the savage features of the country began to soften, and gradually changed to the picturesque beauty of Sicilian scenery. They now discovered at some distance a villa, seated on a gentle eminence, crowned with woods. It was the first human habitation they had seen since they embarked for Italy; and Julia, who was almost sinking with fatigue, beheld it with delight. The captain and his men hastened towards it to make known their distress, while Ferdinand and Julia slowly followed. They observed the men enter the villa, one of whom quickly returned to acquaint them with the hospitable reception his comrades had received.

Julia with difficulty reached the edifice, at the door of which she was met by a young cavalier, whose pleasing and intelligent countenance immediately interested her in his favor. He welcomed the strangers with a benevolent politeness that dissolved at once every uncomfortable feeling which their situation had excited, and produced an instantaneous easy confidence. Through a light and elegant hall, rising into a dome, supported by pillars of white marble, and adorned with busts, he led them to a magnificent vestibule, which opened upon a lawn. Having seated them at a table spread with refreshments he left them, and they surveyed, with surprise, the beauty of the adjacent scene.

The lawn, which was on each side bounded by hanging woods, descended in gentle declivity to a fine lake, whose smooth surface reflected the surrounding shades. Beyond appeared the distant country, arising on the left into bold romantic mountains, and on the right exhibiting a soft and glowing landscape, whose tranquil beauty formed a striking contrast to the wild sublimity of the opposite craggy heights. The blue and distant ocean terminated the view.

In a short time the cavalier returned, conducting two ladies of a very engaging appearance, whom he presented as his wife and sister. They welcomed Julia with graceful kindness; but fatigue soon obliged her to retire to rest, and a consequent indisposition increased so rapidly, as to render it impracticable for her to quit her present abode on that day. The captain and his men proceeded on their way, leaving Ferdinand and Julia at the villa, where she experienced every kind and tender affection.

The day which was to have devoted Julia to a cloister, was ushered in at the abbey with the usual ceremonies. The church was ornamented, and all the inhabitants of the monastery prepared to attend. The *Padre Abate* now exulted in the success of his scheme, and anticipated, in imagination, the rage and vexation of the marquis, when he should discover that his daughter was lost to him for ever.

The hour of celebration arrived, and he entered the church with a proud firm step, and with a countenance which depictured his inward triumph; he was proceeding to the high altar, when he was told that Julia was no where to be found. Astonishment for a while suspended other emotions—he yet believed it impossible that she could have effected an escape, and ordered every part of the abbey to be searched—not forgetting the secret caverns belonging to the monastery, which wound beneath the woods. When the search was over, and he became convinced she was fled, the deep workings of his disappointed passions fermented into rage which exceeded all bounds. He denounced the most terrible judgments upon Julia; and calling for Madame de Menon, charged her with having insulted her holy religion, in being accessary to the flight of Julia. Madame endured these reproaches with calm dignity, and preserved a steady silence, but she secretly determined to leave the monastery, and seek in another the repose which she could never hope to find in this.

The report of Julia's disappearance spread rapidly beyond the walls, and soon reached the ears of the marquis, who rejoiced in the circumstance, believing that she must now inevitably fall into his hands.

After his people, in obedience to his orders, had carefully searched the surrounding woods and rocks, he withdrew them from the abbey; and having dispersed them various ways in search of Julia, he returned to the castle of Mazzini. Here new vexation awaited him, for he now first learned that Ferdinand had escaped from confinement.

The mystery of Julia's flight was now dissolved; for it was evident by whose means she had effected it, and the marquis issued orders to his people to secure Ferdinand wherever he should be found.

CHAPTER XIII

HIPPOLITUS, who had languished under a long and dangerous illness occasioned by his wounds, but heightened and
prolonged by the distress of his mind, was detained in a
small town in the coast of Calabria, and was yet ignorant
of the death of Cornelia. He scarcely doubted that Julia was
now devoted to the duke, and this thought was at times
poison to his heart. After his arrival in Calabria, immediately
on the recovery of his senses, he dispatched a servant back
to the castle of Mazzini, to gain secret intelligence of what
had passed after his departure. The eagerness with which
we endeavour to escape from misery, taught him to encourage a remote and romantic hope that Julia yet lived for him.
Yet even this hope at length languished into despair, as the
time elapsed which should have brought his servant from
Sicily. Days and weeks passed away in the utmost anxiety
to Hippolitus, for still his emissary did not appear; and at
last, concluding that he had been either seized by robbers,
or discovered and detained by the marquis, the Count sent
off a second emissary to the castle of Mazzini. By him he
learned the news of Julia's flight, and his heart dilated with
joy; but it was suddenly checked when he heard the marquis
had discovered her retreat in the abbey of St Augustin. The
wounds which still detained him in confinement, now became intolerable. Julia might yet be lost to him for ever.
But even his present state of fear and uncertainty was bliss
compared with the anguish of despair, which his mind had
long endured.

As soon as he was sufficiently recovered, he quitted Italy
for Sicily, in the design of visiting the monastery of St
Augustin, where it was possible Julia might yet remain. That
he might pass with the secrecy necessary to his plan, and
escape the attacks of the marquis, he left his servants in
Calabria, and embarked alone.

It was morning when he landed at a small port of Sicily, and proceeded towards the abbey of St Augustin. As he travelled, his imagination revolved the scenes of his early love, the distress of Julia, and the sufferings of Ferdinand, and his heart melted at the retrospect. He considered the probabilities of Julia having found protection from her father in the pity of the *Padre Abate*; and even ventured to indulge himself in a flattering, fond anticipation of the moment when Julia should again be restored to his sight.

He arrived at the monastery, and his grief may easily be imagined, when he was informed of the death of his beloved sister, and of the flight of Julia. He quitted St Augustin's immediately, without even knowing that Madame de Menon was there, and set out for a town at some leagues distance, where he designed to pass the night.

Absorbed in the melancholy reflections which the late intelligence excited, he gave the reins to his horse, and journeyed on unmindful of his way. The evening was far advanced when he discovered that he had taken a wrong direction, and that he was bewildered in a wild and solitary scene. He had wandered too far from the road to hope to regain it, and he had beside no recollection of the objects left behind him. A choice of errors, only, lay before him. The view on his right hand exhibited high and savage mountains, covered with heath and black fir; and the wild desolation of their aspect, together with the dangerous appearance of the path that wound up their sides, and which was the only apparent track they afforded, determined Hippolitus not to attempt their ascent. On his left lay a forest, to which the path he was then in led; its appearance was gloomy, but he preferred it to the mountains; and, since he was uncertain of its extent, there was a possibility that he might pass it, and reach a village before the night was set in. At the worst, the forest would afford him a shelter from the winds; and, however he might be bewildered in its labyrinths, he could ascend a tree, and rest in security till the return of light should afford him an opportunity of extricating himself. Among the mountains there was no possibility of meeting with other shelter than what the habitation of man afforded, and such a shelter there was little probability of finding. Innumerable dangers also threatened him here, from which he would be secure on level ground.

Having determined which way to pursue, he pushed his horse into a gallop, and entered the forest as the last rays of the sun trembled on the mountains. The thick foliage of the trees threw a gloom around, which was every moment deepened by the shades of evening. The path was uninterrupted, and the count continued to follow it till all distinction was confounded in the veil of night. Total darkness now made it impossible for him to pursue his way. He dismounted, and fastening his horse to a tree, climbed among the branches, purposing to remain there till morning.

He had not been long in this situation, when a confused sound of voices from a distance roused his attention. The sound returned at intervals for some time, but without seeming to approach. He descended from the tree, that he might the better judge of the direction whence it came; but before he reached the ground, the noise was ceased, and all was profoundly silent. He continued to listen, but the silence remaining undisturbed, he began to think he had been deceived by the singing of the wind among the leaves; and was preparing to reascend, when he perceived a faint light glimmer through the foliage from afar. The sight revived a hope that he was near some place of human habitation; he therefore unfastened his horse, and led him towards the spot whence the ray issued. The moon was now risen, and threw a checkered gleam over his path sufficient to direct him.

Before he had proceeded far the light disappeared. He continued, however, his way as nearly as he could guess, towards the place whence it had issued; and after much toil, found himself in a spot where the trees formed a circle round a kind of rude lawn. The moonlight discovered to him an edifice which appeared to have been formerly a monastery, but which now exhibited a pile of ruins, whose grandeur, heightened by decay, touched the beholder with reverential awe. Hippolitus paused to gaze upon the scene; the sacred stillness of night increased its effect, and a secret dread, he knew not wherefore, stole upon his heart.

The silence and the character of the place made him doubt whether this was the spot he had been seeking; and as he stood hesitating whether to proceed or to return, he observed a figure standing under an arch-way of the ruin; it carried a light in its hand, and passing silently along, disappeared in a remote part of the building. The courage of Hippolitus for a moment deserted him. An invincible curiosity, however, subdued his terror, and he determined to pursue, if possible, the way the figure had taken.

He passed over loose stones through a sort of court till he came to the archway; here he stopped, for fear returned upon him. Resuming his courage, however, he went on, still endeavouring to follow the way the figure had passed, and suddenly found himself in an enclosed part of the ruin, whose appearance was more wild and desolate than any he had yet seen. Seized with unconquerable apprehension, he was retiring, when the low voice of a distressed person struck his ear. His heart sunk at the sound, his limbs trembled, and he was utterly unable to move.

The sound which appeared to be the last groan of a dying person, was repeated. Hippolitus made a strong effort, and sprang forward, when a light burst upon him from a shattered casement of the building, and at the same instant he heard the voices of men!

He advanced softly to the window, and beheld in a small room, which was less decayed than the rest of the edifice, a group of men, who, from the savageness of their looks, and from their dress, appeared to be banditti. They surrounded a man who lay on the ground wounded, and bathed in blood, and who it was very evident had uttered the groans heard by the count.

The obscurity of the place prevented Hippolitus from distinguishing the features of the dying man. From the blood which covered him, and from the surrounding circumstances, he appeared to be murdered; and the count had no doubt that the men he beheld were the murderers. The horror of the scene entirely overcame him; he stood rooted to the spot, and saw the assassins rifle the pockets of the dying person, who, in a voice scarcely articulate, but which despair seemed to aid, supplicated for mercy. The ruffians answered him only with execrations, and continued their plunder. His groans and his sufferings served only to aggravate their cruelty. They were proceeding to take from him a miniature picture, which was fastened round his neck, and had been hitherto concealed in his bosom; when by a sudden effort he half raised himself from the ground, and attempted to save it from their hands. The effort availed him nothing; a blow from one of the villains laid the unfortunate man on the floor without motion. The horrid barbarity of the act seized the mind of Hippolitus so entirely, that, forgetful of his own situation, he groaned aloud, and started with an instantaneous design of avenging the deed. The noise he made alarmed the banditti, who looking whence it came, discovered the count through the casement. They instantly quitted their prize, and rushed towards the door of the room. He was now returned to a sense of his danger, and endeavoured to escape to the exterior part of the ruin; but terror bewildered his senses, and he mistook his way. Instead of regaining the arch-way, he perplexed himself with fruitless wanderings, and at length found himself only more deeply involved in the secret recesses of the pile.

The steps of his pursuers gained fast upon him, and he continued to perplex himself with vain efforts at escape, till at length, quite exhausted, he sunk on the ground, and endeavoured to resign himself to his fate. He listened with a kind of stern despair, and was surprised to find all silent. On looking round, he perceived by a ray of moonlight, which streamed through a part of the ruin from above, that he was in a sort of vault, which, from the small means he had of judging, he thought was extensive.

In this situation he remained for a considerable time, ruminating on the means of escape, yet scarcely believing escape was possible. If he continued in the vault, he might continue there only to be butchered; but by attempting to rescue himself from the place he was now in, he must rush into the hands of the banditti. Judging it, therefore, the safer way of the two to remain where he was, he endeavoured to await his fate with fortitude, when suddenly the loud voices of the murderers burst upon his ear, and he heard steps advancing quickly towards the spot where he lay.

Despair instantly renewed his vigour; he started from the ground, and throwing round him a look of eager desperation, his eye caught the glimpse of a small door, upon which the moon-beam now fell. He made towards it, and passed it just as the light of a torch gleamed upon the walls of the vault.

He groped his way along a winding passage, and at length came to a flight of steps. Notwithstanding the darkness, he reached the bottom in safety.

He now for the first time stopped to listen—the sounds of pursuit were ceased, and all was silent! Continuing to wander on in effectual endeavours to escape, his hands at length touched cold iron, and he quickly perceived it belonged to a door. The door, however, was fastened, and resisted all his efforts to open it. He was giving up the attempt in despair, when a loud scream from within, followed by a dead and heavy noise, roused all his attention. Silence ensued. He listened for a considerable time at the door, his imagination filled with images of horror, and expecting to hear the sound repeated. He then sought for a decayed part of the door, through which he might discover what was beyond; but he could find none; and after waiting some time without hearing any farther noise, he was quitting the spot, when in passing his arm over the door, it struck against something hard. On examination he perceived, to his extreme surprize, that the key was in the lock. For a moment he hesitated what to do; but curiosity overcame other considerations, and with a trembling hand he turned the key. The door opened into a large and desolate apartment, dimly lighted by a lamp that stood on a table, which was almost the only furniture of the place. The Count had advanced several steps before he perceived an object, which fixed all his attention. This was the figure of a young woman lying on the floor apparently dead. Her face was concealed in her robe; and the long auburn tresses which fell in beautiful luxuriance over her bosom, served to veil a part of the glowing beauty which the disorder of her dress would have revealed.

Pity, surprize, and admiration struggled in the breast of Hippolitus; and while he stood surveying the object which excited these different emotions, he heard a step advancing towards the room. He flew to the door by which he had entered, and was fortunate enough to reach it before the entrance of the persons whose steps he heard. Having turned the key, he stopped at the door to listen to their proceedings. He distinguished the voices of two men, and knew them to be those of the assassins. Presently he heard a piercing skriek, and at the same instant the voices of the ruffians grew loud and violent. One of them exclaimed that the lady was dying, and accused the other of having frightened her to death, swearing, with horrid imprecations, that she was his, and he would defend her to the last drop of his blood. The dispute grew higher; and neither of the ruffians would give up his claim to the unfortunate object of their altercation.

The clashing of swords was soon after heard, together with a violent noise. The screams were repeated, and the oaths and execrations of the disputants redoubled. They seemed to move towards the door, behind which Hippolitus was concealed; suddenly the door was shook with great force, a deep groan followed, and was instantly succeeded by a noise like that of a person whose whole weight falls at once to the ground. For a moment all was silent. Hippolitus had no doubt that one of the ruffians had destroyed the other, and was soon confirmed in the belief—for the survivor triumphed with brutal exultation over his fallen antagonist. The ruffian hastily quitted the room, and Hippolitus soon after heard the distant voices of several persons in loud dispute. The sounds seemed to come from a chamber over the place where he stood; he also heard a trampling of feet from above, and could even distinguish, at intervals, the words of the disputants. From these he gathered enough to learn that the affray which had just happened, and the lady who had been the occasion of it, were the subjects of discourse. The voices frequently rose together, and confounded all distinction.

At length the tumult began to subside, and Hippolitus could distinguish what was said. The ruffians agreed to give up the lady in question to him who had fought for her; and leaving him to his prize, they all went out in quest of farther prey. The situation of the unfortunate lady excited a mixture of pity and indignation in Hippolitus, which for some time entirely occupied him; he revolved the means of extricating her from so deplorable a situation, and in these thoughts almost forgot his own danger. He now heard her sighs; and while his heart melted to the sounds, the farther door of the apartment was thrown open, and the wretch to whom she had been allotted, rushed in. Her screams now redoubled, but they were of no avail with the ruffian who had seized her in his arms; when the count, who was unarmed, insensible to every pulse but that of a generous pity, burst into the room, but became fixed like a statue when he beheld his Julia struggling in the grasp of the ruffian. On discovering Hippolitus, she made a sudden spring, and liberated herself; when, running to him, she sunk lifeless in his arms.

Surprise and fury sparkled in the eyes of the ruffian, and he turned with a savage desperation upon the count; who, relinquishing Julia, snatched up the sword of the dead ruffian, which lay upon the floor, and defended himself. The combat was furious, but Hippolitus laid his antagonist senseless at his feet. He flew to Julia, who now revived, but who for some time could speak only by her tears. The transitions of various and rapid sensations, which her heart experienced, and the strangely mingled emotions of joy and terror that agitated Hippolitus, can only be understood by experience. He raised her from the floor, and endeavoured to soothe her to composure, when she called wildly upon Ferdinand. At his name the count started, and he instantly remembered the dying cavalier, whose countenance the glooms had concealed from his view. His heart thrilled with secret agony, yet he resolved to withhold his terrible conjectures from Julia, of whom he learned that Ferdinand, with herself, had been taken by banditti in the way from the villa which had offered them so hospitable a reception after the shipwreck. They were on the road to a port whence they designed again to embark for Italy, when this misfortune overtook them. Julia added, that Ferdinand had been immediately separated from her; and that, for some hours, she had been confined in the apartment where Hippolitus found her.

The count with difficulty concealed his terrible apprehensions for Ferdinand, and vainly strove to soften Julia's distress. But there was no time to be lost—they had yet to find a way out of the edifice, and before they could accomplish this, the banditti might return. It was also possible that some of the party were left to watch this their abode during the absence of the rest, and this was another circumstance of reasonable alarm.

After some little consideration, Hippolitus judged it most prudent to seek an outlet through the passage by which he entered; he therefore took the lamp, and led Julia to the door. They entered the avenue, and locking the door after them, sought the flight of steps down which the count had before passed; but having pursued the windings of the avenue a considerable time without finding them, he became certain he had mistaken the way. They, however, found another flight, which they descended and entered upon a passage so very narrow and low, as not to admit of a person walking upright. This passage was closed by a door, which on examination was found to be chiefly of iron. Hippolitus was startled at the sight, but on applying his strength found it gradually yield, when the imprisoned air rushed out, and had nearly extinguished the light. They now entered upon a dark abyss; and the door which moved upon a spring, suddenly closed upon them. On looking round they beheld a large vault; and it is not easy to imagine their horror on discovering they were in a receptacle for the murdered bodies of the unfortunate people who had fallen into the hands of the banditti.

The count could scarcely support the fainting spirits of Julia; he ran to the door, which he endeavoured to open, but the lock was so constructed that it could be moved only on the other side, and all his efforts were useless. He was constrained, therefore, to seek for another door, but could find none. Their situation was the most deplorable that can be imagined; for they were now inclosed in a vault strewn with the dead bodies of the murdered, and must there become the victims of famine, or of the sword. The earth was in several places thrown up, and marked the boundaries of new-made graves. The bodies which remained unburied were probably left either from hurry or negligence, and exhibited a spectacle too shocking for humanity. The suf-ferings of Hippolitus were increased by those of Julia, who was sinking with horror, and who he endeavoured to support to a part of the vault which fell into a recess—where stood a bench.

They had not been long in this situation, when they heard a noise which approached gradually, and which did not appear to come from the avenue they had passed.

The noise increased, and they could distinguish voices. Hippolitus believed the murderers were returned; that they had traced his retreat, and were coming towards the vault by some way unknown to him. He prepared for the worst— and drawing his sword, resolved to defend Julia to the last. Their apprehension, however, was soon dissipated by a trampling of horses, which sound had occasioned his alarm, and which now seemed to come from a courtyard above, extremely near the vault. He distinctly heard the voices of the banditti, together with the moans and supplications of some person, whom it was evident they were about to plunder. The sound appeared so very near, that Hippolitus was both shocked and surprised; and looking round the vault, he perceived a small grated window placed very high in the wall, which he concluded overlooked the place where the robbers were assembled. He recollected that his light might betray him; and horrible as was the alternative, he was compelled to extinguish it. He now attempted to climb to the grate, through which he might obtain a view of what was passing without. This at length he effected, for the ruggedness of the wall afforded him a footing. He beheld in a ruinous court, which was partially illuminated by the glare of torches, a group of banditti surrounding two persons who were bound on horseback, and who were supplicating for mercy.

One of the robbers exclaiming with an oath that this was a golden night, bade his comrades dispatch, adding he would go to find Paulo and the lady.

The effect which the latter part of this sentence had upon the prisoners in the vault, may be more easily imagined than described. They were now in total darkness in this mansion of the murdered, without means of escape, and in moment-ary expectation of sharing a fate similar to that of the wretched objects around them. Julia, overcome with distress and terror, sunk on the ground; and Hippolitus, descending from the grate, became insensible of his own danger in his apprehension for her.

In a short time all without was confusion and uproar; the ruffian who had left the court returned with the alarm that the lady was fled, and that Paulo was murdered. The robbers quitting their booty to go in search of the fugitive, and to discover the murderer, dreadful vociferations resounded through every recess of the pile.

The tumult had continued a considerable time, which the prisoners had passed in a state of horrible suspense, when they heard the uproar advancing towards the vault, and soon after a number of voices shouted down the avenue. The sound of steps quickened. Hippolitus again drew his sword, and placed himself opposite the entrance, where he had not stood long, when a violent push was made against the door; it flew open, and a party of men rushed into the vault.

Hippolitus kept his position, protesting he would destroy the first who approached. At the sound of his voice they stopped; but presently advancing, commanded him in the king's name to surrender. He now discovered what his agitation had prevented him from observing sooner, that the men before him were not banditti, but the officers of justice. They had received information of this haunt of villainy from the son of a Sicilian nobleman, who had fallen into the hands of the banditti, and had afterwards escaped from their power.

The officers came attended by a guard, and were every way prepared to prosecute a strenuous search through these horrible recesses.

Hippolitus inquired for Ferdinand, and they all quitted the vault in search of him. In the court, to which they now ascended, the greater part of the banditti were secured by a number of the guard. The count accused the robbers of having secreted his friend, whom he described, and demanded to have liberated.

With one voice they denied the fact, and were resolute in persisting that they knew nothing of the person described. This denial confirmed Hippolitus in his former terrible surmise; that the dying cavalier, whom he had seen, was no other than Ferdinand, and he became furious. He bade the officers prosecute their search, who, leaving a guard over the banditti they had secured, followed him to the room where the late dreadful scene had been acted.

The room was dark and empty; but the traces of blood were visible on the floor; and Julia, though ignorant of the particular apprehension of Hippolitus, almost swooned at the sight. On quitting the room, they wandered for some time among the ruins, without discovering any thing extraordinary, till, in passing under the arch-way by which Hippolitus had first entered the building, their footsteps returned a deep sound, which convinced them that the ground beneath was hollow. On close examination, they perceived by the light of their torch, a trapdoor, which with some difficulty they lifted, and discovered beneath a narrow flight of steps. They all descended into a low winding passage, where they had not been long, when they heard a trampling of horses above, and a loud and sudden uproar.

The officers apprehending that the banditti had overcome the guard, rushed back to the trapdoor, which they had scarcely lifted, when they heard a clashing of swords, and a confusion of unknown voices. Looking onward, they beheld through the arch, in an inner sort of court, a large party of banditti who were just arrived, rescuing their comrades, and contending furiously with the guard.

On observing this, several of the officers sprang forward to the assistance of their friends; and the rest, subdued by cowardice, hurried down the steps, letting the trapdoor fall after them with a thundering noise. They gave notice to Hippolitus of what was passing above, who hurried Julia along the passage in search of some outlet or place of concealment. They could find neither, and had not long pursued the windings of the way, when they heard the trapdoor lifted, and the steps of persons descending. Despair gave strength to Julia, and winged her flight. But they were now stopped by a door which closed the passage, and the sound of distant voices murmured along the walls.

The door was fastened by strong iron bolts, which Hippolitus vainly endeavoured to draw. The voices drew near. After much labour and difficulty the bolts yielded—the door unclosed—and light dawned upon them through the mouth of a cave, into which they now entered. On quitting the cave they found themselves in the forest, and in a short time reached the borders. They now ventured to stop, and looking back perceived no person in pursuit.

CHAPTER XIV

WHEN Julia had rested, they followed the track before them, and in a short time arrived at a village, where they obtained security and refreshment.

But Julia, whose mind was occupied with dreadful anxiety for Ferdinand, became indifferent to all around her. Even the presence of Hippolitus, which but lately would have raised her from misery to joy, failed to soothe her distress. The steady and noble attachment of her brother had sunk deep in her heart, and reflection only aggravated her affliction. Yet the banditti had steadily persisted in affirming that he was not concealed in their recesses; and this circumstance, which threw a deeper shade over the fears of Hippolitus, imparted a glimmering of hope to the mind of Julia.

A more immediate interest at length forced her mind from this sorrowful subject. It was necessary to determine upon some line of conduct, for she was now in an unknown spot, and ignorant of any place of refuge. The count, who trembled at the dangers which environed her, and at the probabilities he saw of her being torn from him for ever, suffered a consideration of them to overcome the dangerous delicacy which at this mournful period required his silence. He entreated her to destroy the possibility of separation, by consenting to become his immediately. He urged that a priest could be easily procured from a neighboring convent, who would confirm the bonds which had so long united their hearts, and who would thus at once arrest the destiny that so long had threatened his hopes.

This proposal, though similar to the one she had before accepted; and though the certain means of rescuing her from the fate she dreaded, she now turned from in sorrow and dejection. She loved Hippolitus with a steady and tender affection, which was still heightened by the gratitude he claimed as her deliverer; but she considered it a prophanation of the memory of that brother who had suffered so much for her sake, to mingle joy with the grief which her uncertainty concerning him occasioned. She softened her refusal with a tender grace, that quickly dissipated the jealous doubt arising in the mind of Hippolitus, and increased his fond admiration of her character.

She desired to retire for a time to some obscure convent, there to await the issue of the event, which at present involved her in perplexity and sorrow.

Hippolitus struggled with his feelings and forbore to press farther the suit on which his happiness, and almost his existence, now depended. He inquired at the village for a neighbouring convent, and was told, that there was none within twelve leagues, but that near the town of Palini, at about that distance, were two. He procured horses; and leaving the officers to return to Palermo for a stronger guard, he, accompanied by Julia, entered on the road to Palini.

Julia was silent and thoughtful; Hippolitus gradually sunk into the same mood, and he often cast a cautious look around as they travelled for some hours along the feet of the mountains. They stopped to dine under the shade of some beach-trees;* for, fearful of discovery, Hippolitus had provided against the necessity of entering many inns. Having finished their repast, they pursued their journey; but Hippolitus now began to doubt whether he was in the right direction. Being destitute, however, of the means of certainty upon this point, he followed the road before him, which now wound up the side of a steep hill, whence they descended into a rich valley, where the shepherd's pipe sounded sweetly from afar among the hills. The evening sun shed a mild and mellow lustre over the landscape, and softened each feature with a vermil glow that would have inspired a mind less occupied than Julia's with sensations of congenial tranquillity.

The evening now closed in; and as they were doubtful of the road, and found it would be impossible to reach Palini that night, they took the way to a village, which they perceived at the extremity of the valley.

They had proceeded about half a mile, when they heard a sudden shout of voices echoed from among the hills behind them; and looking back perceived faintly through the dusk a party of men on horseback making towards them. As they drew nearer, the words they spoke were distinguishable, and Julia heard her own name sounded. Shocked at this circumstance, she had now no doubt that she was discovered by a party of her father's people, and she fled with Hippolitus along the valley. The pursuers, however, were almost come up with them, when they reached the mouth of a cavern, into which she ran for concealment. Hippolitus drew his sword; and awaiting his enemies, stood to defend the entrance.

In a few moments Julia heard the clashing of swords. Her heart trembled for Hippolitus; and she was upon the point of returning to resign herself at once to the power of her enemies, and thus avert the danger that threatened him, when she distinguished the loud voice of the duke.

She shrunk involuntarily at the sound, and pursuing the windings of the cavern, fled into its inmost recesses. Here she had not been long when the voices sounded through the cave, and drew near. It was now evident that Hippolitus was conquered, and that her enemies were in search of her. She threw round a look of unutterable anguish, and perceived very near, by a sudden gleam of torchlight, a low and deep recess in the rock. The light which belonged to her pursuers, grew stronger; and she entered the rock on her knees, for the overhanging craggs would not suffer her to pass otherwise; and having gone a few yards, perceived that it was terminated by a door. The door yielded to her touch, and she suddenly found herself in a highly vaulted cavern,* which received a feeble light from the moon-beams that streamed through an opening in the rock above.

She closed the door, and paused to listen. The voices grew louder, and more distinct, and at last approached so near, that she distinguished what was said. Above the rest she heard the voice of the duke. 'It is impossible she can have quitted the cavern,' said he, 'and I will not leave it till I have found her. Seek to the left of that rock, while I examine beyond this point.'

These words were sufficient for Julia; she fled from the door across the cavern before her, and having ran a considerable way, without coming to a termination, stopped to breathe. All was now still, and as she looked around, the gloomy obscurity of the place struck upon her fancy all its horrors.* She imperfectly surveyed the vastness of the cavern in wild amazement, and feared that she had precipitated herself again into the power of banditti, for whom along this place appeared a fit receptacle. Having listened a long time without hearing a return of voices, she thought to find the door by which she had entered, but the gloom, and vast extent of the cavern, made the endeavour hopeless, and the attempt unsuccessful. Having wandered a considerable time through the void, she gave up the effort, endeavoured to resign herself to her fate, and to compose her distracted thoughts. The remembrance of her former wonderful escape inspired her with confidence in the mercy of God. But Hippolitus and Ferdinand were now both lost to her—lost, perhaps, for ever—and the uncertainty of their fate gave force to fancy, and poignancy to sorrow.

Towards morning grief yielded to nature, and Julia sunk to repose. She was awakened by the sun, whose rays darting obliquely through the opening in the rock, threw a partial light across the cavern. Her senses were yet bewildered by sleep, and she started in affright on beholding her situation; as recollection gradually stole upon her mind, her sorrows returned, and she sickened at the fatal retrospect.

She arose, and renewed her search for an outlet. The light, imperfect as it was, now assisted her, and she found a door, which she perceived was not the one by which she had entered. It was firmly fastened; she discovered, however, the bolts and the lock that held it, and at length unclosed the door. It opened upon a dark passage, which she entered.

She groped along the winding walls for some time, when she perceived the way was obstructed. She now discovered that another door interrupted her progress, and sought for the bolts which might fasten it. These she found; and strengthened by desparation forced them back. The door opened, and she beheld in a small room, which received its feeble light from a window above, the pale and emaciated figure of a woman, seated, with half-closed eyes, in a kind of elbow-chair. On perceiving Julia, she started from her seat, and her countenance expressed a wild surprise. Her features, which were worn by sorrow, still retained the traces of beauty, and in her air was a mild dignity that excited in Julia an involuntary veneration.

She seemed as if about to speak, when fixing her eyes earnestly and steadily upon Julia, she stood for a moment in eager gaze, and suddenly exclaiming, 'My daughter!' fainted away.

The astonishment of Julia would scarcely suffer her to assist the lady who lay senseless on the floor. A multitude of strange imperfect ideas rushed upon her mind, and she was lost in perplexity; but as she examined the features of the stranger; which were now rekindling into life, she thought she discovered the resemblance of Emilia!

The lady breathing a deep sigh, unclosed her eyes; she raised them to Julia, who hung over her in speechless astonishment, and fixing them upon her with a tender earnest expression—they filled with tears. She pressed Julia to her heart, and a few moments of exquisite, unutterable emotion followed. When the lady became more composed, 'Thank heaven!' said she, 'my prayer is granted. I am permitted to embrace one of my children before I die. Tell me what brought you hither. Has the marquis at last relented, and allowed me once more to behold you, or has his death dissolved my wretched bondage?'

Truth now glimmered upon the mind of Julia, but so faintly, that instead of enlightening, it served only to increase her perplexity.

'Is the marquis Mazzini living?' continued the lady. These words were not to be doubted; Julia threw herself at the feet of her mother, and embracing her knees in an energy of joy, answered only in sobs.

The marchioness eagerly inquired after her children, 'Emilia is living,' answered Julia, 'but my dear brother—' 'Tell me,' cried the marchioness, with quickness. An explanation ensued; When she was informed concerning Ferdinand, she sighed deeply, and raising her eyes to heaven, endeavoured to assume a look of pious resignation; but the struggle of maternal feelings was visible in her countenance, and almost overcame her powers of resistance.

Julia gave a short account of the preceding adventures, and of her entrance into the cavern; and found, to her inexpressible surprize, that she was now in a subterranean abode belonging to the southern buildings of the castle of Mazzini! The marchioness was beginning her narrative, when a door was heard to unlock above, and the sound of a footstep followed.

'Fly!' cried the marchioness, 'secret yourself, if possible, for the marquis is coming.' Julia's heart sunk at these words; she paused not a moment, but retired through the door by which she had entered. This she had scarcely done, when another door of the cell was unlocked, and she heard the voice of her father. Its sounds thrilled her with a universal tremour; the dread of discovery so strongly operated upon her mind, that she stood in momentary expectation of seeing the door of the passage unclosed by the marquis; and she was deprived of all power of seeking refuge in the cavern.

At length the marquis, who came with food, quitted the cell, and relocked the door, when Julia stole forth from her hiding-place. The marchioness again embraced, and wept over her daughter. The narrative of her sufferings, upon which she now entered, entirely dissipated the mystery which had so long enveloped the southern buildings of the castle.

'Oh! why,' said the marchioness, 'is it my task to discover to my daughter the vices of her father? In relating my sufferings, I reveal his crimes! It is now about fifteen years, as near as I can guess from the small means I have of judging, since I entered this horrible abode. My sorrows, alas! began not here; they commenced at an earlier period.

But it is sufficient to observe, that the passion whence originated all my misfortunes, was discovered by me long before I experienced its most baleful effects.*

'Seven years had elapsed since my marriage, when the charms of Maria de Vellorno, a young lady singularly beautiful, inspired the marquis with a passion as violent as it was irregular. I observed, with deep and silent anguish, the cruel indifference of my lord towards me, and the rapid progress of his passion for another. I severely examined my past conduct, which I am thankful to say presented a retrospect of only blameless actions; and I endeavoured, by meek submission, and tender assiduities, to recall that affection which was, alas! gone for ever. My meek submission was considered as a mark of a servile and insensible mind; and my tender assiduities, to which his heart no longer responded, created only disgust, and exalted the proud spirit it was meant to conciliate.

'The secret grief which this change occasioned, consumed my spirits, and preyed upon my constitution, till at length a severe illness threatened my life. I beheld the approach of death with a steady eye, and even welcomed it as the passport to tranquillity; but it was destined that I should linger through new scenes of misery.

'One day, which it appears was the paroxysm of my disorder, I sunk into a state of total torpidity, in which I lay for several hours. It is impossible to describe my feelings, when, on recovering, I found myself in this hideous abode. For some time I doubted my senses, and afterwards believed that I had quitted this world for another; but I was not long suffered to continue in my error, the appearance of the marquis bringing me to a perfect sense of my situation.

'I now understood that I had been conveyed by his direction to this recess of horror, where it was his will I should remain. My prayers, my supplications, were ineffectual; the hardness of his heart repelled my sorrows back upon myself; and as no entreaties could prevail upon him to inform me where I was, or of his reason for placing me here, I remained for many years ignorant of my vicinity to the castle, and of the motive of my confinement.

'From that fatal day, until very lately, I saw the marquis no more—but was attended by a person who had been for some years dependant upon his bounty, and whom necessity, united to an insensible heart, had doubtless induced to accept this office. He generally brought me a week's provision, at stated intervals, and I remarked that his visits were always in the night.

'Contrary to my expectation, or my wish, nature did that for me which medicine had refused, and I recovered as if to punish with disappointment and anxiety my cruel tyrant. I afterwards learned, that in obedience to the marquis's order, I had been carried to this spot by Vincent during the night, and that I had been buried in effigy at a neighbouring church, with all the pomp of funeral honor due to my rank.'

At the name of Vincent Julia started; the doubtful words he had uttered on his deathbed were now explained—the cloud of mystery which had so long involved the southern buildings broke at once away: and each particular circumstance that had excited her former terror, arose to her view entirely unveiled by the words of the marchioness.—The long and total desertion of this part of the fabric—the light that had appeared through the casement—the figure she had seen issue from the tower—the midnight noises she had heard—were circumstances evidently dependant on the imprisonment of the marchioness; the latter of which incidents were produced either by Vincent, or the marquis, in their attendance upon her.

When she considered the long and dreadful sufferings of her mother, and that she had for many years lived so near her, ignorant of her misery, and even of her existence—she was lost in astonishment and pity.

'My days,' continued the marchioness, 'passed in a dead uniformity, more dreadful than the most acute vicissitudes of misfortune, and which would certainly have subdued my reason, had not those firm principles of religious faith, which I imbibed in early youth, enabled me to withstand the still, but forceful pressure of my calamity.

'The insensible heart of Vincent at length began to soften to my misfortunes. He brought me several articles of comfort, of which I had hitherto been destitute, and answered some questions I put to him concerning my family. To release me from my present situation, however his inclination might befriend me, was not to be expected, since his life would have paid the forfeiture of what would be termed his duty.

'I now first discovered my vicinity to the castle. I learned also, that the marquis had married Maria de Vellorno, with whom he had resided at Naples, but that my daughters were left at Mazzini. This last intelligence awakened in my heart the throbs of warm maternal tenderness, and on my knees I supplicated to see them. So earnestly I entreated, and so solemnly I promised to return quietly to my prison, that, at length, prudence yielded to pity, and Vincent consented to my request.

'On the following day he came to the cell, and informed me my children were going into the woods, and that I might see them from a window near which they would pass. My nerves thrilled at these words, and I could scarcely support myself to the spot I so eagerly sought. He led me through long and intricate passages, as I guessed by the frequent turnings, for my eyes were bound, till I reached a hall of the south buildings. I followed to a room above, where the full light of day once more burst upon my sight, and almost overpowered me. Vincent placed me by a window, which looked towards the woods. Oh! what moments of painful impatience were those in which I awaited your arrival!

'At length you appeared. I saw you—I saw my children— and was neither permitted to clasp them to my heart, or to speak to them! You was leaning on the arm of your sister, and your countenances spoke the sprightly happy innocence of youth.—Alas! you knew not the wretched fate of your mother, who then gazed upon you! Although you were at too great a distance for my weak voice to reach you, with the utmost difficulty I avoided throwing open the window, and endeavouring to discover myself. The remembrance of my solemn promise, and that the life of Vincent would be sacrificed by the act, alone restrained me. I struggled for some time with emotions too powerful for my nature, and fainted away.

'On recovering I called wildly for my children, and went to the window—but you were gone! Not all the entreaties of Vincent could for some time remove me from this station, where I waited in the fond expectation of seeing you again—but you appeared no more! At last I returned to my cell in an ecstasy of grief which I tremble even to remember.

'This interview, so eagerly sought, and so reluctantly granted, proved a source of new misery—instead of calming, it agitated my mind with a restless, wild despair, which bore away my strongest powers of resistance. I raved incessantly of my children, and incessantly solicited to see them again— Vincent, however, had found but too much cause to repent of his first indulgence, to grant me a second.

'About this time a circumstance occurred which promised me a speedy release from calamity. About a week elapsed, and Vincent did not appear. My little stock of provision was exhausted, and I had been two days without food, when I again heard the doors that led to my prison creek* on their hinges. An unknown step approached, and in a few minutes the marquis entered my cell! My blood was chilled at the sight, and I closed my eyes as I hoped for the last time. The sound of his voice recalled me. His countenance was dark and sullen, and I perceived that he trembled. He informed me that Vincent was no more, and that henceforward his office he should take upon himself. I forbore to reproach—where reproach would only have produced new sufferings, and withheld supplication where it would have exasperated conscience and inflamed revenge. My knowledge of the marquis's second marriage I concealed.

'He usually attended me when night might best conceal his visits; though these were irregular in their return. Lately, from what motive I cannot guess, he has ceased his nocturnal visits, and comes only in the day.

'Once when midnight increased the darkness of my prison, and seemed to render silence even more awful, touched by the sacred horrors of the hour, I poured forth my distress in loud lamentation. Oh! never can I forget what I felt, when I heard a distant voice answered to my moan! A wild surprize, which was strangely mingled with hope, seized me, and in my first emotion I should have answered the call, had not a recollection crossed me, which destroyed at once every half-raised sensation of joy. I remembered the dreadful vengeance which the marquis had sworn to execute upon me, if I ever, by any means, endeavoured to make known the place of my concealment; and though life had long been a burden to me, I dared not to incur the certainty of being murdered. I also well knew that no person who might discover my situation could effect my enlargement, for I had no relations to deliver me by force; and the marquis, you know, has not only power to imprison, but also the right of life and death in his own domains; I, therefore, forbore to answer the call, though I could not entirely repress my lamentation. I long perplexed myself with endeavouring to account for this strange circumstance, and am to this moment ignorant of its cause.'

Julia remembering that Ferdinand had been confined in a dungeon of the castle, it instantly occurred to her that his prison, and that of the marchioness, were not far distant; and she scrupled not to believe that it was his voice which her mother had heard. She was right in this belief, and it was indeed the marchioness whose groans had formerly caused Ferdinand so much alarm, both in the marble hall of the south buildings, and in his dungeon.

When Julia communicated her opinion, and the marchioness believed that she had heard the voice of her son—her emotion was extreme, and it was some time before she could resume her narration.

'A short time since,' continued the marchioness, 'the marquis brought me a fortnight's provision, and told me that I should probably see him no more till the expiration of that term. His absence at this period you have explained in your account of the transactions at the abbey of St Augustin. How can I ever sufficiently acknowledge the obligations I owe to my dear and invaluable friend Madame de Menon! Oh! that it might be permitted me to testify my gratitude.'

Julia attended to the narrative of her mother in silent astonishment, and gave all the sympathy which sorrow could demand. 'Surely,' cried she, 'the providence on whom you have so firmly relied, and whose inflictions you have supported with a fortitude so noble, has conducted me through a labyrinth of misfortunes to this spot, for the purpose of delivering you! Oh! let us hasten to fly this horrid abode—let us seek to escape through the cavern by which I entered.'

She paused in earnest expectation awaiting a reply. 'Whither can I fly?' said the marchioness, deeply sighing. This question, spoken with the emphasis of despair, affected Julia to tears, and she was for a while silent.

'The marquis,' resumed Julia, 'would not know where to seek you, or if he found you beyond his own domains, would fear to claim you. A convent may afford for the present a safe asylum; and whatever shall happen, surely no fate you may hereafter encounter can be more dreadful than the one you now experience.'

The marchioness assented to the truth of this, yet her broken spirits, the effect of long sorrow and confinement, made her hesitate how to act; and there was a kind of placid despair in her look, which too faithfully depicted her feelings. It was obvious to Julia that the cavern she had passed wound beneath the range of mountains on whose opposite side stood the castle of Mazzini. The hills thus rising formed a screen which must entirely conceal their emergence from the mouth of the cave, and their flight, from those in the castle. She represented these circumstances to her mother, and urged them so forcibly that the lethargy of despair yielded to hope, and the marchioness committed herself to the conduct of her daughter.

'Oh! let me lead you to light and life!' cried Julia with warm enthusiasm. 'Surely heaven can bless me with no greater good than by making me the deliverer of my mother.' They both knelt down; and the marchioness, with that affecting eloquence which true piety inspires, and with that confidence which had supported her through so many miseries, committed herself to the protection of God, and implored his favor on their attempt.

They arose, but as they conversed farther on their plan, Julia recollected that she was destitute of money—the banditti having robbed her of all! The sudden shock produced by this remembrance almost subdued her spirits; never till this moment had she understood the value of money. But she commanded her feelings, and resolved to conceal this circumstance from the marchioness, preferring the chance of any evil they might encounter from without, to the certain misery of this terrible imprisonment.

Having taken what provision the marquis had brought, they quitted the cell, and entered upon the dark passage, along which they passed with cautious steps. Julia came first to the door of the cavern, but who can paint her distress when she found it was fastened! All her efforts to open it were ineffectual.—The door which had closed after her, was held by a spring lock, and could be opened on this side only with a key. When she understood this circumstance, the marchioness, with a placid resignation which seemed to exalt her above humanity, addressed herself again to heaven, and turned back to her cell. Here Julia indulged without reserve, and without scruple, the excess of her grief. The marchioness wept over her. 'Not for myself,' said she, 'do I grieve. I have too long been inured to misfortune to sink under its pressure. This disappointment is intrinsically, perhaps, little —for I had no certain refuge from calamity—and had it even been otherwise, a few years only of suffering would have been spared me. It is for you, Julia, who so much lament my fate; and who in being thus delivered to the power of your father, are sacrificed to the Duke de Luovo—that my heart swells.'

Julia could make no reply, but by pressing to her lips the hand which was held forth to her, she saw all the wretchedness of her situation; and her fearful uncertainty concerning Hippolitus and Ferdinand, formed no inferior part of her affliction.

'If,' resumed the marchioness, 'you prefer imprisonment with your mother, to a marriage with the duke, you may still secret yourself in the passage we have just quitted, and partake of the provision which is brought me.'

'O! talk not, madam, of a marriage with the duke,' said Julia; 'surely any fate is preferable to that. But when I consider that in remaining here, I am condemned only to the sufferings which my mother has so long endured, and that this confinement will enable me to soften, by tender sympathy, the asperity of her misfortunes, I ought to submit to my present situation with complacency, even did a marriage with the duke appear less hateful to me.'

'Excellent girl!' exclaimed the marchioness, clasping Julia to her bosom; 'the sufferings you lament are almost repaid by this proof of your goodness and affection! Alas! that I should have been so long deprived of such a daughter!'

Julia now endeavoured to imitate the fortitude of her mother, and tenderly concealed her anxiety for Ferdinand and Hippolitus, the idea of whom incessantly haunted her imagination. When the marquis brought food to the cell, she retired to the avenue leading to the cavern, and escaped discovery.

CHAPTER XV

THE marquis, meanwhile, whose indefatigable search after Julia failed of success, was successively the slave of alternate passions, and he poured forth the spleen of disappointment on his unhappy domestics.

The marchioness, who may now more properly be called Maria de Vellorno, inflamed, by artful insinuations, the passions already irritated, and heightened with cruel triumph his resentment towards Julia and Madame de Menon. She represented, what his feelings too acutely acknowledged,—that by the obstinate disobedience of the first, and the machinations of the last, a priest had been enabled to arrest his authority as a father—to insult the sacred honor of his nobility—and to overturn at once his proudest schemes of power and ambition. She declared it her opinion, that the *Abate* was acquainted with the place of Julia's present retreat, and upbraided the marquis with want of spirit in thus submitting to be outwitted by a priest, and forbearing an appeal to the pope, whose authority would compel the *Abate* to restore Julia.

This reproach stung the very soul of the marquis; he felt all its force, and was at the same time conscious of his inability to obviate it. The effect of his crimes now fell in severe punishment upon his own head. The threatened secret, which was no other than the imprisonment of the marchioness, arrested his arm of vengeance, and compelled him to submit to insult and disappointment. But the reproach of Maria sunk deep in his mind; it fomented his pride into redoubled fury, and he now repelled with disdain the idea of submission.

He revolved the means which might effect his purpose— he saw but one—this was the death of the marchioness.

The commission of one crime often requires the perpetration of another. When once we enter on the labyrinth of

vice, we can seldom return, but are led on, through corres-
pondent mazes, to destruction. To obviate the effect of his
first crime, it was now necessary the marquis should commit
a second, and conceal the *imprisonment* of the marchioness
by her *murder*. Himself the only living witness of her
existence, when she was removed, the allegations of the
Padre Abate would by this means be unsupported by any
proof, and he might then boldly appeal to the pope for the
restoration of his child.

He mused upon this scheme, and the more he accustomed
his mind to contemplate it, the less scrupulous he became.
The crime from which he would formerly have shrunk, he
now surveyed with a steady eye. The fury of his passions,
unaccustomed to resistance, uniting with the force of what
ambition termed necessity—urged him to the deed, and he
determined upon the murder of his wife. The means of
effecting his purpose were easy and various; but as he was
not yet so entirely hardened as to be able to view her dying
pangs, and embrue his own hands in her blood, he chose
to dispatch her by means of poison, which he resolved to
mingle in her food.

But a new affliction was preparing for the marquis,
which attacked him where he was most vulnerable; and
the veil, which had so long overshadowed his reason, was
now to be removed. He was informed by Baptista of the
infidelity of Maria de Vellorno. In the first emotion of
passion, he spurned the informer from his presence, and
disdained to believe the circumstance. A little reflection
changed the object of his resentment; he recalled the
servant, whose faithfulness he had no reason to distrust, and
condescended to interrogate him on the subject of his
misfortune.

He learned that an intimacy had for some time subsisted
between Maria and the Cavalier de Vincini; and that the
assignation was usually held at the pavilion on the sea-shore,
in an evening. Baptista farther declared, that if the marquis
desired a confirmation of his words, he might obtain it by
visiting this spot at the hour mentioned.

This information lighted up the wildest passions of his nature; his former sufferings faded away before the stronger influence of the present misfortune, and it seemed as if he had never tasted misery till now. To suspect the wife upon whom he doated with romantic fondness, on whom he had centered all his firmest hopes of happiness, and for whose sake he had committed the crime which embittered even his present moment, and which would involve him in still deeper guilt—to find *her* ungrateful to his love, and a traitoress to his honor—produced a misery more poignant than any his imagination had conceived. He was torn by contending passions, and opposite resolutions:—now he resolved to expiate her guilt with her blood—and now he melted in all the softness of love. Vengeance and honor bade him strike to the heart which had betrayed him, and urged him instantly to the deed—when the idea of her beauty—her winning smiles—her fond endearments stole upon his fancy, and subdued his heart; he almost wept to the idea of injuring her, and in spight* of appearances, pronounced her faithful. The succeeding moment plunged him again into uncertainty; his tortures acquired new vigour from cessation, and again he experienced all the phrenzy of despair. He was now resolved to end his doubts by repairing to the pavilion; but again his heart wavered in irresolution how to proceed should his fears be confirmed. In the mean time he determined to watch the behaviour of Maria with severe vigilance.

They met at dinner, and he observed her closely, but discovered not the smallest impropriety in her conduct. Her smiles and her beauty again wound their fascinations round his heart, and in the excess of their influence he was almost tempted to repair the injury which his late suspicions had done her, by confessing them at her feet. The appearance of the Cavalier de Vincini, however, renewed his suspicions; his heart throbbed wildly, and with restless impatience he watched the return of evening, which would remove his suspence.

Night at length came. He repaired to the pavilion, and secreted himself among the trees that embowered it. Many minutes had not passed, when he heard a sound of low whispering voices steal from among the trees, and footsteps approaching down the alley. He stood almost petrified with terrible sensations, and presently heard some persons enter the pavilion. The marquis now emerged from his hiding-place; a faint light issued from the building. He stole to the window, and beheld within, Maria and the Cavalier de Vincini. Fired at the sight, he drew his sword, and sprang forward. The sound of his step alarmed the cavalier, who, on perceiving the marquis, rushed by him from the pavilion, and disappeared among the woods. The marquis pursued, but could not overtake him; and he returned to the pavilion with an intention of plunging his sword in the heart of Maria, when he discovered her senseless on the ground. Pity now suspended his vengeance; he paused in agonizing gaze upon her, and returned his sword into the scabbard.

She revived, but on observing the marquis, screamed and relapsed. He hastened to the castle for assistance, inventing, to conceal his disgrace, some pretence for her sudden illness, and she was conveyed to her chamber.

The marquis was now not suffered to doubt her infidelity, but the passion which her conduct abused, her faithlessness could not subdue; he still doated with absurd fondness, and even regretted that uncertainty could no longer flatter him with hope. It seemed as if his desire of her affection increased with his knowledge of the loss of it; and the very circumstance which should have roused his aversion, by a strange perversity of disposition, appeared to heighten his passion, and to make him think it impossible he could exist without her.

When the first energy of his indignation was subsided, he determined, therefore, to reprove and to punish, but here-after to restore her to favor.

In this resolution he went to her apartment, and rep-rehended her falsehood in terms of just indignation.

Maria de Vellorno, in whom the late discovery had roused resentment, instead of awakening penitence; and exasperated pride without exciting shame—heard the upbraidings of the marquis with impatience, and replied to them with acrimonious violence.

She boldly asserted her innocence, and instantly invented a story, the plausibility of which might have deceived a man who had evidence less certain than his senses to contradict it. She behaved with a haughtiness the most insolent; and when she perceived that the marquis was no longer to be misled, and that her violence failed to accomplish its purpose, she had recourse to tears and supplications. But the artifice was too glaring to succeed; and the marquis quitted her apartment in an agony of resentment.

His former fascinations, however, quickly returned, and again held him in suspension between love and vengeance. That the vehemence of his passion, however, might not want an object, he ordered Baptista to discover the retreat of the Cavalier de Vincini on whom he meant to revenge his lost honor. Shame forbade him to employ others in the search.

This discovery suspended for a while the operations of the fatal scheme, which had before employed the thoughts of the marquis; but it had only suspended—not destroyed them. The late occurrence had annihilated his domestic happiness; but his pride now rose to rescue him from despair, and he centered all his future hopes upon ambition. In a moment of cool reflection, he considered that he had derived neither happiness or content from the pursuit of dissipated pleasures, to which he had hitherto sacrificed every opposing consideration. He resolved, therefore, to abandon the gay schemes of dissipation which had formerly allured him, and dedicate himself entirely to ambition, in the pursuits and delights of which he hoped to bury all his cares. He therefore became more earnest than ever for the marriage of Julia with the Duke de Luovo, through whose means he designed to involve himself in the interests of the state, and determined to recover her at whatever consequence. He resolved, without further delay, to appeal to the pope; but to do this with safety it was necessary that the marchioness should die; and he returned therefore to the consideration and execution of his diabolical purpose.

He mingled a poisonous drug with the food he designed for her; and when night arrived, carried it to the cell. As he unlocked the door, his hand trembled; and when he presented the food, and looked consciously for the last time upon the marchioness, who received it with humble thankfulness, his heart almost relented. His countenance, over which was diffused the paleness of death, expressed the secret movements of his soul, and he gazed upon her with eyes of stiffened horror. Alarmed by his looks, she fell upon her knees to supplicate his pity.

Her attitude recalled his bewildered senses; and endeavouring to assume a tranquil aspect, he bade her rise, and instantly quitted the cell, fearful of the instability of his purpose. His mind was not yet sufficiently hardened by guilt to repel the arrows of conscience, and his imagination responded to her power. As he passed through the long dreary passages from the prison, solemn and mysterious sounds seemed to speak in every murmur of the blast which crept along their windings, and he often started and looked back.

He reached his chamber, and having shut the door, surveyed the room in fearful examination. Ideal* forms flitted before his fancy, and for the first time in his life he feared to be alone. Shame only withheld him from calling Baptista. The gloom of the hour, and the death-like silence that prevailed, assisted the horrors of his imagination. He half repented of the deed, yet deemed it now too late to obviate it; and he threw himself on his bed in terrible emotion. His head grew dizzy, and a sudden faintness overcame him; he hesitated, and at length arose to ring for assistance, but found himself unable to stand.

In a few moments he was somewhat revived, and rang his bell; but before any person appeared, he was seized with terrible pains, and staggering to his bed, sunk senseless upon it. Here Baptista, who was the first person that entered his room, found him struggling seemingly in the agonies of death. The whole castle was immediately roused, and the confusion may be more easily imagined than described.

Emilia, amid the general alarm, came to her father's room, but the sight of him overcame her, and she was carried from his presence. By the help of proper applications the marquis recovered his senses and his pains had a short cessation.

'I am dying,' said he, in a faultering accent; 'send instantly for the marchioness and my son.'

Ferdinand, in escaping from the hands of the banditti, it was now seen, had fallen into the power of his father. He had been since confined in an apartment of the castle, and was now liberated to obey the summons. The countenance of the marquis exhibited a ghastly image; Ferdinand, when he drew near the bed, suddenly shrunk back, overcome with horror. The marquis now beckoned his attendants to quit the room, and they were preparing to obey, when a violent noise was heard from without; almost in the same instant the door of the apartment was thrown open, and the servant, who had been sent for the marchioness, rushed in. His look alone declared the horror of his mind, for words he had none to utter. He stared wildly, and pointed to the gallery he had quitted. Ferdinand, seized with new terror, rushed the way he pointed to the apartment of the marchioness. A spectacle of horror presented itself. Maria lay on a couch lifeless, and bathed in blood. A poignard, the instrument of her destruction, was on the floor; and it appeared from a letter which was found on the couch beside her, that she had died by her own hand. The paper contained these words:

TO THE MARQUIS DE MAZZINI

Your words have stabbed my heart. No power on earth could restore the peace you have destroyed. I will escape from my torture. When you read this, I shall be no more. But the triumph shall no longer be yours—the draught you have drank was given by the hand of the injured

MARIA DE MAZZINI.

It now appeared that the marquis was poisoned by the vengeance of the woman to whom he had resigned his conscience. The consternation and distress of Ferdinand cannot easily be conceived: he hastened back to his father's chamber, but determined to conceal the dreadful catastrophe of Maria de Vellorno. This precaution, however, was useless; for the servants, in the consternation of terror, had revealed it, and the marquis had fainted.

Returning pains recalled his senses, and the agonies he suffered were too shocking for the beholders. Medical endeavours were applied, but the poison was too powerful for antidote. The marquis's pains at length subsided; the poison had exhausted most of its rage, and he became tolerably easy. He waved his hand for the attendants to leave the room; and beckoning to Ferdinand, whose senses were almost stunned by this accumulation of horror, bade him sit down beside him. 'The hand of death is now upon me,' said he; 'I would employ these last moments in revealing a deed, which is more dreadful to me than all the bodily agonies I suffer. It will be some relief to me to discover it.' Ferdinand grasped the hand of the marquis in speechless terror. 'The retribution of heaven is upon me,' resumed the marquis. 'My punishment is the immediate consequence of my guilt. Heaven has made that woman the instrument of its justice, whom I made the instrument of my crimes;—— that woman, for whose sake I forgot conscience, and braved vice—for whom I imprisoned an innocent wife, and afterwards murdered her.'

At these words every nerve of Ferdinand thrilled; he let go the marquis's hand and started back. 'Look not so fiercely on me,' said the marquis, in a hollow voice; 'your eyes strike death to my soul; my conscience needs not this additional pang.'—'My mother!' exclaimed Ferdinand—'my mother! Speak, tell me.'—'I have no breath,' said the marquis. 'Oh!—Take these keys—the south tower—the trapdoor.— 'Tis possible—Oh!—'

The marquis made a sudden spring upwards, and fell lifeless on the bed; the attendants were called in, but he was gone for ever. His last words struck with the force of lightning upon the mind of Ferdinand; they seemed to say that his mother might yet exist. He took the keys, and ordering some of the servants to follow, hastened to the southern building; he proceeded to the tower, and the trapdoor beneath the stair-case was lifted. They all descended into a dark passage, which conducted them through several intricacies to the door of the cell. Ferdinand, in trembling horrible expectation, applied the key; the door opened, and he entered; but what was his surprize when he found no person in the cell! He concluded that he had mistaken the place, and quitted it for further search; but having followed the windings of the passage, by which he entered, without discovering any other door, he returned to a more exact examination of the cell. He now observed the door, which led to the cavern, and he entered upon the avenue, but no person was found there and no voice answered to his call. Having reached the door of the cavern, which was fastened, he returned lost in grief, and meditating upon the last words of the marquis. He now thought that he had mistaken their import, and that the words ' 'tis possible,' were not meant to apply to the life of the marchioness, he concluded, that the murder had been committed at a distant period; and he resolved, therefore, to have the ground of the cell dug up, and the remains of his mother sought for.

When the first violence of the emotions excited by the late scenes was subsided, he enquired concerning Maria de Vellorno.

It appeared that on the day preceding this horrid transaction, the marquis had passed some hours in her apartment; that they were heard in loud dispute;—that the passion of the marquis grew high;—that he upbraided her with her past conduct, and threatened her with a formal separation. When the marquis quitted her, she was heard walking quick through the room, in a passion of tears; she often suddenly stopped in vehement but incoherent exclamation; and at last threw herself on the floor, and was for some time entirely still. Here her woman found her, upon whose entrance she arose hastily, and reproved her for appearing uncalled. After this she remained silent and sullen.

She descended to supper, where the marquis met her alone at table. Little was said during the repast, at the conclusion of which the servants were dismissed; and it was believed that during the interval between supper, and the hour of repose, Maria de Vellorno contrived to mingle poison with the wine of the marquis. How she had procured this poison was never discovered.

She retired early to her chamber; and her woman observing that she appeared much agitated, inquired if she was ill? To this she returned a short answer in the negative, and her woman was soon afterwards dismissed. But she had hardly shut the door of the room when she heard her lady's voice recalling her. She returned, and received some trifling order, and observed that Maria looked uncommonly pale; there was besides a wildness in her eyes which frightened her, but she did not dare to ask any questions. She again quitted the room, and had only reached the extremity of the gallery when her mistress's bell rang. She hastened back, Maria enquired if the marquis was gone to bed, and if all was quiet? Being answered in the affirmative, she replied, 'This is a still hour and a dark one!—Good night!'

Her woman having once more left the room, stopped at the door to listen, but all within remaining silent, she retired to rest.

It is probable that Maria perpetrated the fatal act soon after the dismission of her woman; for when she was found, two hours afterwards, she appeared to have been dead for some time. On examination a wound was discovered on her left side, which had doubtless penetrated to the heart, from the suddenness of her death, and from the effusion of blood which had followed.

These terrible events so deeply affected Emilia that she was confined to her bed by a dangerous illness. Ferdinand struggled against the shock with manly fortitude. But amid all the tumult of the present scenes, his uncertainty concerning Julia, whom he had left in the hands of banditti, and whom he had been withheld from seeking or rescuing, formed, perhaps, the most affecting part of his distress.

The late Marquis de Mazzini, and Maria de Vellorno, were interred with the honor due to their rank in the church of the convent of St Nicolo. Their lives exhibited a boundless indulgence of violent and luxurious passions, and their deaths marked the consequences of such indulgence, and held forth to mankind a singular instance of divine vengeance.

CHAPTER XVI

In turning up the ground of the cell, it was discovered that it communicated with the dungeon in which Ferdinand had been confined, and where he had heard those groans which had occasioned him so much terror.

The story which the marquis formerly related to his son, concerning the southern buildings, it was now evident was fabricated for the purpose of concealing the imprisonment of the marchioness. In the choice of his subject, he certainly discovered some art; for the circumstance related was calculated, by impressing terror, to prevent farther enquiry into the recesses of these buildings. It served, also, to explain, by supernatural evidence, the cause of those sounds, and of that appearance which had been there observed, but which were, in reality, occasioned only by the marquis.

The event of the examination in the cell threw Ferdinand into new perplexity. The marquis had confessed that he poisoned his wife—yet her remains were not to be found; and the place which he signified to be that of her confinement, bore no vestige of her having been there. There appeared no way by which she could have escaped from her prison; for both the door which opened upon the cell, and that which terminated the avenue beyond, were fastened when tried by Ferdinand.

But the young marquis had no time for useless speculation—serious duties called upon him. He believed that Julia was still in the power of banditti; and, on the conclusion of his father's funeral, he set forward himself to Palermo, to give information of the abode of the robbers, and to repair with the officers of justice, accompanied by a party of his own people, to the rescue of his sister. On his arrival at Palermo he was informed, that a banditti, whose retreat had been among the ruins of a monastery, situated in the forest of Marentino, was already discovered; that their abode had been searched, and themselves secured for examples of public justice—but that no captive lady had been found amongst them. This latter intelligence excited in Ferdinand a very serious distress, and he was wholly unable to conjecture her fate. He obtained leave, however, to interrogate those of the robbers, who were imprisoned at Palermo, but could draw from them no satisfactory or certain information.

At length he quitted Palermo for the forest of Marentino, thinking it possible that Julia might be heard of in its neighbourhood. He travelled on in melancholy and dejection, and evening overtook him long before he reached the place of his destination. The night came on heavily in clouds, and a violent storm of wind and rain arose. The road lay through a wild and rocky country, and Ferdinand could obtain no shelter. His attendants offered him their cloaks, but he refused to expose a servant to the hardship he would not himself endure. He travelled for some miles in a heavy rain; and the wind, which howled mournfully among the rocks, and whose solemn pauses were filled by the distant roarings of the sea, heightened the desolation of the scene. At length he discerned, amid the darkness from afar, a red light waving in the wind: it varied with the blast, but never totally disappeared. He pushed his horse into a gallop, and made towards it.

The flame continued to direct his course; and on a nearer approach, he perceived, by the red reflection of its fires, streaming a long radiance upon the waters beneath—a lighthouse situated upon a point of rock which overhung the sea. He knocked for admittance, and the door was opened by an old man, who bade him welcome.

Within appeared a cheerful blazing fire, round which were seated several persons, who seemed like himself to have sought shelter from the tempest of the night. The sight of the fire cheered him, and he advanced towards it, when a sudden scream seized his attention; the company rose up in confusion, and in the same instant he discovered Julia and Hippolitus. The joy of that moment is not to be described, but his attention was quickly called off from his own situation to that of a lady, who during the general transport had fainted. His sensations on learning she was his mother cannot be described.

She revived. 'My son!' said she, in a languid voice, as she pressed him to her heart. 'Great God, I am recompensed! Surely this moment may repay a life of misery!' He could only receive her caresses in silence; but the sudden tears which started in his eyes spoke a language too expressive to be misunderstood.

When the first emotion of the scene was passed, Julia enquired by what means Ferdinand had come to this spot. He answered her generally, and avoided for the present entering upon the affecting subject of the late events at the castle of Mazzini. Julia related the history of her adventures since she parted with her brother. In her narration, it appeared that Hippolitus, who was taken by the Duke de Luovo at the mouth of the cave, had afterwards escaped, and returned to the cavern in search of Julia. The low recess in the rock, through which Julia had passed, he perceived by the light of his flambeau.* He penetrated to the cavern beyond, and from thence to the prison of the marchioness. No colour of language can paint the scene which followed; it is sufficient to say that the whole party agreed to quit the cell at the return of night. But this being a night on which it was known the marquis would visit the prison, they agreed to defer their departure till after his appearance, and thus elude the danger to be expected from an early discovery of the escape of the marchioness.

At the sound of footsteps above, Hippolitus and Julia had secreted themselves in the avenue; and immediately on the marquis's departure they all repaired to the cavern, leaving, in the hurry of their flight, untouched the poisonous food he had brought. Having escaped from thence they proceeded to a neighbouring village, where horses were procured to carry them towards Palermo. Here, after a tedious journey, they arrived, in the design of embarking for Italy. Contrary winds had detained them till the day on which Ferdinand left that city, when, apprehensive and weary of delay, they hired a small vessel, and determined to brave the winds. They had soon reason to repent their temerity; for the vessel had not been long at sea when the storm arose, which threw them back upon the shores of Sicily, and brought them to the lighthouse, where they were discovered by Ferdinand.

On the following morning Ferdinand returned with his friends to Palermo, where he first disclosed the late fatal events of the castle. They now settled their future plans; and Ferdinand hastened to the castle of Mazzini to fetch Emilia, and to give orders for the removal of his household to his palace at Naples, where he designed to fix his future residence. The distress of Emilia, whom he found recovered from her indisposition, yielded to joy and wonder, when she heard of the existence of her mother, and the safety of her sister. She departed with Ferdinand for Palermo, where her friends awaited her, and where the joy of the meeting was considerably heightened by the appearance of Madame de Menon, for whom the marchioness had dispatched a messenger to St Augustin's. Madame had quitted the abbey for another convent, to which, however, the messenger was directed. This happy party now embarked for Naples.

From this period the castle of Mazzini, which had been the theatre of a dreadful catastrophe; and whose scenes would have revived in the minds of the chief personages connected with it, painful and shocking reflections—was abandoned.

On their arrival at Naples, Ferdinand presented to the king a clear and satisfactory account of the late events at the castle, in consequence of which the marchioness was confirmed in her rank, and Ferdinand was received as the sixth Marquis de Mazzini.

The marchioness, thus restored to the world, and to happiness, resided with her children in the palace at Naples, where, after time had somewhat mellowed the remembrance of the late calamity, the nuptials of Hippolitus and Julia were celebrated. The recollection of the difficulties they had encountered, and of the distress they had endured for each other, now served only to heighten by contrast the happiness of the present period.

Ferdinand soon after accepted a command in the Neapolitan army; and amidst the many heroes of that warlike and turbulent age, distinguished himself for his valour and ability. The occupations of war engaged his mind, while his heart was solicitous in promoting the happiness of his family.

Madame de Menon, whose generous attachment to the marchioness had been fully proved, found in the restoration of her friend a living witness of her marriage, and thus recovered those estates which had been unjustly withheld from her. But the marchioness and her family, grateful to her friendship, and attached to her virtues, prevailed upon her to spend the remainder of her life at the palace of Mazzini.

Emilia, wholly attached to her family, continued to reside with the marchioness, who saw her race renewed in the children of Hippolitus and Julia. Thus surrounded by her children and friends, and engaged in forming the minds of the infant generation, she seemed to forget that she had ever been otherwise than happy.

Here the manuscript annals conclude. In reviewing this story, we perceive a singular and striking instance of moral retribution. We learn, also, that those who do only THAT WHICH IS RIGHT, endure nothing in misfortune but a trial of their virtue, and from trials well endured derive the surest claim to the protection of heaven.

FINIS

EXPLANATORY NOTES

epigraph: from *Hamlet*, I. v. 15. The speaker is the ghost of Hamlet's father:

> But that I am forbid
> To tell the secrets of my prison-house
> I could a tale unfold whose lightest word
> Would harrow up thy soul, freeze thy young blood,
> Make thy two eyes like stars start from their spheres,
> Thy knotted and combined locks to part,
> And each particular hair to stand on end
> Like quills upon the fretful porcupine.

The short epigraph, 'I could a tale unfold', thus signals two things about the following tale. First, it indicates its intention of arousing suspense and terror in its readers, of disarranging them physically in the manner of the sublime effect. Secondly, the message of the ghost is for his son, revealing that he has been murdered, and his place as king and husband usurped by his murderer, Claudius. This is a hint to the truth of the mystery of the haunted tower in *A Sicilian Romance*, to which the reference to 'prison-house' provides a further clue. Radcliffe's plot is a non-supernatural version of *Hamlet*, and even contains a muted reference to incest. In Radcliffe's journal entry describing one of many visits to Windsor (where she later had a rural retreat) she considers that the north terrace of the castle at night evokes the presence of Hamlet's father's spectre (*Gaston de Blondeville, or the Court of Henry III Keeping Festival in Ardenne, A Romance, St Alban's Abbey, A Metrical Tale; With Some Poetical Pieces. By Anne Radcliffe, Author of 'The Mysteries of Udolpho', 'Romance of the Forest' &c. To Which is Prefixed a Memoir of the Author, With Extracts From Her Journals*, 4 vols. (London, 1826), iv. 98).

1 *noble house of Mazzini*: the title of the family, like all the names in the novel, is an invention, but the house's situation near the straits of Messina is realized with some verisimilitude. Its setting allows a view of Etna as well as of Palermo in the far distance. None of the novel's other place-names can be found in contemporary gazetteers, although the de-

scription of the varieties of Sicilian landscape is accurate throughout.

acclivity: 'the upward slope of a hill; an ascending slope' (*OED*).

awe and curiosity: these are the keynotes of the narrator's and the reader's role in the tale. Story (and history) are produced in the intersection between the forward advance of plot, and the stasis that awe and terror engender. The picturesque ruin allows the traveller to read its history in its ruination, but also acts to de-centre and judge the viewer as himself subject to the action of time. In the excerpts from Ann Radcliffe's journal in the biographical memoir by T. N. Talfourd, she makes frequent reference to this idea, most notably in her strong response to the ruins of Kenilworth, about which she was to write more fully in *Gaston de Blondeville*: 'They speak at once to the imagination with the force and simplicity of truth, the nothingness and brevity of this life—generations have beheld us and passed away, as you now behold us, and shall pass away; they spoke of the generations before them as you now think of them, and as future ages shall think of you. We have witnessed this, yet we remain; the voices that revelled beneath us, are heard no more, yet the winds of Heaven still sound in our ivy.' (i. 58)

a manuscript in our library: the device of the 'discovered' manuscript is a common frame for Gothic tales. Horace Walpole's *Castle of Otranto* (1764) is presented in its first edition as no more than such a document, while Sophia Lee's *The Recess* (1785) was, the Advertisement claimed, from an 'obsolete manuscript' dating from the reign of Elizabeth.

2 *convent*: more properly a friary. Radcliffe has the Gothic writer's Protestant vagueness over Catholic ecclesiastical terminology, but here exhibits a more positive picture of monastic life.

4 *entendered*: made tender, weakened (*OED*).

the charms of harmony: the contrast of two sisters, one full of trembling sensibility, the other more governed by the claims of reason, is common to sentimental and Gothic fiction. The heroines of Sophia Lee's *The Recess*, Matilda and Elinor, are one such pair, as are the cousins, Julie and

Claire, in Rousseau's *Julie; ou, La Nouvelle Héloïse* (1761).
Julie is a likely source for Julia's name, as Radcliffe was an
admirer of Rousseau, using *Émile; ou, De l'Education* extens-
ively for the alpine sections of *The Romance of the Forest*. It
has often been suggested that Radcliffe's Sicilian sisters form
a model for the Dashwood pair in Jane Austen's *Sense and
Sensibility*, in which Marianne's excess of sensibility and
Elinor's good sense are demonstrated by their separate devotion to the different arts of music and drawing.

6 *wild and picturesque scenery of Sicily*: compare with Henry Swinburne's description of Taormina in *Travels in the Two Sicilies
. . . in the Years 1777, 1778, 1779, and 1780*, 2 vols. (London,
1783–5): 'Everything belonging to it is drawn in a large sublime
style; the mountains tower to the very clouds, the castles and
ruins rise on mighty masses of perpendicular rock, and seem
to defy the attacks of mortal enemies; Aetna with all its snowy
and woody sweeps fills half the horizon; the sea is stretched
out upon an immense scale, and occupies the remainder of the
prospect.' (ii. 169–70)

Mount Etna: as far back as Longinus's *On the Sublime*, Etna
had been cited as sublime in its power to erupt (ch. 35). In
addition, John Dennis's list in his 'The Grounds of Criticism
in Poetry' (1708) of objects that inspire terror (and are thus
sources of the sublime according to Longinus) includes
'Thunder, Tempests, raging Seas, Inundations, Torrents,
Earthquakes, Volcanos . . . ' (*Works*, ii. 460).

they had never passed the boundaries of their father's domains:
this seclusion accords less with Sicilian custom, and more
with Rousseau's theories of the proper manner of female
education as exhibited in *Émile*, and such novels as Charlotte
Lennox's *The Female Quixote* (1752) and Eliza Fenwick's
Secresy; or, The Ruin on the Rock (1795). In *The Present State
of Sicily and Malta, Extracted from Mr Brydone, Mr Swinburne,
and Other Modern Travellers* (London, 1788), the liberal
upbringing of the young women of Palermo is particularly
stressed: 'Instead of being immured within the gloomy walls
of a convent, the young ladies are in general educated in the
houses of their parents, and mix there in society with the
utmost freedom' (pp. 146–7).

7 *the poetry of Tasso*: Torquato Tasso (1544–95), Italian poet
and author of the epic of the Crusades, *Gerusalemme Liberata*,

was immensely influential for sixteenth and seventeenth-century English verse. His *Aminta*, a pastoral drama of great beauty and extensive natural descriptions, was still frequently being translated into English in the eighteenth century. One of its scenes takes place in the cavern of Aurora. With Ariosto, Tasso was the proper courtly reading for an Italian noblewoman of the period.

the familiar and the sentimental: 'sentimental' in this context is used in its meaning of 'refined and elevated feeling' (*OED*), so that the conversation described precludes the personal and anything of self-interest. The closest model in the fiction of the period is the discourse of Sir Charles Grandison, in the novel of that name by Samuel Richardson. Such talk eschews the tittle-tattle of 'female' gossip but also the persuasive eloquence of the masculine public debate.

8   *Vincent*: an abrupt introduction—one of several in this novel—of the name of one of the Marquis's servants.

10   *Hippolitus*: as Melvin D. Palmer has made us aware ('Madame D'Aulnoy in England', *Comparative Literature*, 27/3 (Summer 1975), 237–53), the name for Radcliffe's hero is derived from a novel by Marie d'Aulnoy, translated as *Hypolitus Earl of Douglas, Containing some Memoirs of the Court of Scotland* (London, 1708). This work went into seven editions in the eighteenth century, four between the years 1766 and 1778. It charts the frustrated love of Hypolitus and Julia of Warwick, for 100,000 words through England, France, and Italy. There are strong connections between the two novels. Like Radcliffe's heroine, d'Aulnoy's Julia is promised in marriage to a villain whom she flees, and is briefly taken in at a convent, only to run away. Both plots involve a storm and a sea-journey. The name Hippolitus also suggests the beautiful young man for whom Phaedra conceives an incestuous passion in Euripides's tragedy. Unlike Radcliffe's hero, the classical Hippolytus does indeed die, but Pierre Arnaud sees a parallel between the murderous passion of Radcliffe's Maria de Vellorno and that of the self-destructive Phaedra, both of whom kill themselves (see *Ann Radcliffe et la fantastique: Essai de psychobiographie* (Paris, 1976), 121). Arnaud does not remark on the fact that Phaedra's husband is away, helping to rescue Persephone

from the underworld, to which she had been abducted from her home in Sicily.

11 *repulsive*: 'repellent; intended or tending to repel by denial, coldness of manner, etc.' (*OED*).

15 *saloon*: a large apartment or hall for public assemblies and gatherings, especially for entertainment.

17 *bandellets*: 'a small band, streak, or fillet' (*OED*). The word has an additional architectural reference, applying to a band encircling a column, and Radcliffe may have wished to suggest the appearance of the idealized classical costume of the figures in a Poussin or Dughet painting.

20 *various*: 'complex', perhaps, rather than 'various' in its then common sense of 'changeable'.

22 *violoncello . . . flute . . . piana-forte*: these are, of course complete anachronisms. Later Radcliffe novels avoid such obvious mistakes, and *Gaston de Blondeville* in particular is loaded with what was then considered accurate historical detail.

23 *by which the darkness of its general shade is contrasted*: this sentiment is also to be found in Radcliffe's private journal (*Gaston de Blondeville*, ii. 50): 'Yet even here life is still a FLEETING VISION! As such it fades, whether in court or convent, nor leaves a gleam behind—save of the light of good works.'

Sonnet: in the eighteenth century, the sonnet need not necessarily consist of exactly fourteen lines, but could refer to any short lyrical poem.

Charlotte Smith, Radcliffe's respected contemporary, also included poetry in her novels, but it is in Radcliffe particularly that verse is important both as expressive of individual feeling and as part of a claim for high literary status for the novel. Rather more of her poems are put in the mouths of female characters. The first lines of this sonnet echo the opening sentiment of Walpole's drama of 1768, *The Mysterious Mother*:

> What awful silence! How these antique towers
> And vacant courts chill the suspended soul,

which is spoken by the hero, Florian, once the victim of his mother's incestuous desires. More generally, the poem is of a piece with the eighteenth-century allegorical treatment of evening. The skilful modulation of 'still' from motionless tranquillity in the first line to its dual use as 'continues' and also as block to the lover's desire for repose in the last lines suggests the movement of the Gothic novel itself, with its alternate sublime moments of pensive tranquillity, and its extreme use of plot and the resultant frustration until the mystery is unravelled.

26 *croud*: crowd.

an ever-moving scene: Radcliffe may have in mind the illustration of Messina in Swinburne's *Travels in the Two Sicilies* (iv. 217), which also includes a lighthouse, a feature of one of the later scenes of *A Sicilian Romance*.

29 *Orlando*: perhaps named for the emotional hero of Ariosto's *Orlando Furioso*—a suitable choice for one about to die as a result of his strong passions.

36 *he, therefore, can make unembodied spirits*: this discussion is again taken up in *Gaston de Blondeville*, the work written by Radcliffe for her own pleasure, and left unpublished at her death. In that later work, the worthy characters, such as the Archbishop of York, believe in the existence of ghosts as agents of God's judgement, while the villains attribute any supernatural events either to a magician's trickery, or to demonic possession.

42 *insensibly sunk her mind into a state of repose*: see Charlotte Smith, *Emmeline: The Orphan of the Castle* (London, 1788), in which the heroine, avoiding the unwelcome attentions of Lord Delamere's valet, walks to the sea-shore to be soothed by the scene: 'Seating herself on a fragment of rock, [she] fixed her eyes insensibly on the restless waves that broke at her feet. The low murmurs of the tide retiring on the sands; the sighing of the wind among the rocks which hung over her head, cloathed with the long grass and marine plants; the noise of the sea fowl going to their nests among the cliffs; threw her into a profound reverie.' (Chapter III) Smith's is the more particularized description, while she completely eschews the moves Radcliffe makes to aestheticize the experience, and render it sublime.

Evening: a traditional topic for verse of the period, as in Thomas Gray's 'Elegy in a Country Churchyard' and Joseph

Warton's and William Collins's 'Ode to Evening'. Radcliffe's debt to the latter is even clearer in her separately published poem 'Scene on the Northern Shore of Sicily', which follows Collins in its evocation of the pastoral sights and then the sounds of a dying day from the terrace of a ruined castle:

> Then let me rove some wild and heathy Scene,
> Or find some Ruin 'midst its dreary Dells,
>   Whose walls more awful nod
>   By thy religious Gleams.

In Radcliffe's 'Evening', the elements of Collins's Ode, such as the hours, the car, the figure of evening as a woman, her fingers drawing the veil of obscurity that is dusk, are re-orchestrated so as to foreground the role of the speaker's imagination in re-creating the lost scene with 'Fancy's eye'.

43 *car*: chariot.

illapses: 'a gentle gliding movement' (*OED*).

46 *An air of proud sublimity*: the text here illustrates the contrast between 'high' sublimity and 'low' 'sullen groan'—an axis to which the Introduction draws attention and associates with male and female viewpoints respectively.

52 *exordium*: 'the beginning of anything: especially the introductory part of a discourse, treatise, etc.' (*OED*).

53 *banditti who sought protection in his service*: see Patrick Brydone, *A Tour Through Sicily and Malta. In a Series of Letters to William Beckford*, 2 vols. (London, 1775), i. 74–5, on the use made of banditti by local princes and noblemen, whose livery they even affected.

55 *finesse*: 'delicacy of manipulation or discrimination; refinement, refined grace' (*OED*). There may also be a suggestion of the word's other main meaning of artifice or stratagem in the Marquis's stern address to his daughter.

57 *revolved*: 'to turn over (something) in the mind' (*OED*).

sopha: a now obsolete rendering of sofa.

58 *wean*: probably intended in the obsolete medieval sense of 'beautiful'.

69 *unlimited power of life and death*: see Brydone, *A Tour Through Sicily and Malta*, i. 109, about the barons, 'each of whom has the power of life or death in his own domains,

[which] is an evil of very enormous magnitude, of which the lower orders of the people universally complain'.

72 *habiliments*: garments.

77 *Anthony*: here is an example of Radcliffe's adoption of the Shakespearian 'mechanical' to lighten the tone of the narrative. When used humorously, such characters are given English names, in contrast to their intriguing Sicilian masters.

84 *party of the banditti . . . infested*: the scene evoked is a re-creation of the paintings of the seventeenth-century artist and satirist Salvator Rosa, whose sombre caverns and rocky promontories infested with sinister little figures of banditti were enormously popular with the British in the eighteenth century.

85 *early Romans . . . softened them*: Aeneas, the legendary Trojan founder of Rome, was popularly considered to have founded cities in Sicily during his wanderings. However, the benign view of banditti as primitives rather than criminals derives from the eighteenth-century interpretation of Rosa's etchings of soldiers as banditti, leading to a fashion for depicting such figures as picturesque relics in exotic landscapes in the work of such artists as John Hamilton Mortimer (the 'Salvator of Sussex') and Joseph Wright of Derby.

90 *and could scarcely credit his senses*: this effect of distant jollity in what should be an ascetic institution is used to satiric effect by the Marquis de Sade in *Justine* (1791), when the heroine seeks refuge from bandits and is directed by a charmingly pastoral shepherdess to a depraved Benedictine monastery.

103 *the obscurity which involved them*: see Edmund Burke, *A Philosophical Enquiry*, pt. 2, sect. 3, on the necessity of obscurity to render anything very terrible: 'When we know the full extent of any danger, when we can accustom our eyes to it, a great deal of the apprehension vanishes'.

104 *romantic*: 'grotesque' in the first edition.

from Nature up to Nature's God: a misquotation from Pope's *Essay on Man*, Epistle 4, line 332, 'But looks thro' Nature up to Nature's God'. The verse continues: 'Pursues that Chain which links th' immense design / Joins heav'n and earth, and mortal and divine'. Madame de Menon's desire to follow the meandering path is thus associated with the religious study of the chain of being of eighteenth-century natural theology.

117   *Superstition. An Ode*: the model is, as in 'Evening', William Collins's series of odes on abstract subjects, such as fear, pity, and liberty. The 'Ode to Fear' appears to be a direct influence here, with its train of demons, personified Vengeance, and associated spectres. Collins also wrote an ode 'On the Popular Superstitions of the Highlands of Scotland', but this poem is far less pejorative in its approach to the subject than Radcliffe's allegory. Joseph Warton's 'Ode IV' is entitled 'To Superstition', and similarly invokes terrors, fear, and ignorance, as well as phantoms.

Alverna's: Roger Lonsdale and Jasper Griffin have identified this as a Latinization of the Auvergne region in France, which was often a site of religious extremism. Another possible location is Mount Alvernia or La Vernia in the Casentino east of Florence, where St Francis founded a friary, and where he received the stigmata.

121   *noviciate*: novice.

125   *vermil*: vermilion.

136   *Last came the friars*: like other Gothic novelists, Radcliffe is often inclined erroneously to unite nuns and monks or friars in one order, or in one institution. Such propinquity of the sexes in a place dedicated to the sublimation of sexual passion emphasizes the importance such texts place on sexual difference, which the supposedly sexless convent or monastery somehow produces.

149   *the various and secret caverns of the place*: Swinburne, in his *Travels in the Two Sicilies* (iv. 93), describes the extensive subterranean gardens of the Capuchin monastery at Syracuse, consisting of caverns formed by channels of lava.

152   *coup d'œil*: 'a view as it strikes the eye at a glance' (*OED*).

Far on the rocky shores the surges sound: quotation unidentified. It is possible that the lines are by Radcliffe herself.

171   *beach-trees*: the modern spelling is 'beech'.

172   *a highly vaulted cavern*: compare this architectural feature of what might appear a natural formation with Swinburne's

description of a cave called 'the ear of Dionysus', which he believed to have once been used as a prison or listening place: 'the sides are very smooth, and the roof covered, gradually narrowing almost to as sharp a point as a Gothic arch' (*Travels in the Two Sicilies*, iv. 104).

173 *struck upon her fancy all its horrors*: see Horace Walpole's Gothic tale of 1764, *The Castle of Otranto*, in which the heroine is pursued through the passages under the castle: 'An awful silence reigned throughout those subterranean regions, except, now and then, some blasts of wind that shook the doors she had passed, and which, grating on the rusty hinges, were re-echoed through the long labyrinth of darkness. Every murmur struck her with new terror.'

176 *its most baleful effects*: the first edition has 'the more baleful effect of its influence'.

179 *creek*: 'crack' in the first edition.

186 *in spight*: in spite. The contending emotions of vengeance and affection towards a (supposedly) erring wife are reminiscent of the response of Leontes, also a Sicilian, in *The Winter's Tale*. In Shakespeare's play the Queen is also brought back to life, after a hidden existence of many years' duration.

189 *ideal*: imagined

197 *flambeau*: 'a torch; esp. one made of several thick wicks dipped in wax' (*OED*).

THE WORLD'S CLASSICS

A Select List

ÉMILE ZOLA:
The Attack on the Mill and Other Stories
Translated by Douglas Parmée

Nana
Translated and Edited by Douglas Parmée